Peter Watt has spent time as a soldier, articled clerk, prawn trawler deckhand, builder's labourer, pipe layer, real estate salesman, private investigator, police sergeant, surveyor's chairman and advisor to the Royal Papua New Guinea Constabulary. He speaks, reads and writes Vietnamese and Pidgin. He now lives at Maclean on the Clarence River in northern New South Wales. He has volunteered with the Volunteer Rescue Association, Queensland Ambulance Service and currently with the Rural Fire Service. Fishing and the vast open spaces of outback Queensland are his main interests in life.

Peter Watt can be contacted at www.peterwatt.com.

Author Photo: Shawn Peene

Also by Peter Watt

Excerpts from emails sent to Peter Watt

'Dear Peter, just finished *While the Moon Burns*. Enjoyed it immensely. Hope another one is in the pipeline. Keep up the good work.'

'Can you please tell me whether there are any more books planned in the Frontier series? After reading the first ten books over the last four weeks, I am really looking forward to the next instalment.'

'Once I get started on your books I just can't put them down. I love all the books that you have written, they are so entertaining and so full of Australian history.'

'I have been following the Duffy/Macintosh saga from the beginning. They have kept me enthralled. I am now halfway through *While the Moon Burns* and loving it . . . Looking forward to your next book.'

'Don't write such compelling stories, I cannot put them down once I start them, consequently nothing gets done . . . I am just glad you don't write three – four books a year.'

'Thanks for the terrific reads . . . Great research! Just finished *Beneath a Rising Sun*. Is there another following this one? I would love to know how Sarah Macintosh finishes up!'

'I would like to congratulate you for taking on the telling of Australia's history through fiction . . . I have never contacted an author before but couldn't resist this time! Thank you so much and good luck with future writings.'

'Just finished it, excellent as always and not long enough as always. Waiting anxiously for the next one.'

'Mate, you are truly like a good bottle of red – the older you get the better you get . . . Mate, not ever being in the military, my stomach and heart turn over with what our boys had to endure in their service to this wonderful country of ours. Always waiting impatiently for the next edition of the Macintosh and Duffy historical journey; absolutely love your books.'

'Just to let you know I have read and enjoyed all your books . . . can't wait for the follow-up to *While the Moon Burns*.'

'Have just finished reading *While the Moon Burns* and again was totally enthralled with the Duffy/Macintosh saga. Everything here just had to wait – couldn't put the book down!!! So my pet rabbit, my Persian cat, chooks (who conveniently kept laying eggs) and dog just HAD to be patient. I love the storyline including the Aussies in the Pacific and can't wait for Sarah to get what's coming to her!'

'A really great series, thanks mate. I have loved them all so far and will continue to the end.'

'Pete, I just re-read *And Fire Falls, Beneath a Rising Sun* and then your latest, *While the Moon Burns*. It is fantastic how you interweave facts and fiction. You know, I'm the first genera-tion in my family that has not experienced war . . . One cannot imagine the suffering the boys went through at a young age. You describe that so well; every now and then I had tears in my eyes . . . Anyway, thanks for the wonderful stories . . . can't wait until the next book lies under the Christmas tree!!!'

'I so love the Duffy/Macintosh saga. You give me a closeness to my late father with your writing of the Pacific at war. Thank you again for *While the Moon Burns*. I thoroughly loved it.'

PETER WATT

From THE Stars Above

PAN
Pan Macmillan Australia

First published 2017 in Macmillan by Pan Macmillan Australia Pty Ltd
This Pan edition published in 2018 by Pan Macmillan Australia Pty Ltd
1 Market Street, Sydney, New South Wales, Australia, 2000

Cataloguing-in-Publication entry is available
from the National Library of Australia
http://catalogue.nla.gov.au

Typeset in 13/16 pt Bembo by Post Pre-press Group
Printed by McPherson's Printing Group

For my beloved wife, Naomi.

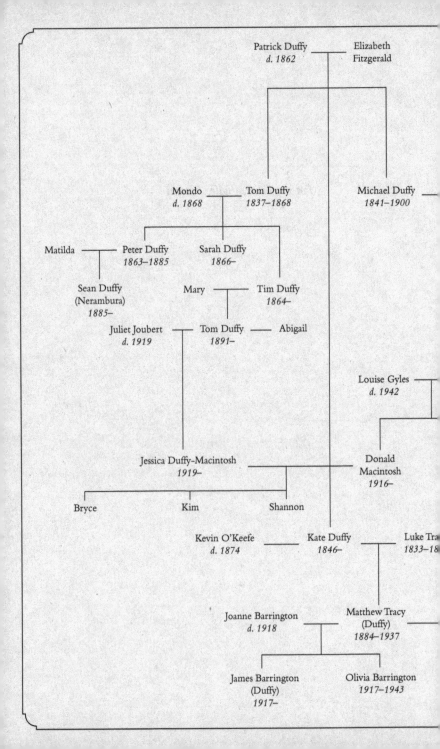

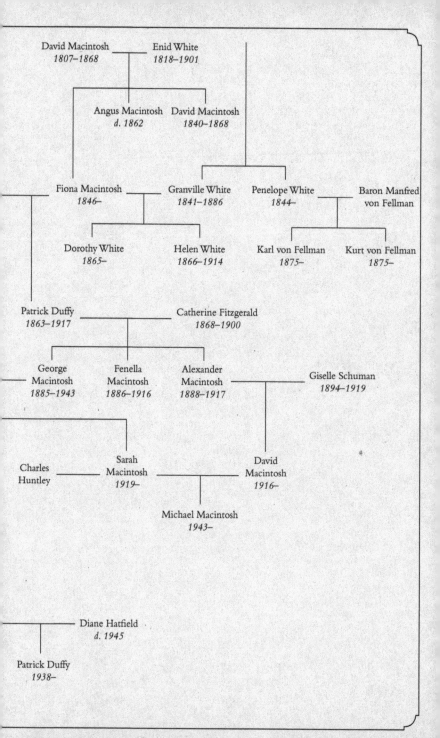

PROLOGUE

Central Queensland, Australia

My name is Wallarie and I am a Darambal man. It has been many generations since the whitefellas came to my lands and killed my people in the shadow of our sacred cave. I do not hate the whitefellas because one was my brother, and when we were young we roamed the colony of Queensland as free men.

But we are all now gone to the sky an' can only watch over those who have come after us. Some of the whitefellas have my blood. Jessica Duffy and her children carry my blood. Jessica is an old woman now, but she never forget ol' Wallarie. She tell the stories of her ancestors – and me – to her children an' grandchildren an' great-grandchildren. But they do not listen and soon I will be forgotten. They will not hear my voice on the wind in the brigalow scrub or see me floating above them on the wings of the great wedge-tailed eagle who is my totem brother.

Whitefella war has always bin in the blood of the Duffy and Macintosh families. Even now some of them are fighting in wars that the whitefella will one day forget.

I am almost gone from your world, my bones lie in the red earth of my traditional lands – as do those of many who came after me, both whitefellas and blackfellas. Very few of them lived as long as I did on the earth.

So, before you also forget me, I will continue telling you the story of two families.

One family called the Duffys and the other the Macintoshes.

But you get me some baccy first, before I sit with you under the ol' bumbil tree an' continue their story.

Part One

The Malayan Emergency

1958

ONE

The two soldiers dressed in jungle-green field uniform lay side by side behind their self-loading rifles. Gone were the Lee Enfield bolt-action .303 rifles of past conflicts; the new Belgium-designed FN SLR with its 20 round magazine was now issued to Aussie soldiers.

Neither man spoke or moved as together they covered a clearing in front of a Chinese settlement. They had been on watch since midnight the previous evening; it was now near midday and the tropical sun blazed down on the carefully camouflaged Australian troops. The two men were not alone: other members of the platoon were hidden not far away in the line of heavy rainforest opposite the settlement houses.

For Private Patrick Duffy, the landscape was familiar as he had spent his very young days growing up in Malaya, until he and his mother had been forced to flee in the face of the advancing Japanese army. Patrick had been able to reach Australia, but his mother had died in Changi prison on the last day of the Pacific war.

The soldier beside Patrick was Aboriginal. Terituba had grown up alongside Patrick on Glen View cattle station in central Queensland. They were as close as brothers could be and had enlisted in the Australian Army together two years earlier. Terituba was accepted by his fellow soldiers for his uncanny tracking abilities and quick sense of humour, while Patrick was a natural leader despite his lowly military rank.

Sweat trickled down the faces of the two men and both were fighting the urge to drink water from their canteens because that would involve movement. The strict rules of ambush meant absolute self-discipline.

'The boss has ordered us out,' said a quiet voice from behind them.

'Okay, sarge,' Patrick answered.

'Is there something dead near here?' the sergeant asked, wrinkling his nose at the putrid smell.

'Bloody whitefella smell,' Terituba said in disgust. 'Bloody Pat bin eating a curry last night and bin making that smell all the time we bin here.' Patrick had acquired a taste for Malaya's spicy and exotic curries.

The platoon sergeant glanced at Patrick, who was attempting to smother his laughter. 'Sorry, sarge,' he said.

'No sense apologising to me, Private Duffy. You should be apologising to Terituba. Poor bastard, having to put up with that for the last twelve hours.'

Both soldiers eased themselves to their feet, their muscles stiff from lying prone for most of the ambush. Cautiously, they made their way through the thick scrub to rejoin the rest of the platoon crouching in a circle around the platoon commander, Lieutenant Stan Gauden.

'Gentlemen,' he said quietly, 'the intelligence on our target seems to be incorrect. Comrade Sam did not enter our killing ground. Maybe next time.'

The men understood. This counterinsurgency war was a matter of patience and luck. The Communist terrorists – CTs as they were known – had been decimated by military and police operations in the years since 1950. Now only a handful of very dangerous leaders remained at large – to be killed or captured. No one underestimated the very experienced guerrilla fighters who were mainly of Chinese nationality. It was a strange war – more like a police action. But it was a war where soldiers under British command died in short, sharp skirmishes in the mountains and jungles of the former British colony.

The platoon boarded trucks waiting for them on a rutted dirt road an hour's march away. They had been fortunate that the operation had only lasted overnight; now they could return to a hot meal and showers back in their barracks, which had once been home to a sultan's harem. The harem was long gone now, but after the long night all the Australian soldiers cared about was standing down and enjoying the luxuries of good food and sleep.

*

The two men sitting opposite each other in the coolness of the lounge of the Raffles Hotel in Singapore were very much opposites. One was slightly built and short, the other tall and broad-shouldered. Both men were in their early forties and wearing civilian tropical dress of white slacks and shirt. They were drinking gin and tonic, surrounded by the trappings of colonial Britain in the sumptuous hotel.

'I am sorry to hear that your marriage did not work out,' the smaller man said, sipping his drink.

'I guess life in the army is not all that conducive to being in a marriage, Sir Rupert.' Major Karl Mann shrugged.

'Well, old chap, it is good to see you again after such a long time,' Sir Rupert Featherstone said. 'I think the last time was when you were here back in '47, collecting intelligence on the Malayan Communist Party. You and I came to the right conclusion when we said they would emerge as a threat to the country, but that information seemed to be put on file until it was too late. I propose a toast to us working together again.' He tipped his glass in a salute.

'Last time we worked together you almost got me killed,' Karl answered with a wry smile. 'I heard a rumour that you are now a bigwig with MI6.'

Featherstone shrugged. 'I have been sent out here to the Emergency. The Foreign Office has decided to call it an emergency rather than a war to play down the situation. I was able to track you down and have you seconded to us for sensitive operations with your colonial comrades.'

'And I am truly grateful that you saved me from a desk job in Canberra. I was starting to worry about getting paper cuts filing documents.'

'What do you know about the situation up north?' Featherstone asked, leaning forward.

'What I know is that some of our former allies in the Malayan National Liberation Army are now our enemies. They want to throw you Poms out of Malaya and install a Communist-style government. The armed insurgency is mostly dominated by local Chinese, with a few Indians and Malays in their ranks. They rely on the goodwill of other ethnic Chinese to supply them with provisions and intelligence in rural villages. Since confronting the insurgency in the early 50s, we have been able to decimate their ranks, and now it is just a matter of mopping up.'

Featherstone nodded. 'Britain has granted Malaya its independence, but this still leaves the Communists' aspirations to establish a Communist government. Chairman Mao has been a great inspiration to their cause, but our intelligence suggests that he has not given much logistical support to them. I will be appointing you as a liaison officer with the local police working alongside your colonial comrades around the Perak and Kedah districts. The 3rd battalion have that as its area of operations, and our intelligence indicates that one of the most dangerous leaders operating there is a young Eurasian man we know as Comrade Sam. It is rumoured that he fired the shots that killed Sir Henry Gurney back in '51, and in order to deliver a decisive blow to the CTs we must capture or kill him. If anyone can do that, I think you can.'

'I am at a disadvantage as I don't speak Chinese,' Karl said. 'At least in the Middle East I was able to speak the language of our enemies.'

Featherstone had had Karl reassigned to him from his duties as an infantry platoon commander during the Allied force's Syrian Campaign against the Vichy French. Ironically, Karl had faced the same enemies his father had fought against as an officer in the Imperial German Army. Karl had been born in Germany but had grown up in New Guinea and had adopted Australia as the country he was loyal to. With the help of a former Australian Army officer, Jack Kelly, Karl had been able to convince the officers board that he was not an enemy alien.

'We do have interpreters,' Featherstone said, 'but we need to recruit more to assist with interrogations of the surrendering enemy. It appears our strategy of isolating the Chinese population in the new settlements is working. We are cutting off the CTs from their main sources of supply.'

'I'll take the job,' Karl said. 'I presume that you have already completed the paperwork.'

'All is in place, old chap,' Sir Rupert replied. 'You will be on a transport aircraft tomorrow to fly north. Now that's out of the way, it will be my pleasure to buy you lunch.'

Karl raised his gin and tonic in a toast. 'Chin-chin, Sir Rupert,' he said with an affected upper-class English accent.

*

He was a head taller and much heavier than Patrick as they faced off in the long barracks room. Patrick had sensed the confrontation was coming from the moment the two men had first met in training back at Holsworthy camp in Australia. For some reason the large private had taken a dislike to Patrick and Terituba.

'What's up your arse?' Patrick growled, inches from his adversary's face.

'I think you and the blackfella are pooftas,' said Private Ted Morrow. 'We never see you apart. Next thing you'll be holding hands.'

The other members of the platoon fell silent; the only noise was the whirring of the overhead fans.

'I hear you went to a fancy school and got your leaving certificate,' Morrow said. 'So what are you doing here with us? I suppose you couldn't bear to be apart from your black bum-buddy.'

Patrick's sudden punch came hard and fast. Morrow's eyes bulged and he buckled as the air was forced from his lungs. He went down on one knee and Patrick unleashed a rapid barrage of punches to his head, flooring him.

'Attention!' one of the men called. Patrick's timing could not have been worse.

'What is going on here?' the angry voice of the platoon's commander shouted down the barracks room. 'Why aren't you men standing by your beds for inspection?' His eyes settled on Private Morrow, curled into a ball on the shiny floor, Patrick standing over him, nursing his bruised fists.

Lieutenant Gauden marched towards the two men with the platoon sergeant trailing behind him. 'What is going on here? Are you two men fighting?'

Patrick was standing to attention; Morrow struggled to his feet and also attempted to stand to attention. Neither man replied.

'I asked a question, Private Duffy,' Lieutenant Gauden said in a cold voice. 'If you do not reply I will have you charged with conduct to the prejudice of good order and discipline. The same with you, Private Morrow.'

Still neither man answered, and the platoon commander turned to his sergeant. 'Have both of these men charged, sergeant. I want them paraded before the CO today, as we will be going out on ops tomorrow.'

'Yes, sir,' the sergeant replied, glowering at the two offenders. The members of the platoon remained silent and fell in beside their beds for the morning inspection. Patrick and Morrow followed suit. Morrow was dripping blood from his nose and was ordered to present himself at the battalion regimental aid post to have his injury seen to.

When the inspection was over, the platoon commander called to Patrick to fall out and report to him outside the barracks.

'Private Duffy,' said Lieutenant Gauden, 'I am disappointed in you. Until now you have had a spotless service record, and I was on the verge of recommending you for your first stripe in Corporal Hastings's section. Instead I should be recommending the serious charge of assault.

We are a tight-knit platoon and I cannot afford to have any ill feeling in the ranks. As you know, field punishment on active service can be very harsh.'

'Yes, sir.' Patrick knew that the sometimes brutal field punishment was far worse than imprisonment. He cursed himself for his hot-tempered reaction.

'Report to BHQ at 1400 hours, Private Duffy. You are dismissed.'

Patrick saluted his officer and returned to the barracks. He would have to put on his best uniform for the parade before the battalion's commanding officer.

'What did the boss want to see you for?' Terituba asked.

'Nothing much,' Patrick replied. 'Just that I have to be at BHQ this afternoon.'

'Bloody wrong you get charged when Morrow start it,' Terituba said in disgust. 'You sure got him a good one but.'

'Yeah, all those hours in Harry's gym paid off,' Patrick said, sitting carefully on the end of his bed so that the bedcover was not wrinkled. 'I'm just sorry that Uncle David will hear about me copping a charge. He served with the battalion in Korea and got a gong for his part at Kapyong.'

'Not your fault, Pat. That bastard Morrow caused this.'

At 2 pm Patrick presented himself to the orderly room of the battalion headquarters where he was escorted by two soldiers and the regimental sergeant major into the CO's office. He was commanded to salute and remove his head-dress. Standing to attention, Patrick stared straight ahead over the sitting senior officer's head.

'Private Duffy,' the CO said after the charge was read out, 'I am disappointed in your behaviour. I have reports of your leadership amongst the diggers of your platoon, and with your education I have always been mystified as to why you did not apply for officer training at Duntroon.'

'Sir, I always promised my cobber, Private Terituba Duffy, that we would enlist together and stick together in the army.'

'He has the same family name as you, I see,' the commanding officer said. 'Are you related?'

'Yes and no, sir,' Patrick replied. 'We grew up together on a cattle station in Queensland and he has always been my best mate. Terituba adopted my family name and my Aunt Jess and Uncle Donald formalised it for him so that he could enlist.'

The CO reflected on Patrick's explanation and nodded. 'Then I can see how you would consider him a brother. I have been informed that the stoush was provoked by Private Morrow, and I think if I had been in your boots I would have reacted in the same way. I am going to drop this charge on the provision that you and Morrow settle your argument for the sake of good order and discipline within the unit. You are dismissed.'

Patrick quickly replaced his headgear, snapped his best salute and, under barked orders from the RSM, about-turned and marched out of the office.

On the verandah of BHQ, Patrick breathed a deep sigh of relief.

'I'll be watching you, Private Duffy – and your brother.'

For a second Patrick swore he saw the hint of a smile on the most senior non-commissioned officer's face. But that was not possible: RSMs were selected because they had been born without a sense of humour.

Outside the barracks, Patrick was greeted by the grim-faced members of his section.

'What's the sentence, Pat?' one of the members asked.

'Not guilty,' Patrick grinned. 'I'll be going out with the platoon tomorrow.'

'You beauty!' a couple of men chorused, and there was much back-slapping. Getting off a charge was next to impossible – but somehow Patrick had done it.

'The boss must have told the CO about that bastard Morrow calling you a poofta,' Terituba said.

'Who told the boss what happened?' Patrick asked in surprise.

'All the platoon lined up and marched down to Gauden's office an' told 'im,' Terituba said. 'He went an' saw the CO.'

'Thanks, fellas,' Patrick said.

That night the platoon was assembled for a briefing on the next operation. This time they would be out for at least a week patrolling, gathering intelligence and laying ambushes – the bread and butter of counterinsurgency warfare.

TWO

He was struggling, entangled in barbed wire, shrapnel tearing at his uniform as he attempted to untangle himself.

David Macintosh woke up screaming and slowly realised he was in the bedroom of his cottage overlooking the Tasman Sea in northern New South Wales. He was aware that he was not alone; a woman was standing in the doorway.

'I heard you screaming when I arrived early this morning and thought that you were in trouble,' Gail Glanville said as she moved towards David.

'Just a memory of Africa,' David said, sitting up. 'It happens when the dreams come, and nowadays I'm not sure which war I'm in.'

Gail knew that David had fought in the Spanish Civil War, the Middle East and North Africa, as well as in New

Guinea and Korea where shrapnel damage to his leg had resulted in him living with a walking stick. They had met seven years ago when he returned from the Korean War, and in all that time he had not made a pass at her. She was a widow with a teenage son, Craig, who had come to think of David as his father. Gail knew that she was attractive to men and had always wondered why David had not seen that, as she had come to love this quiet man who mostly kept to himself.

In the small community where they lived, he had proven to be generous to those in need and was highly respected. David sometimes drank at the local pub and former veterans gravitated to him; he was at home in their company. On the nights Gail had accompanied him, she would sit with the other women in the hotel's saloon bar. Her friends would be forever questioning her about her relationship with the tall, broad-shouldered and ruggedly handsome man she was so often seen with in public. Her reply was always the same: they were neighbours and good friends – nothing more. And that was the truth, although she wished it were not. Why couldn't David see how she felt about him?

David swung his feet over the single bed. He was wearing boxer shorts and at the sight of his muscled body Gail felt a yearning to have him hold her. She looked away as he slipped on shorts and an old army shirt with its sleeves cut out. Outside the sun shone in the subtropical skies and a gentle breeze stirred the tops of the banana trees near the cottage's tank stand.

'I can make us breakfast,' Gail suggested.

'That would be nice.' David followed her to his tiny kitchen where she stoked the cast-iron wood combustion stove. David sat down at the table, forcing the vivid memory of the nightmare from his mind. He had even given up his desire to create art in paintings and drank more often.

When the fire was lit and the stove began to heat up, Gail took out a frying pan, some eggs from the kerosene-powered refrigerator and loose tea leaves from a tin on a sideboard.

'I brought the local paper for you to read,' Gail said, unfolding the paper to reveal the headlines.

David glanced at the front page and a black-and-white photo of a familiar young man stared back at him. *WAR HERO STANDS FOR FEDERAL PARLIAMENT IN BY-ELECTION.* The article explained that former lieutenant Angus Markham was the son of a prominent federal politician who had served with distinction in the coalition parliament during the war.

'That gutless bastard!' David snarled. 'I should have had him court-martialled.'

'So it is the same man,' Gail said. 'The one you once told me was responsible for you losing your commission.'

'That's him, and he was no bloody hero. He was a down-right coward who almost got his men killed.'

'Now that my father-in-law is vacating his seat for the district, he thinks you should stand against Markham,' Gail said.

David knew John Glanville; the two men, introduced by Gail, had formed a soldier's bond. John had served in the Great War as a company commander with the infantry. Often they talked politics when John was not in Canberra, and David always listened with interest. He had once raised the issue of having lost his commission because of the influence of Markham's father in response to David having his son returned to Australia for an act of cowardice during the war in northern New Guinea. John Glanville had also informed David that the federal politician had made a small fortune profiting from the war and was not even respected by members of his own party.

'I don't have any experience in politics,' David said.

'John will be your mentor.' Gail said. 'He has enough influence in the party to have you nominated as the candidate for his old seat when he retires. I think you should seriously consider his offer. At least go and see him.'

David sat staring at the photo of the man who had been responsible for stripping him of his commission. Eventually he glanced up at Gail hovering at the end of the table. 'I will do it,' he said. 'From what I have seen, even a used-car salesman could get a seat in parliament these days.'

*

John Glanville's house reflected his status in the community. It was a sprawling brick house atop a manicured hill, surrounded by a white-painted fence, and it had a view over rolling green fields and the ocean a few miles away.

David drove his old Model T Ford up the fine gravel driveway to the house and was met outside by John – a big, burly man with a ruddy complexion and balding head. He was in his early sixties but walked with the step of a much younger man.

'Hello, Dave,' he greeted.

'John,' David responded, stepping from his old 1920s sedan.

'Why don't you get a new car?' John asked, staring at the Model T held together with wire.

'Maybe if I get into politics I might be able to afford a new car – or do they give you one for nothing?'

John Glanville broke into a smile and, gesturing for

David to follow him inside, called out, 'Nancy, put on the billy and break out the scones.'

John's wife appeared, wiping her hands on her apron. 'I made those scones for the CWA meeting this afternoon, so you can only have a couple of them. Hello, David.'

'Damned woman,' John growled softly when his wife disappeared back into the kitchen. 'She's trying to starve me to death since the doctor told her I was due for a heart attack and should lose weight and quit working. Take a seat.'

David sat down on a lounge next to the radio in its ornate timber cabinet.

'One day television is going to dominate the living room and politicians will no longer be simply a voice but also a face. Dave, you have the kind of face that inspires confidence.'

'So that's all it takes, hey? Easier than I thought,' David grinned.

'Well, there is a bit more to being a politician,' John said, easing himself back into a big leather chair. 'Gail has already informed me that you and Angus Markham have a bit of history.'

'The bastard was one of my platoon commanders when we were fighting up around Wewak. He panicked in front of his men, and when I found out I had him shipped back to Australia.'

'In my day on the Western Front I would have just shot him,' John said. 'It's different if a soldier panics, but it cannot be allowed for a commander. It's just too dangerous.'

David was quite sure that the big man sitting opposite would have carried out that kind of punishment. 'You do know that I am a Jew,' David said. 'There is a bias against us even in Australia.'

'The finest officer on the Western Front was General John Monash,' John said as Nancy brought a tray with a teapot, small jug of milk, container of sugar – and just two scones adorned with rosella jam.

'David, the scones are for you,' Nancy said sweetly, and departed the living room to go to her Country Women's Association meeting.

John leaned over and took a scone. 'As I was saying, Monash should have been commander of all Allied forces on the Western Front, but he had four things against him. He was of German heritage, a Jew, colonial and not even a regular officer – he was from the militia. Even Churchill supported him, but men like war correspondent Bean opposed his promotion. Bean was a good chap but a bit short-sighted about Monash. Anyway, enough of memories of other wars, I already knew that you were Jewish.'

'How will that go down in a conservative party?' David asked.

'Well, we even have a few Roman Catholics in the ranks these days.' John shrugged, wiping away a few scone crumbs from his ample stomach. 'And we have been swamped with immigrants from Europe – no doubt one or two Jews have come over with them.'

'Okay, how about the fact I fought in the Spanish Civil War with a Communist International Brigade?' David said.

'Were you a Communist?' John asked, leaning forward.

'No. I had been thrown into Dachau and was full of hatred for the Fascists. I was just young and stupid.'

'Good enough,' John said, leaning back in his chair. 'You will attend our next local party meeting, sign up and give a rousing speech as to why you wish to stand for election as a Country Party representative. Just don't mention you are out to sabotage Markham's plans.'

David sipped his tea and the talk turned from politics to soldiering. Both agreed that what Australia was doing in Malay would prevent the dominoes falling in South-East Asia. If the country fell to Communism it was possible the dominoes would continue to fall right up to the coast of Australia.

Eventually it was time for David to return to his small macadamia plantation. He rose and John thrust out his hand. David felt its strength: it was the hand of a farmer before that of a politician.

'You know I also have another good reason to nominate you as my replacement,' John said.

'What is that?'

'My grandson,' John said. 'Since the death of my son – who should never have been a soldier – I have seen how Craig has taken to you, and in return how you have guided him with care and wisdom. You have become like a father to him, and for that I thank you. I am surprised that my daughter-in-law has not made a play for you. I know that she loves you. You have to admit she is a beautiful woman, and I also know every single man in the district would give anything to have her. But she only has eyes for you. Do you prefer men?'

'Definitely not,' David replied. 'It's just that every woman I have loved has had a tragic end. Maybe I'm cursed. I swore a long time ago I would not allow another woman into my life for that reason.'

'Do you have feelings for Gail?' the former politician asked bluntly.

David did not answer but released his grip and walked away. Did he have feelings for Gail? He knew the answer to that question.

★

Michael Macintosh, son of Sarah Macintosh and Charles Huntley, was at that awkward age when he was no longer a boy but yet to become a man. He stood staring vacantly across a land of scrubby trees stretching as far as the eye could see. The sun was a red ball on the horizon and this time of day brought a kind of serenity to the vast and ancient plains of central Queensland. Soon the stars would appear in a countless blaze from horizon to horizon and the sound of the nocturnal birds and animals would fill the night. Glen View Station would be an oasis in the endless plains of scrub and red earth. Michael was on holidays at Glen View, but he felt down. His old mates, Patrick and Terituba, were in Malaya fighting a war Michael's friends hardly knew about. Patrick occasionally sent him letters filled with their escapades as soldiers in a foreign land. He had shown the letters to his friends at his expensive private school but they had little interest in the lives of private soldiers. Their eyes were on the world of banking and finance.

Michael felt very much alone as he stared across the scrub at the setting sun.

Behind him was the ever-expanding Glen View homestead. A packed-earth road brought wheeled vehicles to the property these days, and a telephone line brought instant messages to this remote part of the country. There was even electricity provided by a bank of batteries powered by a windmill, and a big radio in the living room.

'Are you coming in for dinner? called his Aunt Jessie from the verandah.

'Yes, Aunt Jessie,' Michael replied and dawdled back to the homestead with his hands in his pockets. Over the years of travelling to Glen View at his father's insistence, Michael had grown very fond of his Uncle Donald and Aunt Jessica. He had grown used to his Uncle Donald's badly scarred face, which he knew was an injury from the war. Their kids were younger than Michael, and although he was fond of them, he did not have the same bond with them as he had with Patrick and Terituba. As it was, this would be his last visit to Glen View for a long time as his mother had organised for him to be sent to England to finish his schooling at one of the prestigious private schools there. She had told him this was his opportunity to make contacts with the rich and powerful families of the Old Country. As he was highly intelligent and good-looking with a quiet charm, she felt that he would fit in and establish bonds with some important families. Michael was not so sure.

'What's on your mind, Michael?' Jessica asked when she saw the expression on the young man's face.

'I was just thinking how much fun it used to be when Pat, Terituba and I would go out in the bush to hunt for goannas with spears. That seems a lifetime ago now,' he sighed.

'It was only about five years ago,' Jessie smiled. 'Time is different when you grow older. It just seems to fly.'

Michael looked at her and she could see that he was struggling with something.

'Why does my mother hate you so much?' he blurted.

'It's a long story,' Jessica replied quietly. 'The land you stand on now is sacred to both her and me. Many of your ancestors are buried here in the little cemetery – and so are many of mine. Around the time you were born, your uncles Donald and David voted that the property be sold to my father, Tom Duffy. Your mother was enraged by the sale, and my father gave his life defending his right to own this land.'

'I didn't know that,' Michael said. 'My mother has never mentioned it.'

'I suspect that your mother has not told you a lot of things, but all the ill will between your mother and me has nothing to do with you. Your father is a fine man and understands that you need to know your extended family. You are your own person.'

'I have to return home on Thursday,' Michael said. 'Do you think I could ride out to the hill tomorrow?'

'I can't see why not,' Jessica replied. 'I will pack you some sandwiches to take with you, but be back by nightfall. It is easy to get lost out there.'

The following morning Michael saddled a horse, packed the sandwiches and canteens of water. He rode in the direction of the sacred hill and reached it just on midday. He dismounted, tethering his horse to a scrubby tree, retrieved his wrapped sandwiches, a canteen of water and a torch and proceeded to climb the well-worn trail to the top. In all the times he had visited Glen View for his holidays he had never been to the mysterious hill. Whenever he had asked Patrick and Terituba to take him there they had always refused. Terituba had simply said it was a *baal* place haunted by ghosts of the old ones killed many years earlier by the Native Mounted Police. Michael did not believe in ghosts and saw only an ancient volcanic plug eroded over millions of years.

He struggled up the old trail under a fireball in the sky, sweating as he went and sipping from his water canteen. Eventually he reached the top where a great flat panorama of red earth and spindly scrub revealed itself to him. He sat down under the tiny sliver of shade provided by an overhang of rock and opened the beef and chutney sandwiches. He devoured them and sighed with contentment. A great wedge-tailed eagle drifted overhead on the thermals and Michael gazed at its majestic flight.

Eventually he stood up to go in search of a cave he had been told was on the hill. He quickly found the entrance beside a gnarled old tree. Michael flicked on the torch, shining its beam into the dark opening. It bounced off internal walls of rock, and he stepped inside to see what the cave held. Very few on Glen View talked about the cave on the hill and Michael was curious to see why.

Inside it was cooler. The cave had a musty smell he recognised as coming from ancient, charred wood. At the centre of the cave he could see a place that had been used to light fires. When he directed the light beam to the walls, a mosaic of Aboriginal drawings revealed itself: stick figures in ancient hunts of giant kangaroos and other creatures he did not recognise. One stick figure with a raised spear caught his attention as it seemed to be desecrated by a sharp instrument. The white warrior fascinated him and he did not know why.

Suddenly the hairs on the back of Michael's neck rose. He felt that he was not alone and that someone was standing behind him. He had never experienced such intense fear before and he stood frozen to the spot. He fought to reassure himself that it was his imagination. If he turned around the fear would go away. With every ounce of his physical and mental strength, Michael forced his attention to the entrance of the cave, and there he saw the outline of a wedge-tailed eagle staring at him. His scream echoed around the cave wall and the giant eagle hopped away to take flight.

Michael could feel his heart beating like a hammer in his chest and his legs were so weak he slumped to his knees. In his mind he was trying to convince himself that the event was natural. But then a voice came to him: *Why are you here, Michael Macintosh?* It had to be his own thoughts, Michael told himself, and rose unsteadily to his feet. The circle of daylight beckoned to him from the entrance.

A second wave of fear suddenly swamped him. Again, he was not alone. He swung around and saw the hazy figure of an old Aboriginal man standing at the back of the cave. He was armed with a long spear and wooden clubs tucked into the string band around his waist.

Michael bolted from the cave into the reassuring sunlight, his heart beating violently in his chest. He ran and stumbled down the trail until he reached his mount grazing on the desiccated native grasses.

Michael untethered the reins and swung into the saddle, urging his horse into a canter until he was satisfied that the hill was well behind him. He reached the Glen View homestead just before last light, the events in the cave still ringing in his mind.

When he finished unsaddling and rubbing his horse, he made his way from the stables to the lights of the house. Jessica was in the kitchen preparing a beef stew on the big cast-iron combustion stove.

'Hello, Michael,' she greeted. 'Did you have a good day?'

Michael did not know how to answer. How could he tell his aunt that he'd seen an apparition?

'Did you visit the sacred cave?' Jessie asked, seeing how pale Michael looked.

He nodded and slumped into a chair in the kitchen. 'I think I saw a ghost in the cave,' he said finally.

Jessica wiped her flour-covered hands on her apron and sat down at the wooden table opposite Michael. 'Was he an Aboriginal man with a grey beard, and armed with a long spear?'

He looked up at his aunt in surprise. 'How did you know that?'

'Because if you were in the cave it was probably Wallarie,' she answered with a gentle smile. 'You are fortunate because it has been such a long time since anyone has seen him.'

'Is Wallarie that man my mother sometimes mentions?' Michael asked in an awed voice. 'I have heard her say he haunts our family.'

'Wallarie is the spirit of these plains,' Jessica answered. 'He protects us, and sometimes we see him when the big eagles fly above Glen View. For him to appear to you is a good sign because it means he will always protect you.'

Despite what he had seen with his own eyes, Michael still found it hard to believe what Jessie was saying. And yet . . .

That night Michael's dreams were haunted by the spectre of an ancient Aboriginal warrior. The following day he left Glen View Station for the next stage of his life in England, where wedge-tailed eagles did not soar in the low grey skies.

THREE

Under the canopy of the rainforest giants on the Thai-Malay border, a group of six men armed with a motley collection of small arms sat in a semicircle facing a young man standing before them. Sam Po was their leader and legendary for having assassinated the high commissioner of British Malaya. Sam Po was of Eurasian heritage but identified as Chinese. He was a good-looking young man, but close inspection revealed a cruel darkness in his eyes. For years he had led raiding parties, executing Malay police and government officials in remote kampongs. His fanatic dedication to the Communist cause was not disputed amongst his small band of followers, and he had sworn that he would never be taken alive.

The dim light filtering through the jungle canopy in the rugged hills of the border region hid the despairing looks of one or two of the Communist guerrillas. Their lives had been hell as they were pursued by the Australian troops and their allies in the district assigned to Sam Po. Short on food and medical supplies, they had seen their number reduced by typhus and malaria, and those remaining were secretly considering the generous terms of the amnesty offered by their enemy.

'We are not beaten,' Sam said in a strong voice. 'The British have deployed an army to hunt us, and yet we have been able to strike at the place and time of our choosing. Under the leadership of Comrade Chin Peng we will prevail, just as the Vietnamese have prevailed against the French and just as Mao has prevailed against the American-backed imperialist forces. We will prevail and you will be remembered as heroes of the struggle.'

His speech did not seem to inspire his group, and he glared at them.

'Comrade Tek, I have an important mission for you,' he said, looking directly at one of the men sitting before him. 'You are to travel to Kuala Lumpur to deliver a message to our party members there. I will brief you on the contents of the message after we have eaten, and you will be issued with supplies for the difficult trip south.'

The young Chinese man nodded his head without looking at Sam. Comrade Tek had come to the end of his tether with the cause and had been considering desertion. Now Sam had given him the opportunity. He would surrender himself to the British and be paid generously to do so. He'd get more if he could also hand over a weapon. Even more valuable still was the information he had about the whereabouts of Britain's enemy on the Thai border.

Sam took his handful of cooked rice seasoned with curry powder and sat with his back against the trunk of a forest giant, his Sten submachine gun across his lap. He ate slowly, savouring every grain of rice in his meagre meal, and thought about the only woman he had ever loved. She had been four years older than he, and the daughter of the merchant who had taken him in from a life of begging on the streets. The girl had been a nurse and a committed member of the Malayan Communist Party. The Malay police had captured her with compromising documents when she had been a courier between the armed fighters in the jungles and the party cadre in the cities. In captivity she had taken her own life, and Sam had never forgiven his enemy for what he perceived as her murder. It helped to drive him through the torrential rain, humidity and harsh conditions in the field over the long years of leading his band of guerrilla fighters. So long as he had a heartbeat he would fight for the cause, and to avenge her death.

*

Almost four thousand miles south in the Australian city of Sydney, a detective sergeant sat at his desk staring at a battered folder. Detective Senior Constable Brendan Wren had finally been granted status after his plainclothes service under the notoriously corrupt Detective Inspector Lionel Preston who had recently retired to his coastal home north of Sydney. Preston had been an arrogant pig of a man, and the source of his wealth was no secret to those who worked for him. Preston had always singled out Brendan for ridicule and made his life miserable. But he was now gone, and the detective had recovered the file that had haunted him for all those years since he had been a newly appointed uniformed constable, investigating a hit-and-run on the night Australia celebrated the end of the Pacific war.

Preston had forced Brendan to drop his investigations into the death of a Miss Allison Lowe when the eager young constable had tracked the offending vehicle to the Macintosh Enterprises. Brendan had joined the force believing all were equal before the law, but that day Preston had taught him a lesson: those in high places were beyond justice.

'What you got there, Brendan?' asked a fellow detective constable, leaning over his shoulder.

'Just a case I had when I first got into the job,' Brendan answered, pushing the file into the top drawer of his desk.

'Anything in it?' asked Detective Constable Mick Prowse.

'Not a real lot,' Brendan answered, closing the drawer, picking up his hat and rising from behind his desk. 'Nothing I can act on. Come on, there are a couple of break and enters we have to go out and check on.'

Brendan kept to himself that he intended to eventually solve the case, and by doing so he'd reveal his old mentor, Detective Inspector Preston; the well-known underworld figure, William Price; and the head of a financial empire, Sarah Macintosh, as an unholy trinity. He intended to have them brought before a court on charges of conspiracy to murder, and murder.

Brendan and his partner stepped out onto the busy streets of the inner city. One of the break and enters had been on a deserted boxing gym belonging to someone Brendan knew, Harry Griffiths. It was not of great importance as whoever had broken in had just carried out acts of vandalism, but it was an excuse for Brendan to contact the man who had once been a good friend of his policeman father and who had ears and eyes throughout the city's underbelly.

After a short walk along the busy streets filled with cars and trams, the two police officers came to a building marked for demolition. It was to make way for a multi-storey building in this prosperous city that had been booming in the years following the war. Brendan knew that Harry Griffiths still lived in his small rooms above what had once been a popular boxing gym. But many of its star fighters had gone to war and not returned. Boxing was losing its appeal amongst the new generation of young men who found themselves in full-time work and too busy to fit lives around the long hours and tough programmes Harry insisted his pupils follow. He was now a war pensioner, occasionally working for his old friend Sean Duffy to supplement his pension.

Brendan pushed aside the front door barely hanging from its hinges and entered the musty-smelling building. Pigeons scattered in flight from the rafters above a raised dais that had once held a boxing ring.

'Harry, you here?' Brendan called, and his voice echoed around the empty building.

'Who's that?' a distant voice responded.

'Detective Senior Constable Brendan Wren, Harry. I met you a few years back. You used to work with my dad before the Great War.'

Harry appeared wearing a singlet and old trousers held up with braces. He had not shaved in days and his eyes were rheumy, probably from a heavy night of drinking, Brendan thought. Harry had once been a big and powerfully built man, but now he looked old and shrunken. He made his way down the rickety stairs to stand before Brendan and his partner. For a moment he squinted at them, but then he broke into a slow smile, extending his hand in the process.

'Bloody hell, it has been years,' Harry said. 'How are you, young fella? How's your dad?'

'Sad to say the old man died a few years back,' Brendan replied, realising with surprise how powerful the older man's grip was. 'We got the message that you had a break-in last night.'

Harry glanced around at his gym. 'Not much in it – except they took a few old photos of my former fighters that were still hanging on the wall. They don't have much value other than sentimental. I just wanted to report the matter in case any of the photos ever turned up. Probably only knocked them off for the frames they were in.'

Harry described the photos and Brendan's partner duly took down their descriptions. When they were finished, Brendan turned to his partner. 'Mick, duck across the street to the cafe and order us a couple of sandwiches. I'll catch up with you.'

'Harry,' Brendan began when Mick had left, 'do you remember a young woman called Allison Lowe who was killed on VJ Night?'

The question caused Harry's eyes to mist and he pulled out a dirty handkerchief to wipe them. 'Bloody dust around here gets in your eyes,' he said. 'I remember Allison well. She was a beautiful girl who was going to marry a young man called David Macintosh who was like a son to me.'

'Macintosh,' Brendan echoed. 'Is he related to a woman called Sarah Macintosh?'

'She's his first cousin,' Harry said. 'Why do you ask?'

'It's just that the hit-and-run never went over well with me as an accident, and Sarah Macintosh's name cropped up in my initial investigation. I was stopped from interviewing her by Detective Inspector Preston.'

'That bastard,' Harry spat. 'I hear he's retired and living in the lap of luxury, thanks to all the payoffs he got. I know Preston and Billy Price had something to do with Allison's murder. But proving it is just about impossible after all these years.'

'Not if I can help it,' Brendan said quietly. 'I still have the file in my desk, although it's light on evidence, and now I don't have Preston around to stop me investigating the incident.'

Harry looked closely at the young man. 'You do that, son,' he said. 'You need to talk to my old cobber, Sean Duffy.'

'I know Mr Duffy,' Brendan grinned. 'He and I have been up against each other often in the magistrates court. He's as cunning as a sewer rat, and a tough man when it comes to defending his crims.'

'That's Sean,' Harry agreed. 'But you wouldn't find a more fair-dinkum bloke if you searched the entire world. Allison was his law clerk when she was killed. He knows a lot about the case.'

'I'll look him up as soon as I can,' Brendan said, extending his hand. 'It was good to catch up with an old cobber of my dad.'

Brendan exited the building into the bright sunshine of the day and walked across the road to join Mick Prowse, who was sitting at a table with a cup of tea and two lots of sandwiches.

'I got you devon and sauce. So what's going on, Brendan?' he asked.

'Old Harry was once a copper with my dad before the Great War,' Brendan said, slipping into a seat at the formica table. 'We were just catching up on the times they spent together on the beat around here.'

'Yeah, and pigs can fly,' Mick said, sipping his tea. 'I know you, cobber. You're up to something. It's written all over your face.'

The trouble with working a long time with one partner was that they got to know you even better than your own family did, Brendan thought, and ordered a cup of tea. At least he knew he could trust his partner. But he would have to hide his investigation from the department. Sarah Macintosh and Billy Price were still in the game – even if Preston was out of it – and they were influential players.

*

The following day Brendan was due at the magistrates court in the city to give evidence in a case of petty theft. He had arrested a well-known pickpocket who worked the horse tracks. The defending solicitor was Sean Duffy, and after the case was decided in favour of the prosecution, Brendan intercepted Sean on the courthouse steps as he was leaving.

'Detective, you did a good job in there,' Sean said when Brendan fell into step with the older man. The solicitor walked stiffly, aided by a walking cane, as he had two artificial legs, a legacy of his service in the trenches on the Western Front of the Great War. Brendan knew all who were close friends called him the Major, although he did not encourage the name.

'You knew as well as I that the little weasel was guilty,' Brendan said. 'Major Duffy, I did not come to gloat over justice prevailing, but on the suggestion of an old friend of yours, Harry Griffiths. It's about a case I know you are well and truly familiar with, the death of Miss Allison Lowe.'

Sean stopped walking and looked at the policeman. 'I think we should afford ourselves some privacy at a pub around the corner from my office. They have a good ale and counter lunch. I thought the investigation into Miss Lowe's death had long ago been stifled by Inspector Preston.'

'True,' Brendan replied. 'I won't ask how you know.'

Sean smiled and gestured to Brendan to go inside the cool confines of the hotel. They took a seat in the corner and Brendan purchased two glasses of beer.

Both took a long sip and then Sean opened the conversation.

'You know she was murdered on the orders of Sarah Macintosh,' Sean said. 'Sarah gave the order to Preston, who in turn passed on the job to Billy Price to have her run down. The only mistake Price made was using a Macintosh company car which, I believe, you discovered in a repair shop.'

'You are well informed, Major,' Brendan said. 'But it is all hearsay and speculation. And it happened a long time ago.'

'There is no statute of limitations for murder,' Sean said. 'If the investigation is being reopened, I will provide every assistance I can.'

'My superiors would never reopen the case when the coroner made a finding of death by accident. The nearest thing the coroner could recommend was that the driver of the vehicle – if ever apprehended – be charged with culpable driving causing death. To top it all off, you and I both know that if I went after Sarah Macintosh, those above me would ensure I was out on George Street in uniform directing the morning traffic.'

'Ah, there is the law and there is justice and never the twain shall meet,' Sean said, taking a sip of cold beer. 'I understand your predicament. However, we can fight fire with fire. I just happen to know someone who might be willing to assist us with political clout and financial resources.'

'May I ask who?' Brendan queried.

'The person I am thinking of has good reason to wish to bring to justice the person responsible for Miss Lowe's murder,' Sean said quietly. 'She has a very strong suspicion that Sarah Macintosh gave orders to have her father murdered around the same time that Allison was killed. Jessica has friends in high places.'

'God almighty!' Brendan said. 'Who is this woman Sarah Macintosh?'

'One of the most dangerous people you will ever come across in your police career,' Sean replied with a grim smile. 'She has no human feelings of empathy and views killing as a legitimate means to an end.' Sean explained the incident at Glen View when Tom Duffy was killed defending his land. To the world, Sarah Macintosh was a successful businesswoman who had made her name in the chauvinistic world of commerce. She was well known as a philanthropist for her work with popular charities.

'So that is what you are up against,' Sean concluded. 'Thankfully there is one woman who is more than a match for her, and that is Jessica Duffy-Macintosh. Unlike Sarah, who needs to have other people do her dirty work, Jessie did her own killing during the war and was rewarded with military decorations from our government and the Yanks. Not that Jessie would resort to killing outside the field of war. I think I will inform the dear girl of your interest in seeing justice done. I am sure she will contribute to the successful outcome of your covert investigation.'

Sean raised his glass to his lips and Brendan followed suit. His mind was spinning with revelations about the absolutely ruthless woman he was investigating. How different was the world of the rich and powerful to the petty criminals he encountered, day in, day out, on the grimy backstreets of Sydney.

FOUR

The men filed into the village hall, taking off their hats. Their wives were with them, dressed in long summer skirts, hats and white gloves. They were a typical cross-section of David Macintosh's rural community. David sat on the stage beside John Glanville, watching them enter. The party had endorsed David overwhelmingly as their candidate. John would occasionally greet one or two members of the audience with a nod and smile. David was feeling nervous as this was his debut into the world of federal politics and he wanted to do well. Although he had initially been motivated to accept the nomination simply to stand in the way of the man who had ended his military career, he now felt that he could use his leadership skills to help the people of this district who had welcomed him into their fold. Politics was a way to fight a new war, this time on the front of social and economic issues for the betterment of his local community.

'There's a good crowd,' John said, leaning towards David. 'And I reckon you will have most of them on your side.'

'I see Markham is not here yet,' David said. 'But the representative of our local paper is.'

'I heard Markham will be here with his father,' John said. 'I am looking forward to his reaction when he spots you.' John nodded as the entrance of two men at the back of the hall caused a few heads to turn.

David stared at the younger man he had last seen in the jungles of New Guinea thirteen years earlier. Angus Markham's veiled threat to take revenge on David's decision to strip him of his command had not been empty. David had lost his commission after the war, thanks to Markham's father's political influence in Canberra. David guessed the older man beside Markham was his father. Henry Markham left his son's side and walked up to the stage.

'Ah, John, I see that you have not left politics entirely,' Henry Markham said, ignoring David.

'You are looking at the man who will take over my seat, Henry,' John said, stepping down from the stage to shake the hand of his former political adversary.

Markham Senior glanced up at David. 'It is time that the good people here had a change of parties. Your protégé has no experience in politics, whilst my son has grown up with it.'

'Dynasties in this business are not guaranteed.' John released Markham's hand. 'I believe Angus and David have already met,' he added with a wicked smile. 'Is it true that Angus had a nervous breakdown in New Guinea during the war?'

Henry Markham's face clouded. 'There are two sides to every story,' he said, and stalked away.

John returned to the stage and resumed his seat beside David. 'Young Angus's military record is clearly a touchy issue,' he grinned. 'He had better not come on as the war hero here.'

'Do I question him on his record of service?' David asked, and John frowned.

'Not a good idea to slur your opponent in this business – unless absolutely necessary. We have to act like gentlemen.'

David glanced down at the sheaf of notes trembling in his hands. The shaking he had known since combat had remained with him. He looked up and saw Gail enter the hall. Their eyes met and she smiled, giving a little wave of her hand before taking a seat at the back.

Angus Markham walked up to the stage and, without any greetings, sat down on a chair a few feet away from John and David.

John turned to the new arrival and said quietly, 'Are you ready?'

Angus gave a nod of his head, and John took centre stage, introducing both men and then calling on Angus to deliver his speech. Angus made the usual political promises of a better future. It was a long, polished speech and Angus spoke well. Polite but muted clapping followed him as he sat down and David took centre stage. He would not allow his nerves to show and he forced his trembling hands down by his sides. John had written notes for him but David crushed them into a ball in his fist.

'I had written notes to read from,' he opened his address, 'but all I am going to say is that, unlike my opponent, I live here, drink here, work here and go fishing here. Most of you know me and know I struggle to make a living out of my macadamias, like so many others in primary production in this district. But I know that I live in the best part of the world, and if you vote for me, I will do my best to see that the government gives us a fair go. I don't make any promises, but I will work my guts out on behalf of this community. Thank you, ladies and gentlemen.'

David returned to his seat and a short silence followed. Then suddenly the audience broke into loud clapping and even whistles of approval.

John shook his head. 'That was the shortest – and worst speech – I have ever heard,' he said quietly with a smile. 'But it bloody well worked!'

When David glanced down at Henry Markham he could see fury in his face.

At question time Henry Markham sprang to his feet. 'Mr Macintosh,' he said in an educated tone. 'I would like to clarify a couple of things about your past for those who are here today. Is it true that you served in an international Communist brigade in the Spanish Civil War?'

David remained seated to answer. 'I enlisted in a brigade to fight Fascism,' he said.

'A *Communist* brigade,' Markham stated. 'Is it true that you were a member of the Communist Party?'

David glanced at the journalist sitting in the front row and could see how eager he was to score some dirt on the upstart with aspirations to compete with the professional politicians in Canberra.

'I have *never* been a member of the Communist Party,' David replied firmly. 'At the time I could see the danger Fascism posed to the world and felt it was better to destroy it before it spread.'

'You must realise, Mr Macintosh, that to the average person in this room your service with the Communists opposing Franco makes you guilty by association. Surely your time with them influenced your political thinking.'

'Maybe I should have joined your party, Mr Markham,' David retorted. 'It has more in common with communism than my party.'

David's reply raised a few cries of 'Hear, hear' from the audience, and the senior politician switched to the next item in his bag of dirty tricks.

'Could you explain how you were arrested in Palestine by the British administration after the war?' he asked, and the audience fell silent.

'I was arrested by an overzealous British officer who had just been responsible for shooting a young woman in the back,' David said. 'I tried to protect her and was arrested. I was detained in a prison in Acre before being released – without charge.'

'What reason did you have to be in that situation in the first place, Mr Macintosh? It was hardly a holiday destination.'

'I was in Israel to visit the land of my mother's religion,' David said.

'So you are a Zionist,' Markham said smugly.

'No, I am a Jew by birth, but I love my bacon and eggs too much to be a practising Jew.'

David's answer brought a few chuckles from the audience and Markham realised that David was getting the better of him.

'I would like to say something.' Gail's voice echoed from the back of the hall and heads turned. 'Mr Macintosh fought Fascism as a young man because he had been imprisoned in Dachau concentration camp and had seen first-hand what Fascism was capable of. He confronted it in Spain as Britain and France should have done. His service to Australia in two wars has seen him decorated for bravery, and fighting in the Korean War is why he now needs to use a walking stick. Maybe your son could talk about his service to the country, Mr Markham.'

Angus Markham paled, but his father quickly came to his rescue.

'Ladies and gentlemen, you have had an opportunity to hear from both candidates now. My son and I want to thank you for taking time out of such busy lives to be here today.' With that, Angus left the stage and joined his father to stride out of the hall.

The audience broke up to make their way to tables laden with scones, jugs of cream and pots of tea prepared by the local CWA, whose contribution to local rural communities was highly valued by all, leaving David and John alone on the stage.

'Next time you give a speech, stick with the notes,' John growled but not without humour. 'Next time it won't be in front of people you know from the district.' He glanced down at Gail, standing with a cup of tea in hand. 'My daughter-in-law should be your campaign manager. Or you could just do the right thing and marry her.' John put his hat in his head and walked off the stage.

David followed down the steps, using his cane for balance, and walked over to Gail. 'How did you know I was in Dachau?' he said.

'You told me one night when you were drunk,' she said. 'I was not going to allow that arrogant man to attack someone of great worth and courage.'

'Thank you for your intervention,' David said with a smile. 'You're truly a wonderful woman.'

'Maybe one day your eyes will open and you will see what is right in front of you,' Gail said, briefly touching David on the cheek as Mrs Robinson, the town gossip, strode forward to have a word with the man she was going to vote for – even if he was a Jew!

★

The years had not been kind to the old Macintosh mansion standing above Sydney Harbour. The garden was overgrown and the climbing ivy covering the walls needed pruning. Inside was little better, the furnishings faded and the carpets worn and tatty. Most of the staff who had been employed to look after the house had been let go as the Macintosh Enterprises declined. War taxes had taken a great chunk out of profits to expand. Michael's nanny doubled as cook, and a gardener only worked twice a week.

Michael Macintosh pressed his clothes into the suitcase, closed it and stood back to look around his room to see if there was anything else he should pack for his trip to England. Nanny Keevers would know. He would go and ask his beloved nanny what he should take with him.

But his mother was standing in the doorway. Michael could see that she had been drinking, although not to the point of being drunk as his father usually was.

'Hello, Mother,' he said, and Sarah Macintosh stepped into the room.

'I can see that you have packed,' she said. 'How was your visit to Glen View?'

Michael heard the hostility in his mother's tone. 'It was a bit lonely without Patrick and Terituba, but I finally got to go to the sacred hill on the property.'

'Is that bitch Jessica gloating over owning our property?' Sarah asked.

Michael frowned. 'No, Mother. She is always very nice to me when I stay.'

'How about my brother?' she asked.

'Uncle Donald is fine,' Michael answered, feeling uncomfortable at his mother's bitter questions. He had grown to be very fond of his family in Queensland who had accepted him without rancour.

Sarah took a cigarette from a silver case and lit it, blowing smoke into the confines of the room.

'I have great hopes for you when you return from England. You will be a major catalyst in restoring the Macintosh companies to their pre-war glory,' she said, taking a seat on the edge of Michael's bed, the cigarette dangling in her hand.

'What if I don't want to join the family business?' Michael questioned, looking directly at his mother. 'What if I want to do something else?'

Sarah glared at her son. 'I have spent the last sixteen years rearing you, and you owe it to me to take your place in the family enterprise.'

'I think Nanny Keevers raised me, not you,' Michael answered coldly.

'Nanny Keevers is a paid servant,' Sarah said. 'She is not your flesh and blood.'

Michael shook his head. He could not remember his mother ever hugging him or showing affection. It had always been Val Keevers who had cared for him; she had dried his tears and hugged him when he yearned for a gentle touch. He was not about to listen to anything else his mother had to say, and he stalked towards the bedroom door.

'Don't you walk away from me, young man,' Sarah said in a raised voice. 'No man walks away from me.'

Michael stopped in the doorway. 'Is that why I have never met your cousin David?'

Sarah stood up from the bed.

'What do you mean?' she asked sharply.

'I have heard rumours that you were once very keen on him and that he walked away from you,' Michael said. 'Uncle Donald told me that David is a war hero, yet you told Father I was never to meet him. Why?'

Sarah slumped back on the edge of the bed as if punched in the stomach. 'It was I who walked away from him,' she lied. 'He is a stupid and arrogant man who could not see that we were destined to be together. That was years ago and now he is nothing to me.'

Michael knew she was lying, and he almost pitied her because he could see the pain in her face. Nevertheless, he did not want to hear any more from her. He walked out of his room in search of his nanny.

FIVE

The men of Patrick Duffy's platoon knew what to expect as they moved out into the hills.

First they had to navigate the dense head-high spear grass known as *lalang*. Inside the long grass the humidity was extremely high, and water rationing did not help the men carrying heavy loads of weapons, backpacks and water canteens. Once spear grass was traversed, the platoon was up against the plantations of rubber trees in their neat hillside rows. If they were lucky it was 'clean rubber' that had been well maintained, and the canopy would provide just a little protection from the tropical sun. Next came the lush rainforest giants, and if the area had been logged the thick undergrowth would be agony to negotiate.

Thankfully this time the men struggled up the hills under untouched canopies that provided a dim world of sickly sweet rotting vegetation underfoot and welcome shade above. There was only one drawback, and that was the enemy had a clear view of those entering their territory between the tall trees.

Patrick was forward scout and was carrying an Owen submachine gun. The Australian–designed weapon had proven itself in two wars, and Patrick liked the feel of it. He moved cautiously with the weapon pointed forward. All communication within the platoon was by hand signal alone. He knew that Terituba's sharp eyesight was scanning the ground for anything out of place. He was around ten paces behind Patrick.

Patrick did not see the signs but Terituba did. A sharp hiss brought Patrick to a stop. He turned to see his platoon commander signalling for Patrick to return. Patrick did and squatted down beside his friend. Terituba pointed to barely discernible tracks in the rotting vegetation.

'Three men bin come this way a short time ago. They go across our track that way,' Terituba whispered, pointing at a right angle to the platoon's advance.

The platoon commander nodded and signalled for his section commanders to join him for an impromptu orders group. Once briefed, the corporals returned to their sections, which had taken up all-round defensive positions in case of attack. The platoon swung around on its new axis of advance in an arrow formation. This time Terituba took the forward scout position to follow the footprints that only he seemed to see. His father Billy had taught him to track on Glen View.

The platoon advanced with even more caution, and just before last light they were rewarded by the sight of three armed men hunkered down around a temporary campsite about fifty yards away. The men went to ground and the platoon commander quickly worked out a plan to cut off any escape. He would deploy his three sections in an

L formation to avoid crossfire casualties. The light was rapidly failing and all knew they must act quickly. It would not be possible to call on the Communist terrorists to surrender, as in the dim light they had a chance to flee and escape.

Patrick was fully aware that the weeks of fruitless patrols had now come to a point where he was going to earn his pay as a soldier on active service. He lay behind his sub-machine gun with the sights centred on the shadowy three men he could see moving around in the near darkness. He knew it would be a long shot for his lighter calibre weapon designed for close-quarters fighting, but the heavy SLRs of the section would easily make the distance with accuracy. His hands were sweating as he considered this might be the first time he killed a fellow human. It was not easy looking down the sights of his weapon at three men whose lives were now measured in minutes – if not seconds.

Suddenly one of the three enemy appeared to have spotted their ambush and swung around to run. But the platoon commander gave his order to fire, and the rain-forest silence was shattered by the explosive sound of small arms. Patrick fired a long burst, ignoring his training to fire in short bursts, and he could see two of the men jerk as a fusillade of bullets ripped into them. The man who had begun to run ducked behind trees, and Patrick was aware that two more of the enemy had suddenly appeared in that location. They fired off a Sten gun in the direction of Patrick's section without causing any casualties, and then disappeared into the darkness.

On shouted orders from the platoon commander, the men were on their feet pursuing the escaping terrorists, but they were quickly ordered to halt to prevent being caught in their own crossfire from the flank.

Patrick was ordered to return to the bodies of the two men caught in the ambush to search them, while the platoon commander radioed in a sitrep to BHQ. The other sections returned to their rendezvous point and spread out in a defensive perimeter.

Terituba joined Patrick kneeling by the bodies. One of the dead enemy had his face shot away and his elbow shattered. The smell of blood was as strong as the scent of the rotting vegetation. The second body had been riddled with bullets to the torso and had a smashed leg. The 7.62 millimetre rifle rounds caused horrific wounds as they travelled at thousands of feet per second before hitting yielding flesh and bone.

Patrick stared at the undamaged face of the second man and experienced a twinge of guilt. He was very young – maybe fifteen – he thought. The boy's eyes were open and his expression dulled by death. Patrick could see how malnourished the dead boy was and he had nothing on him but a pair of chopsticks and a tattered party membership card.

'How did you go, Private Duffy?' the platoon sergeant asked over his shoulder.

'Just these,' Patrick said, holding up the two items. 'The poor bastard looks as if the chopsticks didn't get much of a workout.'

The sergeant produced a camera to photograph the dead enemy for future identification purposes. A burial party was quickly organised and the two bodies were committed to a common, shallow grave.

The order from battalion headquarters was for the platoon to continue the next day and pursue the survivors; there was no sense attempting this during the night. Patrick saw the platoon commander praising Terituba for spotting the tracks earlier in the afternoon. He had just earned a new name from the members of his platoon – Tracker – which he accepted with beaming pride.

*

Sam Po had been stunned by the ambush on his small party. He had been about to join them when the gunfire had erupted in the gloom of the rainforest giants. His reaction had been quick, and he had turned with his companion to escape the hail of bullets raining down on the three men at their rendezvous point in the rainforest.

He ran as hard as he could and hoped that the growing darkness would hide him and his comrade. He ran until his lungs gave out and he collapsed on the soft bed of rotting vegetation. The man with him stopped too and fought for breath.

'What do we do, Comrade Po?' he gasped.

'We keep going until we reach the shallow creek not far from here, and then we use it to cover our tracks,' Sam finally said when he had been able to get his breath back. 'Then we make our way back to our main base on the border.'

Sam and the other guerrilla soldier stood up and began to jog towards the creek in a gully below them. They entered the water and waded upstream until Sam was satisfied he had broken the trail they had left. It would take him two days to reach his main base, and he knew that the British would call for reinforcements to pursue him. He also knew they had helicopters and light reconnaissance aircraft to fly over the rainforest in search of him. Every step he took was a step closer to death.

*

The following day Patrick's platoon continued the pursuit with Terituba leading the way. By mid-morning they reached a fast-flowing but shallow creek where Terituba said the enemy's trail disappeared into the water. He guessed they had used the creek to break the trail and knew time would be required to beat a way through the heavy scrub at the edge of the creek to find where the two men had exited the water.

He explained the situation to his platoon commander who pulled a pained face. 'It looks like they're leading us towards the Thai border,' Lieutenant Gauden said and turned to his radio operator. However, he was unable to contact BHQ and guessed that the radio was not strong enough over the distance and hilly terrain they had covered in the pursuit.

The platoon used the opportunity to replenish water canteens. Each man had to chlorinate the water as even clean running water could carry deadly diseases such as leptospirosis. No matter how thirsty they were, they knew that they could not take a drink for at least thirty minutes in order to allow the foul-tasting chemical to take effect. Thirty minutes was a long time for such thirsty men.

'Sergeant, we will backtrack and get into a position to contact BHQ,' Lieutenant Gauden finally said after his assessment of the situation. Radio communication was vital for the safety of his men and he would let his commanding officer make the decision as to the future of the patrol. They could return in the knowledge that they had struck a blow against the local insurgents with only the regret that two had got away.

When radio comms were re-established, the order came down from BHQ to terminate the patrol and return to base. Three days later the weary men of the platoon were taking hot showers and drinking cold beer. It was a relief from the arduous conditions of the rainforest where leeches, deadly disease-carrying mites, heat exhaustion and never-ending thirst were part of the day-to-day life of jungle patrols. They had at least returned in the knowledge that their patrol had eliminated two more CTs, and Terituba was recommended for a Mentioned in Dispatches for his skill in locating the enemy campsite. The recommendation was not greeted with great delight by the Aboriginal man from central Queensland because it meant he had to shout the members of his platoon at the other ranks' canteen.

★

Major Karl Mann was head and shoulders above the Malay police gathered in the small compound. They stood either side of a thin Chinese man whose bedraggled appearance spoke of a harsh life.

'He is giving himself in,' said a young Chinese man.

'How much has he said?' Karl asked his interpreter.

'He say he come all way from Thai border,' the Chinese interpreter replied. 'He say Sam Po his boss.'

Karl gave the interpreter a look of interest. 'You are sure he said Sam Po?'

'Yes. I don't think he tell lie.'

Karl Mann had been tasked with hunting down the man reputed to have killed the British high commissioner and who had risen through the ranks to command a unit infamous for its savage treatment of isolated villagers, both Malay and Chinese.

'Tell the officer in charge to have our man brought to the office. I want to question him further about Comrade Po,' Karl said, and the interpreter switched to Malay to pass on the order.

The frightened man was escorted inside and sat down on a rickety chair beside an equally battered table. Karl sat behind the table and two Malay policemen and his interpreter stood beside the door of the tiny room. Behind Karl was a large coloured map of Malaya.

'Ask our man if he can point out where he last saw Sam Po,' Karl said and carefully watched the demeanour of the prisoner as he was questioned.

'He say he can show us on map where Sam Po has his main camp.'

'Good,' Karl nodded. 'Get him to point it out on the map behind me.'

The frightened prisoner studied the map for a moment and then placed his finger on a spot just above the Thai border. He said something in Chinese and Karl indicated to him to resume his seat.

'Interesting,' Karl mused. Po's main camp was in an isolated area of rugged terrain. Karl remembered reading in the Australian battalions intelligence summary a few days earlier about a contact one of the platoons had made only a few miles south of this position. Apparently they had killed two CTs but a couple had escaped. Karl knew they had taken photographs of the dead men and wondered if they had killed the notorious leader. The only man he knew who could positively confirm Po was one of the dead was sitting trembling opposite him.

'Tell our man that he will not be harmed and that, in fact, he is a special guest of the Malayan government and will be rewarded for his co-operation. However, he will have to stay with us for a little longer before he is released.'

The interpreter passed on the message meant as reassurance. Yet, as the man looked up, Karl could see absolute fear in his eyes. Sam Po was a very dangerous enemy, and if he got wind of the fact this man was informing against him, his retribution would be cruel and deadly.

*

Detective Senior Constable Brendan Wren removed his hat when he entered Sean Duffy's office. Harry Griffiths was sitting in a chair, smoking a cigarette, and Brendan nodded a greeting. The meeting had been arranged discreetly so that Brendan's superiors would not be aware of his relationship with the formidable criminal lawyer.

'Good that you could get time off to make this meeting,' Sean said. He did not get up from behind his desk as the joints with his artificial legs were giving him some pain today. 'Take a seat. So, do you have anything new in your investigation?'

Brendan shook his head. 'Before he retired, Preston had many files disappear concerning the hit-and-run,' he said. 'About all I have is my own memory and a few sketchy notes I was able to write in my notebook. I did learn that Miss Macintosh's father died of an accidental fall at her home before the death of Miss Lowe.'

'I am surprised you were not aware of that,' Sean said. 'It was all over the news at the time.'

'I was in my last year of school when it happened,' Brendan said. 'About all I was interested in then was the comic section of the newspapers. I liked Ginger Meggs.'

Sean smiled. He also liked the Ginger Meggs cartoons. 'I know Sir George's death was ruled as accidental by the coroner, but Harry and I are naturally cynical people, and it just so happened that he died the day before he was going to announce his heir to the throne. Knowing the man as we did, we would never have bet on him appointing his daughter as head of the Macintosh companies. We have always suspected that Sarah Macintosh killed her own father.'

Brendan swore quietly.

'You can bet that without Preston on her side she would

not have been able to get away it. But the old bastard was too smart to leave any evidence.'

'You know,' Harry said with a smile, 'retired coppers have a habit of keeping bits of their past with them in their retirement. Old files – and one or two pieces of evidence that always seem to disappear after a case is closed. I bet if we could get into his house up the coast we'd find something interesting.'

Sean grinned at Harry.

'There's not a hope in hell that we could get a warrant to search his place,' Brendan said. 'He still has a lot of friends in high places.'

'In my world,' Harry said, 'a warrant is a jemmy and torch.'

'You mean a break-in?' Brendan said aghast.

'You didn't hear that from me,' Harry replied. 'Besides, I am too old to go climbing through windows in the middle of the night. But I do know a couple of young blokes who might be up to it.'

'I don't suppose you're going to mention their names in front of me,' Brendan grinned.

'Not likely,' Harry said. 'You'd go out and arrest them.'

'How much to hire them?' Sean asked.

'Gentlemen, I think this is my cue to say adieu and let you get on with your conversation,' said Brendan. 'As they say, *I was never here.*' He rose and shook hands with the two old villains, then left the office.

'Let's do it,' Sean said. 'After all, what have we got to lose? We still have Jessie working at her end to assist but no results at this stage.'

Harry beamed at him. It would be like old times when they were young men.

SIX

Sean and Harry sat in a corner of the bar of the hotel they had frequented for as long as they could remember.

'They pulled out,' Harry said over his beer. 'When I told them whose place I wanted them to go after, they said it would be suicide. Preston's name still inspires fear.'

Sean Duffy stared bleakly into his empty glass. 'Then it looks like you and I will have to do the break-in.'

'Look at us!' Harry exclaimed. 'A couple of old coots with medical problems – you with your dicky legs and me with my dicey ticker. Breaking into houses is a young man's job.'

'It doesn't seem so long ago we were crawling around no-man's-land under fire in the dark,' Sean said.

'Cobber, that was forty years ago,' Harry said, finishing his beer in one swallow.

'It's so bloody strange that our bodies age but our minds

stay young,' Sean reflected. 'All we have to do is get into Preston's place when we know he and his missus are not home, have a look around, then leave. It won't matter if he discovers his place has been burglarised. We wear gloves to leave no fingerprints and cover our tracks. It is the only hope of possibly finding anything that may prove to be useful. As you said, retired coppers have a habit of keeping old files of cases they were involved in.'

'I'm not convinced this is a good idea,' Harry said. 'What if we get caught?'

'That doesn't sound like the Harry Griffiths I've always known,' Sean said. 'After all, you'll have your legal brief with you if you're caught.'

Sean's attempt at humour raised a smile on Harry's face. 'Okay, let's do it,' he sighed. 'What plan do you have?'

Sean leaned forward across the small table, taking out his fountain pen and a sheet of blank paper. 'Preston's house is just up from Palm Beach,' Sean said, commencing a sketch of his plan. 'There is a dirt track leading to it, but we will not be approaching from the land. I have a little cabin cruiser at Avalon Beach near my beach shack. We will be making a seaward approach on our target, preferably on a moonless or cloudy night. We beach the cruiser and make our way from there to his house.'

'Bloody hell, Major, you make it sound like a military operation.'

'Old habits die hard,' Sean smiled. 'I reckon that even a legless man could get up the beach, into the house and out before you can say Jack Robinson. The only thing we have to know is when Preston is likely to be away from his residence for a good period of time.'

'Well, I can tell you that,' Harry said. 'A mate of mine who knows Preston from the old days told me that Preston is driving up to Queensland for a holiday with his missus in a couple of weeks' time.'

'Perfect,' Sean said. 'All I have to do is check the phases of the moon. When the time is right, you can pack your fishing rod and we will depart just before last light to motor north. The only thing that could stop us is bad weather.'

'I get seasick,' Harry said. 'That's why I never joined the navy in 1915, although I suspected then they might not see a lot of action like we saw on the Western Front.'

'You will be too exhilarated to get seasick,' Sean reassured. 'This is a lot easier than being sent into the trenches. It's just a simple beach landing.'

'Yeah, they said that about Gallipoli,' Harry noted miserably.

The two men ordered another round of beers. They might have convinced themselves that the operation was no big deal, but they both knew the best laid plans of battle often went to pieces when the first shot was fired.

*

With Preston confirmed on his way to Queensland and the house deserted, Sean waited in the late afternoon at his beach shack. The conditions could not be better: calm seas and a new moon. Sean's beach retreat was no mansion – a fibro house with one bedroom and very little in the way of furniture – but it was in the dunes overlooking the beach and a good place to do some beach fishing. His small clinker-built cabin cruiser was on a rail system and winch to allow him to let the boat rattle down to the water's edge.

He was loading a couple of fishing rods when he heard a car pull into his driveway behind the house. Two doors slammed closed and Sean watched as Harry appeared around the corner with his son in tow. Sean knew Harry's son well. He had helped Daniel get his commission in the Royal Australian Navy during the war, for which Harry had been extremely grateful. Daniel was tall and slim and owned a successful real estate business in the expanding city suburbs.

'Hello, Major,' Daniel greeted, and Sean cast a quizzical look at Harry.

'I figured we could do with some naval help,' Harry shrugged.

'Dad told me what you two were up to,' Daniel grinned. 'I reckon you're both a couple of galahs, but I think the army will be in need of help from the navy on this mission.'

'You must realise that what we are doing is illegal.'

'Yeah, I know,' Daniel replied. 'Selling real estate is not exactly adrenaline-pumping work. Besides, he's my old man and I can do no less than have his back. Maybe after this you might be able to convince him to come and live with me and the family.'

Harry had always fought offers to live with his son as he liked the culture of the inner city where his gym had once been a very important meeting place for young men learning to become boxers. But the gym was destined to be bulldozed to make way for the city's unrelenting progress.

'I promise you that when we pull off this job I will personally drag your old man kicking and screaming to your place,' Sean said with a smile. 'Welcome aboard the team.'

The boat was launched and the three men boarded. The engine kicked over and Sean gave Daniel the wheel to steer the boat out through the surf. They turned north and, as the sun began to set over the hills on their portside, the boat pitched and rolled in the swell. Harry was already hanging over the side being sick, and cursing Sean and his son. Both laughed at Harry's suffering.

Eventually they found themselves off the beach below Preston's house. The night was pitch black and all that could be seen were a couple of electric lights burning in houses neighbouring Preston's residence.

'Okay, we switch off our navigation lights,' Sean ordered, and the red and green side lights were turned off. Both Sean and Harry had blackened their faces and wore dark clothing. It brought back memories of their youth on the Western Front before they went on a trench raid. Sean was relying on Daniel's naval skills to guide the boat towards their target. He did so cautiously and soon they could see the white of the waves breaking on the sandy beach. Daniel eased the boat nose in and leaped over the side, running out the anchor in the sand to secure his mooring. When he returned, Sean and Harry were already out of the boat with the items they needed for the break-in.

'You stick with the boat,' Sean said to Daniel. 'If anything goes wrong, you up anchor and get away from here. I don't want anyone to know you were involved.'

Daniel protested but his father backed Sean, and Daniel backed down.

'If you see three flashes of light from our torches, that means you make your escape,' Harry added.

With that, he and Sean made their way up the beach, knowing that when the tide came in a few hours later it would wash away their prints in the sand.

They reached the darkened house, towering above them, and climbed the dunes to its front entrance.

'Where do we start?' Sean whispered to Harry, pulling on gloves so as not to leave fingerprints.

'The garage,' Harry answered.

The two men made their way along the front section of the house to the garage. To their surprise it was unlocked.

Clearly Preston had no fear of anyone attempting to break in to his house.

They stepped inside and turned on their torches. The garage storage was a jumble of tools, fishing rods and tea chests. Sean took the lid off one chest and used his torch to illuminate the contents. He could see a mixture of items that held no interest.

'Hey, Sean, look at this,' Harry said, going through the contents of another tea chest.

Sean shone his torch at something Harry was holding up. It appeared to be a couch pillow. 'It looks like the Shroud of Turin.'

Sean moved over to Harry and looked closer at the pale cream pillow with a brownish outline of what could be clearly seen as a human face. It was eerie and Sean experienced a touch of fear.

'What do you make of it, Harry?' he asked.

'It looks like someone had this over their face and the brown stuff we can see was blood,' he replied. 'It gives me the creeps.'

'We take it,' Sean said. 'I don't know if it has anything to do with what we are looking for, but maybe it could be useful.'

The two men continued to riffle through the many files they found in the tea chests, throwing aside anything that did not have any bearing on their search.

'Eureka!' Sean finally exclaimed. He held in his hands a file stamped with the name of Sir George Macintosh, and under that another file with Allison Lowe's name on it. For some reason Preston had packed both together.

Sean flipped open the file and found a pile of black and white photos taken inside Sir George Macintosh's home the night he had 'accidentally' fallen down the stairs and died.

Amongst the photos were a few of Sir George's body. Sean shone his torch on a close-up of Sir George's dead face. 'God almighty!' he hissed, staring at the photo. 'Harry, get over here and look at this.'

Harry stared at the photo. 'What? The photo looks like Sir George Macintosh.'

'Yes, but look at the blood on his face,' Sean said.

Harry looked closer. 'The blood has been smeared. Like someone attempted to wipe his face . . . Bloody hell!' Harry turned his torch on the pillow lying on the floor of the garage a few feet away. 'Or maybe put a pillow over Macintosh's face to smother him.' He looked at Sean. 'Surely any investigator worth his salt would have picked that up at the scene.'

'Preston was in charge of putting the evidence before the coroner,' Sean said quietly. 'I don't ever remember any pillow being mentioned in the evidence.'

Their speculation was interrupted by the sound of a car engine approaching the house. Both men snatched the items of interest they had collected and turned off their torches.

'I forgot to mention that Preston has a couple of the local boys drop out from time to time to keep an eye on his place. I didn't think they would come tonight,' Harry said just as car lights came into view at the other side of Preston's residence.

'C'mon,' Sean said. 'We have to get out of here.'

Carrying the pillow and the old files, both men exited the garage to the sound of voices and the beams of flash-lights approaching. Sean and Harry were stumbling in the dark down the sand dunes when Sean felt himself yanked off his feet. His wooden leg had jammed in the branches of a heavy piece of driftwood he had not seen in the dark.

'Sean,' Harry hissed. 'Where are you?'

'Up here,' Sean hissed back. He could hear the voices of the two uniformed policemen only about fifty yards away and coming in his direction. They did not sound as though they had found anything suspicious, but they had a torch and the beam was moving around in the darkness.

Harry scrambled up beside his friend. 'What's up?'

'My bloody left leg is caught in something,' Sean whispered.

'Disconnect it,' Harry whispered back, and Sean twisted to release his artificial leg. It came loose.

The voices were only yards away now, and both men lay very still as the two police officers stood almost on top of them. They were discussing coming down to the beach on the weekend to do some fishing. What seemed like forever went by before the two turned and disappeared.

'We have to get out of here,' Harry said. 'Just untangle your leg and lean on me until we get to the boat.'

Sean tugged at the leg and it eventually came loose. Gripping it in one hand, he allowed Harry to guide him down the dunes to the relative flat of the beach. Harry still had the evidence they had stolen from Preston's garage.

'Dad, that you?' Daniel's voice came softly from the darkness.

'Yeah, son,' Harry answered. 'Get the anchor up,' he said as he dragged Sean towards the water.

Daniel had the boat afloat on the rising tide and Harry helped Sean into the cabin cruiser. The three aboard, Daniel turned over the engine and pointed the bow south. When the boat was a good distance from the shore he turned on the navigation lights. It was now safe to turn on the cabin light for Sean to reattach his leg. When he had done so, he reached into the cabin and produced two long-necked bottles of beer.

'Well, we got away with it,' Sean said, knocking the top off one of the bottles and handing it to Harry. 'It's not real cold but it will do the job.'

Harry took a long swig and handed the bottle to his son at the helm. 'For a moment back there it was just like old times.'

'Most fun I've had in years,' Sean said, gulping back his beer. 'It makes you feel alive again.'

They glanced at each other in the dim light of the navigation guides and held up their bottles in salute.

'I don't want to know what you pair of reprobates did back there,' Daniel grinned, 'but it wasn't necessary to bring me a cushion to sit on.'

'That's not a cushion,' Harry said. 'That's evidence – and don't sit on it.'

By morning all three men were back in Sydney, weary but elated by the success of their crime. And the next day Brendan was back in Sean's office staring at the blood-stained cushion. Beside it were the file and photos of the Sir George Macintosh investigation. Sean briefed the detective on his suspicions, and Harry filled in any details Sean had missed.

'Unfortunately, even if you are right, the pillow is useless as evidence. There's the broken chain of custody, for a start, never mind proving it came from the crime scene. Preston would never admit to taking it without entering it into evidence,' Brendan said.

'Why would he keep it?' Sean asked, and it was Harry who came up with an answer.

'Maybe to blackmail Sarah Macintosh. If it had been produced at the time, no doubt a more careful autopsy would have been done to look for traces in Sir George's mouth or lungs of pillow fibres, which may have led to a coroner's finding of homicide.'

'But it proves nothing,' Brendan said. 'Even if you both are right, I can't just have the case reopened on the strength of a stolen piece of potential evidence.'

Both men reluctantly agreed. All Sean could do now was carefully store the pillow and examine Preston's notes of his investigation. It did not help them with Allison's case, but it was on the verge of something just as dangerous to Sarah Macintosh. Maybe one day forensic science would advance and the cushion would become a critical item. Harry and Sean both felt that it was an imprint of Sir George Macintosh's face in the last moments of his life.

SEVEN

The hours on the campaign trail were exhausting and David always looked forward to returning to his house overlooking the ocean. There he could sit on the hill and gaze at the great breakers rolling in from the ocean. His political future was uncertain but John Glanville thought the signs were promising that he would be elected as the federal member for the local electoral division.

David heard the sound of a car engine and knew it was Gail driving up to join him, as she often did when he was home from campaigning.

'Hello, David,' she said and sat down on the grass beside him, staring out over the ocean rolling gently under a warm sun on a cloudless day.

For a short time, they both simply gazed at the ocean.

'I have something to tell you,' Gail said in a strained voice. 'I have decided to start seeing someone else.'

For a moment her words did not sink in, then David realised what she was telling him.

'That's good,' he said, struggling to hide the pain he suddenly felt.

'I know that we are friends,' Gail said, 'and that we will always remain that way. You have been a positive influence in my son's life, and I will always be grateful for that. I didn't want to tell you on the eve of the election, but this is a small town and you were bound to hear rumours.'

'I will miss our times together,' David said, plucking at a blade of grass. 'I wish you all the happiness in the world.'

'Is that all you have to say?' Gail said angrily, turning to face David. 'You hope I'll be happy?'

'What else should I say?' David said, forcing back the rush of emotion swirling up in him. He knew he wanted Gail, and had from the time he had first seen her standing on the railway station platform when he returned from the Korean War, but he had denied himself any expression of his real desires. How many women had he loved and lost to violent ends? He did not want this to happen to Gail.

'If that is it,' Gail said, standing up and brushing down her skirt, 'then I wish you all the best in the election and hope you find what is missing from your life.'

She walked away and left David alone again, watching the ocean. After a moment he felt tears on his cheeks. For the first time in as long as he could remember, he broke down into sobs of grief for what he had lost. He had led men into battle and lost, but losing Gail was different. He felt that he had just lost the most important battle of his life, and suddenly, winning a seat in parliament meant nothing much to him at all.

★

Slacks and shirts were a welcome change from jungle greens for the men of Patrick's platoon who were going on leave from their base. The three-hour truck drive to Butterworth military base and then the ferry across to Georgetown held the promise of booze and bar girls. Lieutenant Stan Gauden had his married quarters on Penang Island. With a broad grin, he warned the men about the dangers of venereal disease as he waved them goodbye.

'Let's go get an ice-cream,' Patrick said to Terituba as the party of happy soldiers fanned out to explore the carnal and material delights of the town. They headed towards a large shop, Singapore Cold Storage, and walked inside into the cool, a welcome relief from the baking sun of the tropical town. They purchased a couple of cones and stepped back onto the street to join the din of traffic and honking horns and cries of merchants peddling their wares in the narrow, twisting streets. They were staying overnight in a hotel that smelled of curry spices. The room had two single beds, simple but clean, with a view over the cramped street filled with Chinese, Malays and Indians going about their daily lives. It was a long way from the screeching of monkeys in the jungle, the eerie silence of the rainforest, and the ever-present threat of danger from the elusive enemy.

'I reckon we should go and find a bar with some good-looking sheilas in attendance and consume as much as we can until we fall down drunk,' Patrick said, and they set off in search of such a paradise, as soldiers had done for as long as there had been armies.

They found a promising-looking bar and pushed their way inside. The place was crowded and immediately they spotted some of their comrades from the platoon. There were also other Aussie soldiers in the bar, probably artillery gunners from the base at Butterworth.

'Hey, Pat, Tracker, over here!' one of the platoon members stood and shouted above the din.

Ted Morrow glared at them as they joined the small group sitting around the small wooden table, glasses of beer in front of them.

They dragged up chairs and ordered extra beers from a stony-faced Chinese girl carrying a tray of empty glasses. Patrick could see from Ted's scowl that the knockdown in the barracks was not forgotten, and the man was spoiling for a fight. Patrick did not want to fight; all he wanted was a day of drinking cold beer and chasing women.

Terituba stood to make a trip to the toilet and a stranger from a table nearby bumped into him, spilling the beer he was carrying.

'Bloody Abo,' the man snarled. 'Bloody useless anywhere you go.'

Terituba was about to apologise and buy the man another beer but was shoved in the chest. He was sent sprawling across the table, scattering glasses of beer and knocking Patrick from his seat.

It was Ted Morrow who was on his feet while Patrick untangled himself from the floor.

'No one speaks to Tracker that way,' the big man roared and launched himself at the offending man, shoving him so hard that he fell onto the table of his companions, causing the same amount of damage.

By now Patrick had scrambled to his feet and watched as Ted waded into the other party yelling, 'Bloody drop shorts. You don't insult the infantry.'

It was an evenly matched brawl, and above the screams of the bar ladies, smashing of furniture and grunting of the combatants, a high-pitched voice could be heard yelling, 'I call police.'

The warning sobered both gunners and infantrymen alike, and the punches and kicks ceased as they hurried for the entrance to escape the possibility of either military or civil police turning up. Outside, Terituba and Patrick ran as hard as they could down the crowded street until they felt they had put enough distance between themselves and the destroyed establishment of pleasure.

Catching their breath, they looked back to see Ted Morrow puffing his way up to them. 'Bloody drop shorts,' he gasped.

'Thanks, Ted,' Patrick said, extending his hand.

'What for?' Ted asked, eyeing Patrick's outstretched hand suspiciously.

'For sticking up for Tracker back in the bar.'

'Tracker is one of our mob,' Ted grunted, accepting the hand of friendship. 'No one goes messing with one of the best diggers in the platoon. You know anywhere else we can get a cold beer?'

The three men found another bar and little else was remembered until Patrick awoke the next morning fully dressed on his bed. He felt sick and his head was pounding, but he didn't want to waste the few hours left of his leave. Maybe a dip might help ease his pain. Terituba lay on his back, also fully dressed, happily snoring away the hours.

Patrick scooped up his swimming trunks and an army towel. There was a swimming pool reserved for Europeans not far from his hotel; once inside the grounds he dropped his towel on the manicured lawn adjoining the clear waters of the pool. It was virtually deserted. He walked to the edge where a young woman wearing a one-piece swimsuit was lying on a towel. Patrick didn't dive so much as fall in, causing a great splash of water. He descended to the bottom and resurfaced to see the girl sitting up and looking at him with anger in her eyes.

'You splashed me,' she said in an educated voice.

'Sorry,' Patrick replied, swimming to the edge of the pool. 'My balance is a bit off today.'

He looked up into her face and saw how pretty she was. He guessed that she was around his own age. 'You sound like a Pom.'

'You act like a colonial.'

'My name is Patrick, and I once again offer my apologies for disturbing the lady of the lake at her repose,' Patrick said with a grin.

'Are you a soldier?' the young woman asked.

'Would it make a difference if I were not?'

'Well, you're obviously an Australian, but you have almost an English accent.'

'Yeah, a few of my friends have told me I sound like a Pom. I guess that's a result of a decent education.'

'So you must be an officer?'

'If you tell me your name I'll answer your question.'

'You Australians have a very forward manner, but I will tell you my name. It's Sally.'

'Hello, Sally, pleased to meet you,' Patrick said, extending his hand. She moved closer to take it and he immediately yanked her into the pool.

'You, you . . .' she spluttered as she resurfaced.

'It's a hot day and you looked like you were baking,' Patrick laughed. 'The lady of the lake appeared in need of rescue. As to your question about me being an officer, the answer is no, I am just a simple infantry soldier.'

'Yet it is obvious that you know the chronicles of King Arthur,' Sally said. 'And you don't sound like a simple soldier.'

'I'm not sure if that's a compliment,' Patrick replied. 'Are you a nurse from Butterworth?'

'Why would you presume that?' Sally countered. 'Have you had a lot of experience with nurses?'

'Not really,' Patrick replied quickly. 'It's just that there are not that many pretty young women over here who are not in the armed forces.'

'Well, I am not a nurse. I work for my father's import-export business in Malaya.'

'Kind of nice meeting a civilian.'

'Is this your first time in Malaya?' Sally asked.

'I was here as a very young kid when the Japs invaded. My mother owned an aircraft business operating out of Singapore. She was a pilot.'

'Your mother sounds like a very interesting woman. Is she still in Singapore?'

'My mother died in Changi,' Patrick answered. 'So I guess, yes, she is still in Singapore.'

'I am sorry to hear that,' Sally said. 'I lost my mother in London in the Blitz. My father has raised me and I have travelled the world with him. Have you travelled widely?'

'Only to places where you have to carry a gun,' Patrick said. 'This is the first so far.'

Patrick realised that he found Sally very attractive. Her cascade of red hair complemented her emerald green eyes. But with a sinking heart he knew this might be the only time they met, as she was obviously from a wealthy background and leave from military operations was a rare thing. Soldiers in war zones tended to snatch love for brief moments, knowing that it was fleeting. This felt different to Patrick.

They climbed out of the pool and made their way to the shade of a great mango tree, spreading their towels on the lawn under its shade. Conversation seemed to come easy between Patrick and Sally, and he noticed that he could make her laugh. He sensed that she felt comfortable in his company.

Midday drifted into late afternoon and Patrick realised that he would have to take the ferry back to the mainland or be charged with being absent without leave.

'I would like to see you again,' he said, holding his breath and waiting for the rejection.

'I would like that,' Sally said. 'I'll give you a telephone number where I can be contacted next time you get leave.'

For a moment it did not sink in that the beautiful young woman had accepted his invitation. Sally took a small notebook from the bag beside her, scribbled down her number and handed it to Patrick. 'You be very careful out in the jungle, Patrick,' she said. 'I am expecting you to take me out to dinner next time we meet.'

Patrick walked away as if floating on air, clutching the scrap of paper that linked him to the enchanting lady of the lake.

When he met up with the members of his platoon waiting for the ferry, Terituba asked him, 'Where you bin?'

'To Camelot,' Patrick grinned.

'Is that near Rockhampton?' Terituba asked.

'Try England,' Patrick replied.

For a moment Terituba stared at Patrick. 'Only ol' Wallarie could fly to England on the wings of an eagle,' he said, suddenly serious.

The order came to board the ferry and the men of Patrick's platoon shuffled aboard. The two-day leave had done damage to many and a rest back at the barracks was a welcome thought. But when they finally returned, they were met by a grim-faced Gauden and an equally stern-looking company sergeant major.

'Welcome home, men,' Lieutenant Gauden greeted them. 'Tomorrow morning at 0500 hours you are to assemble outside my office for a briefing. You will parade sober, healthy and ready for a very important mission. Full patrol kit.'

Patrick noticed the impressively built Australian major walk up behind Lieutenant Gauden, who turned to salute him. Patrick had never seen this officer before, but he could tell from the rows of ribands on his chest that he had seen action in both the last war and Korea.

Lieutenant Gauden turned to address his platoon. 'Men, this is Major Mann. He will be working with us on our next op.'

Patrick could see that the major was scanning the faces of each and every soldier. When the major's gaze settled on Patrick, he could sense the fire and steel in this new officer. Major Mann was as big as Private Ted Morrow, but he struck Patrick as far more menacing. Patrick instinctively knew that the attachment of the unknown officer meant something big was in the air and he felt a shiver of both excitement and fear.

Sally's words echoed in his mind . . . *Be very careful out in the jungle, Patrick.*

EIGHT

Sarah Macintosh had just walked out of a dismal meeting with the principal accountants of the Macintosh enterprises. Some of the investments to expand had gone wrong and the overall profit had taken a hammering. As she drove her Bentley into the driveway of the Macintosh mansion overlooking Sydney Harbour, her mind was on a stiff gin and tonic.

There was no longer a butler to greet her at the entrance to the home that had been in her family's possession for over a century. At least Miss Keevers would have cooked a fine meal for her and Charles – not that Sarah had much of an appetite as she went over the losses the companies were suffering even in this time of economic boom.

The confidence that always glimmered in her eyes had dimmed as the years had gone by, and she knew she looked as tired as she felt. She slept badly at nights, haunted by ghosts of her father and the woman who had once been her best friend. In public she was always elegant and confident, but out of the spotlight she felt her life was a hollow shell.

'Bad day by the look on your face,' said her estranged husband, Charles Huntley, who was sitting at the end of the long polished dining table, drink in hand.

Sarah went to the liquor cabinet to pour herself a gin and tonic. 'You could say that,' she said, retrieving a cigarette from a silver case. 'Profits are down across the board and we are badly in need of new strategies.'

'I read in today's financial section of the paper that your sister-in-law is looking at investing in mining exploration in Western Australia,' Charles said.

Sarah glanced at the newspaper spread out on the table and noticed that Charles had been filling in a crossword. She tolerated him under her roof for her son's sake but otherwise he was virtually useless in her life. As a decorated fighter ace he was a good handbag at social occasions, but Sarah sought her pleasure in the arms of other lovers.

'Mining,' she said. 'Most of the gold in WA has been taken out of the ground. I doubt she will do any good in that sector.'

'From what I read,' Charles said, 'she is more interested in locating deposits of iron ore and other metals. You have to remember that her father got the jump on you investing in wool after the war, so maybe you should keep a close eye on what she is up to.'

Sarah picked up the paper and saw a black and white photo of Jessica Duffy-Macintosh staring back at her with a smug expression. Even after giving birth to three children she still looked youthful. Donald, Jessica's husband and Sarah's brother, was rarely seen in her company, no doubt because of his grotesquely scarred face. Apparently he preferred to work the Glen View cattle station and from what Sarah had heard, the years had only strengthened the love her brother and Jessica had for each other.

'Have you ever considered a company merger with your sister-in-law?' Charles said.

'That will never happen,' Sarah snapped. 'If anything, the bitch will overextend herself in this fruitless venture in WA, and I will make an offer on her companies when she comes grovelling on her knees to me.'

She flipped the pages of the paper and froze. There was an article about a federal by-election in northern New South Wales and attached was a photo of David Macintosh, her cousin. Almost a quarter of a century had passed since she had first laid eyes on him in a Berlin cafe, and yet he was still as desirable to her as ever.

'I see that you have noticed David is running for a seat in parliament,' Charles said, reading the shocked expression on her face. 'I think he will make a fine representative for his electorate.' Charles was aware of his wife's obsession with David, although they had not spoken about it for many years.

'I don't care what he does,' Sarah said, closing the paper.

'Oh, a letter came from Michael,' Charles said and passed her the opened envelope.

Sarah took it and began to read. Michael wrote that he was settling in to his new school and that he had made contact with the White family in London. The Whites were relatives of the Macintosh family, as many years earlier Granville White had married Fiona Macintosh. Sarah only knew of his existence because she had read Lady Enid's diary. The White family had made a fortune in trade with the East India Company in the eighteenth and nineteenth centuries and had only grown richer in the years since.

The London residence was just one of many the White family owned across Britain. Michael said they had received him warmly. He had made the rowing team and was in the Seconds rugby team. He had included an academic record in his letter and Sarah could see it was excellent. He said the boys were a bit snobby, but his distant connection to the White family helped break down the barriers between a colonial and the sons of the English upper class.

Sarah felt a strong link with her son when she read the letter. After all, it would be he who would one day inherit the family business. Sometimes it frightened Sarah to think all her aspirations were centred on her son. What if he rejected taking over the Macintosh Enterprises and sought another life? How much had he inherited of his real father, David Macintosh? David had always been a restless soul. Sarah shook away the thoughts; there was no question of Michael not obeying her in this – he was her son and he would do as she demanded.

Sarah finished her drink, refilled the glass and took it upstairs to the library, leaving Charles to his crossword puzzle.

*

Major Karl Mann sat in the small room allocated to him beside the officers' mess. In the dim light he read the top-secret file on Comrade Sam Po that had been sent to him by Featherstone from Singapore.

Karl learned that Sam Po had been a prisoner in Changi during the war. His European father and Chinese mother had both died, and a British woman, Diane Duffy, had assumed the role of foster mother in the infamous Japanese prison. She had also died in Changi, and the boy had disappeared, reappearing on the back streets of Singapore, where he was taken in by a Chinese merchant and his family – now revealed as members of the Malayan Communist Party. Their daughter, a nurse, had died whilst in British custody, and it was known that Sam Po had sworn vengeance. It was rumoured that, when he was barely more than a kid, he had killed the British high commissioner in a road ambush, and that this had helped him rise through the ranks of his district party. His group had proved to be the most vicious and effective insurgent force in the area of operations currently under the control of the Australian battalion. Now the intelligence placed Sam Po just over the Thai border.

Karl had requested the best platoon in the battalion be seconded to him, and the CO had nominated Patrick's platoon under the command of one of his most capable officers, Mr Gauden.

Karl checked his field equipment and cleaned the non-issue 1911 Browning semi-automatic pistol. He liked the weapon because the hard-hitting .45 rounds were known to be knockdown killers at close range. He then destroyed the thin sheets of paper in the file with his lighter, dropping the burning pages into a metal waste-paper bin. Satisfied, he turned off the light to snatch a few hours' sleep before the mess batman came to wake him with a cup of tea in the very early hours of the morning. The only thing that played on his mind was the last directive in the file for his eyes only. Should Sam Po be tracked to Thai territory, he was to lead the searchers across the border in an unauthorised intrusion of Thai sovereignty. He very much hoped it would not come to that.

*

An early breakfast was provided for the men of Patrick's platoon and the company sergeant major had organised their rations, ammunition and other bits of kit. Patrick had his Owen replaced with a heavy FN 7.62 semi-automatic rifle. He could see that Ted had been issued with a Bren gun. They would be carrying around eighty pounds of weight, although that would reduce as they used up their rations.

'Attention!' Lieutenant Gauden called, and Patrick rose to his feet.

'Stand easy,' commanded the big Australian major who had just entered the hut, and the men relaxed. 'Trucks will arrive to take us to our jump-off point. From the intelligence I received, I believe that it was you men who almost caught up with a much sought-after member of the CTs, Sam Po, on one of your patrols. This time we are going to finish the job and either capture or kill him. You will be out in the scrub for an indefinite time, and if necessary we will be resupplied by air. Are there any questions?' There were no questions and the major turned to the platoon commander. 'Mr Gauden, your parade.'

The platoon commander saluted the major as he strode out of the hut.

Before sunrise the trucks arrived and the men piled in. Within hours they leapt out at the edge of one of the new settlements and proceeded to navigate towards the primal forests of the mountain range. As usual it was exhausting under the tropical sun and soldiers' thoughts turned inward to take their minds off the arduous conditions they were suffering. For Patrick, it was a case of trying to remember Sally's every feature as the sweat rolled down his face and the leeches from the swamp they were crossing attached themselves to his body.

Beside him, big Ted grunted with each step carrying the Bren gun and extra ammunition. On the other side of Patrick, Terituba softly hummed a popular Elvis Presley tune. Patrick could not shake the feeling he had that this patrol was not going to go well.

*

Sam Po lay on his back staring up at the few stars he could see through the canopy of branches above his camp. Not far away his small group of men slept after the exhausting trek through the jungles and mountains into southern Thailand. They could rest without sentries because the British were forbidden to undertake military operations in this part of the world.

The Thai army was not interested in hunting them down – so long as they caused no trouble in Thailand – and this was their sanctuary.

Unfortunately they had little in the way of food, as it was difficult to obtain in Thai territory – unless there was money to purchase it from the local villagers. His comrades had suffered too much privation, and they were rapidly becoming a non-functional force, but at least one of the men who had recently joined his party had brought with him a captured Bren gun and a good supply of ammunition. It was now very precarious to raid villages in the area of operations of the Australian battalion. The Australians were extremely active in long-range patrols, setting up ambushes along trails and watching kampongs and villages for any strangers coming or going.

Sam knew that he had to obtain money to continue his guerrilla campaign. As reluctant as he was to leave his men, he could trust his second-in-command, Comrade Ching, while he made a journey south to contact party HQ and request money for food and medical supplies.

The following morning Sam briefed his men. He wondered as he scanned their thin faces which of them would take advantage of his absence to desert and surrender.

Armed with nothing more than a Webley Scott revolver and twelve rounds of pistol ammunition, Sam set out through the forests alone. He knew it was a dangerous journey as this was a land of tigers and elephants and the pistol was not much protection against the big predator cats. But years of living the life of an insurgent had toughened him in body and soul. The pocketful of cooked rice would sustain him and he would supplement it with rainforest fruits.

*

On the third day of the long-range patrol, Patrick's platoon had reached its first RV point. Navigation had been with map and compass, carefully making magnetic adjustments to the bearings. Appointed soldiers kept count of paces taken on the bearing in this world with no clear landmarks to march to.

Lieutenant Stan Gauden sat in the dim light of the forest in a small clearing where a storm had brought down a few of the older, rotten tree giants. The men could see the sky and the tropical clouds brewing into a storm. Two-man hoochies – small tents – were quickly erected in a defensive perimeter to be on guard against any possible attack.

Major Karl Mann and Lieutenant Gauden conferred on their position and their locstat was radioed to the rear support. Soon a small single-engine Auster was flying towards the grid reference they had transmitted. The sound of the aircraft overhead confirmed that their navigation was spot on and both officers were relieved.

It was then that a strange coded message was sent for Major Mann. Only he had the special codebook to decipher the message and Lieutenant Gauden watched curiously as the major translated the message by torchlight hidden by a ground sheet. When he was finished he took a map and placed it on the ground between himself and Gauden.

'There has been a change in coordinates for the CT camp,' Karl said. 'The new grid reference from the latest intelligence places it approximately here.' He pointed to an area on the map.

'But that is in Thailand,' Gauden said. 'Standard operating procedure says that we cannot cross the border.'

'I will be fully responsible for the decision, Mr Gauden,' Karl said. 'The authorisation comes from beyond your CO's level of command. If anything should eventuate it will simply be put down to bad navigation, and not an intention to trespass on Thai sovereignty.'

'With respect, sir, do I brief my section commanders on our incursion?' Lieutenant Gauden asked.

Karl looked at the young officer. 'No,' he answered. 'That would be admitting we all knew. This is a need-to-know operation, so you don't even tell your sergeant. From here on in, just you and I are responsible for knowing where we are on the map. I'm afraid the next airdrop we get will be our last until we are back across the border in our own area of operations.'

Lieutenant Gauden folded the map against the gentle rain-drops that had started to fall, knowing that within seconds they would turn into a torrential downpour, making his soldiers' lives miserable as it soaked them to the bone. The two-man hoochies were no real protection against fierce tropical storms. But, worse still, should things go pear-shaped in Thai territory, Lieutenant Gauden knew his military career was well and truly over. The Australian government would never sanction such an intrusion into an ally's territory.

NINE

Huddled over the map, Lieutenant Gauden and Major Mann ascertained that they were a mere few hundred yards from the Thai border. It was just on midday and above them the thick canopy of intertwined branches cast an eerie light on the forest floor of decomposing vegetation.

'What do we do now, sir?' Lieutenant Gauden asked in a hushed voice.

For a moment Karl frowned. 'I want your best section to go with me across the border on a recce,' he said. 'I gather Private Terituba Duffy is an excellent tracker, so I will require his services.'

'He is in my best section,' Lieutenant Gauden said. 'Do I tell them they are going across the border?'

'That will not be necessary,' Karl said. 'At this stage we need to locate Sam Po's camp, and when that is done, bring up the rest of the platoon.'

'Why not all of us go?'

'Because if things go wrong there will be fewer of us to account for,' Karl said grimly. 'Not that I am expecting any appearance by the Thai army this far south.'

'Okay.' Lieutenant Gauden shrugged. 'I will brief the section that they will be directly under your command for the recce.'

Patrick and Terituba listened as they were instructed to go with Major Mann on a scouting mission to locate the CT camp. There were no questions at the end of his briefing, and the infantrymen forced themselves to their feet. They were to leave their big packs behind and patrol with just their weapons. They followed Major Mann away from their platoon location deep into the forest. Each soldier moved slowly and silently as they had been trained. Terituba took the lead. His eyes constantly scanned the ground around them until about an hour into the patrol when he signalled a stop and requested Major Mann to move up to his position.

'Tracks,' Terituba whispered, pointing to the ground. 'Fresh tracks of three men. They go that way.' He pointed to the north.

Karl nodded and placed his hand on the soldier's shoulder. 'Well done, digger,' he said and moved back to gather his section for a situation report. He could see that the men were exhausted and he called a short break so that they could drink water and recover before proceeding. They would have to be particularly alert as the enemy might have sentries out, although Karl was hoping that in their sanctuary in Thai territory they might be less alert.

Patrick squatted beside Terituba.

'I could do with a fag,' Terituba sighed. But they both knew this was impossible so close to their target.

'You know,' Patrick said, 'I've been counting paces and, according to my calculations, we are no longer in Malaya. I saw the boss's map just before we left, and from where we were last at camp to where we are now, puts us in Thailand. I always thought that one day I would go to Thailand as a tourist, not carrying a gun.'

'Is that bad?' Terituba asked.

'It is if we get caught,' Patrick said. '*Baal*.'

The signal was given to continue the patrol and it was late in the afternoon when Terituba smelled the first sign of human activity. He calculated it was a campfire and signalled to the rest of the section the direction the smell came from. Safety catches came off rifles and every man felt the adrenaline beginning to rise. So far they had the element of surprise as they crept forward, eyes and ears straining in the gloom.

Patrick saw the first CT. He was standing with a rice bowl in his hand, chatting to someone out of view behind the trunk of a large tree. He signalled to the rest of the section who slowly lowered themselves to the forest floor. The signal reached Major Mann and he indicated to Patrick and Ted, carrying the Bren, to flank the site. Terituba and another soldier were given field signals to go around the other flank.

Patrick and Ted had gone about fifty feet when a sudden burst of machine-gun fire tore into them. The enemy might have been surprised but they had reacted quickly. Patrick saw Ted fall and cursed. Just as Patrick hit the ground with his rifle pointed in the direction of the unseen machine gunner, he felt a searing pain along the length of his right arm. It was as if he had been electrocuted. Ignoring his wound, Patrick yelled out to Ted about ten yards from him.

'Cobber, are you okay?'

At first the big man did not answer. 'Caught one in the hip,' he groaned. 'The bastard hurts like hell.'

More bullets ripped up the forest floor inches from both men, and Patrick realised the unseen gunner had them pinned down. Patrick was sure, though, that the enemy could not see him because the trunk of an ancient forest giant lay beside him, concealing his position. Some instinct told him the shots on Ted were meant to lure him out. It was a ruse often used by snipers – wound a man and shoot those attempting to rescue him.

All around him Patrick could hear the constant crash of small-arms fire and even an exploding hand grenade. The fight was on with the rest of his section engaging the guerrillas. But for Patrick the only piece of the fire-fight that mattered was the few feet around him and Ted. This was their battleground and they were up against formidable firepower. From what Patrick could discern, they were being fired upon by a Bren gun. He realised that a bullet had grazed the length of his forearm and opened up a nasty wound that was bleeding profusely. He also felt a numbness in his fingers, along with the searing pain of his wounded arm. But Ted was worse off with a wound to the hip. If the bullet had pierced the femoral artery, the big man would probably die from blood loss before he could be retrieved.

Patrick did not hesitate. He left his rifle and wriggled forward to Ted. Within moments bullets sped towards him, spraying earth in his face. But the enemy gunner must have been forced to redirect his attention to a more immediate threat because the bullets stopped coming in their direction.

With all his strength, Patrick proceeded to drag Ted back to his position. Ted did not let go of the Bren, and suddenly the CT machine gunner redirected a burst in their direction, chipping chunks off the rotten tree trunk. Patrick swore under his breath.

'Thanks, Pat,' Ted said through gritted teeth.

Patrick examined Ted's wound and applied a battle bandage to the bloody thigh. He was not a medic, but was relieved to observe that the femoral artery had not been severed.

'Hey, cobber, it looks like you copped one too,' Ted said when he noticed Patrick's bloody forearm.

The gunfire stopped and the voice of Major Mann came to them from around fifty yards away.

'Private Duffy, Private Morrow. Are you men okay?'

'We copped a couple,' Patrick replied. 'We might need a couple of extra bandages.'

Within seconds the two wounded men were joined by Terituba and the section corporal. Patrick could see the relief in Terituba's face when he saw that his best friend had not been mortally wounded.

'How did it go?' Patrick asked Terituba.

'Two got away, we got the rest,' Terituba answered. 'Major Mann is looking to see if Sam Po is one of the dead. You want a fag?'

Patrick shook his head but Ted piped up, 'I'll have one, Tracker.' Terituba rolled one for Ted and one for himself.

A quick sweep of the area and the bodies of three dead CTs was confirmed. Any papers and documents were collected along with weapons. Major Mann organised a litter to be made from the camp tent poles. Ted was placed in the improvised litter, and his comrades carried him south to rendezvous with the platoon HQ. It was dark when they were challenged at its perimeter and allowed through.

Ted's face was grey but the bleeding had been stopped with bandage compressions. Patrick applied more bandages to his arm, peppered with antiseptic.

Major Mann brought Patrick a mug of hot tea and squatted beside him. 'Private Morrow told me you exposed yourself to gunfire to rescue him,' he said. 'A brave act worthy of official recognition.'

'But that won't happen, will it, sir,' Patrick said, taking a sip of the hot, sweet black tea. 'We were in Thai territory, and I somehow reckon we were not supposed to be.'

'Mr Gauden told me that you should be in officer training,' Karl said with a grim smile.

'Did we get Sam Po?' asked Patrick.

'I'm afraid not,' sighed Major Mann. 'Our intelligence was good, so I think he was one of the CTs who got away. But the papers we recovered from the bodies will possibly be of importance to people higher up. You should consider Mr Gauden's recommendation that you apply for a commission. If you do, I will support your application. The army needs officers like you in this war.' Major Mann placed his hand on Patrick's shoulder and rose to walk away.

Patrick considered the major's suggestion, but to apply for a commission meant leaving his best friend behind in the ranks, and he was not prepared to be separated from the man who was as close to him as any brother.

The platoon withdrew to an area that had been cleared by the CTs for a vegetable patch. The men carrying Ted's litter groaned and stumbled under his weight, cheerfully cursing him for being so heavy. They knew he was in bad shape but kept up his spirits with their constant chiding.

They located the clearing and in a short time heard the whop-whop of an approaching helicopter.

Patrick looked up to see the dragonfly-shaped Sycamore chopper descending into the clearing. It was a tight fit but the skill of the pilot brought it to the ground safely. Ted was loaded aboard and Patrick was ordered to join him as walking wounded. Within minutes the chopper was in the air and Patrick was gazing down at a sea of rainforest trees.

★

The Eastern and Oriental Hotel in Penang was an elegant colonial-style building on the water. It was a place where those who could afford it went to dine or drink.

Major Karl Mann, wearing a civilian suit, sat opposite Sir Rupert Featherstone at a dining table covered with the finest linen cloth. Only days earlier Karl's hands had been covered in blood from searching the bodies of the dead CTs. To the other diners he looked like any other businessman at a luncheon meeting.

'Do you know, old chap,' Featherstone said, 'many famous and infamous people have dined here.'

'Like who?' Karl asked, sipping a gin and tonic.

'Rudyard Kipling, Charlie Chaplin, Douglas Fairbanks, Somerset Maugham. Now you and me.'

'I hope your civil service salary is paying for lunch,' Karl said.

'Always for my favourite agent,' Featherstone replied.

'I am not a spy,' Karl said. 'I am a major in the Australian Army.'

'Who broke one or two international laws crossing the border into Thailand,' Featherstone said quietly. 'Publicly, the British government would never have sanctioned that. Privately, we would have got around any repercussions to you and the men with you.'

'I saw an opportunity to capture or kill Sam Po and I took it,' Karl said.

'From our intel sources in KL it seems you missed him by a day,' said Featherstone.

'Why is the British government so determined to catch up with Po?' Karl asked.

'Let us say that it is a matter of honour. One does not kill a high-ranking servant of Her Majesty and get away with it. Did any of the men you led across the border suspect they were in Thailand?'

'One of the soldiers caught on,' Karl said. 'A very bright and brave digger. However, I reminded him of the Secrets Act. I am sure he will say nothing. We left the CTs' bodies in situ for any tigers in the area.'

'It is a damned pity that you were unable to settle the matter of Po. I have since been given intelligence that he is travelling to a meeting with one of the more important people in the insurgency. We have yet to learn where and when, but when that happens you will be on call to have another crack at him. I will be contacting the CO of the Aussie battalion to second a section of men to you. I want you to use the same section that you used to cross the border as you spoke very highly of their conduct in your report.' Featherstone picked up the menu. 'Now, I think it is time to order lunch. I hope I can afford it as a simple civil servant on my meagre stipend from Her Majesty.'

Karl broke into a broad smile. He knew that Sir Rupert Featherstone was no simple civil servant in the British administration but a ruthless, highly placed spymaster who also happened to have a substantial private income from old family estates.

★

Patrick was very bored sitting around the hospital in Penang. He had protested to doctors that he was fit to return to his unit, but they had countered that his arm needed to heal a little more so that infection was no longer a threat to his health, reminding him that the tropics were a breeding ground for all kinds of exotic bacteria and viruses.

At least he was not bed-bound, but the only other men he could talk to were British soldiers wounded in action up-country and he found little in common with them. Ted had been evacuated back to Australia and Patrick had to admit that he would miss the big boof-headed soldier.

At least he was able to sit out on the verandah and catch up with happenings from home in newspapers flown over. He was reading an article about eight firefighters burned to death in a bushfire in South Australia when he heard a voice behind him call his name.

Startled, Patrick turned to see Sally standing in the entrance to the verandah.

'Sally,' he said in surprise. 'How did you find me here?'

She took a couple of steps towards him, and he rose from his cane chair, self-conscious that he was wearing hospital pyjamas.

'Your name was in the local paper,' she said, staring at his heavily bandaged arm. 'It said that you and another Australian soldier had been wounded in a clash with CTs just south of the Thai border, and I thought I would come to check whether that Patrick Duffy was you. I decided to come and visit a soldier wounded in battle.'

'I would hardly call it a battle,' Patrick said. 'More a brief moment of confusion when I was stupid enough to get in the way of a bullet.'

'I suspect that you're being modest,' Sally said with a warm smile. 'The newspaper article said that you rescued another soldier under fire.'

Patrick had been informed by Major Karl Mann that the newspapers would report the clash, although the location would be shifted back over the border into Malaya. It was important that the destruction of the Communist infra-structure be reported to reassure the Malayan population that Britain and its allies were winning the war.

'You know the papers exaggerate,' Patrick said with a smile. 'Do I strike you as someone stupid enough to put himself in the line of fire?'

'Yes, you do,' Sally said. 'I sense you're not just a simple soldier serving his country. But I won't say any more because you will get a swollen head. I can't stay long as my father wants me at a business function. I am to act as the hostess and impress a local dignitary with my beauty and charm.'

'Your father made a good choice for your role,' Patrick said.

'I was being facetious about the beauty and charm bit,' Sally said, glancing at her expensive wristwatch. 'Well, I must go. I only came to wish you all the best in your recovery, and to see for myself what a wounded warrior looks like.'

Sally turned and walked away, leaving Patrick's thoughts in turmoil. It had been as if an angel had come to visit him and all he had left was the hint of her perfume lingering in the humid air of the tropical afternoon. It was a scent now burned into his brain. He had not even asked if he could see her when he was next granted leave. Patrick cursed himself. She was as elusive in his life as gossamer floating in the breeze.

TEN

Much to his surprise, Sally visited Patrick the next day, and the day after that. They talked about their lives, and Patrick told her that he had been reared by a distant relative, Sean Duffy, in Sydney and had done so well at school he could have applied for medicine, although he had opted to join the army with his best friend Terituba, instead. Sally tried to imagine Patrick's holidays spent on a cattle station in central Queensland, mustering cattle on horseback and hunting wild animals with his Aboriginal friend. It was so far from her own life, she had difficulty picturing it.

Sally informed Patrick that she had been educated in a Swiss ladies' college, and that her holidays had been spent between her father's English mansion and various Asian countries where her father conducted his import-export business.

Patrick was finally cleared as fit for active service. The wound had healed well, leaving a long scar along his forearm. He applied for a day pass before returning to the battalion, and was granted his request.

He stepped into the warm sunlight to find Sally waiting for him by an expensive open-top MG sports car.

'Does that belong to your father?' he asked, impressed.

'No,' she replied. 'It's mine. Hop in and we can go for a spin.'

Patrick settled into the car. Sally put her foot down and pulled into the traffic.

'Where are we going?'

'Somewhere nice,' she said with a smile. 'I think you have earned a reward for your brave service to the Queen.'

Sally drove until they had left the city behind and were on country roads passing through little towns bustling with commerce. Eventually they reached the water. There Sally parked and produced a picnic hamper, spreading out a blanket under the shade of tall trees swaying in the tropical breeze. The blue sky was dotted with fluffy white clouds and off the beach a fishing boat drifted as the men aboard hauled in a net.

Sally spread out cheeses, chutneys, pâtés, thin slices of roast beef and wafers, as well as a bottle of good champagne crusted with ice and two crystal goblets. After Patrick had poured the wine, they sat side by side, gazing out at the tranquil waters.

'You know,' Patrick said, 'I think I have just died and gone to heaven in the company of a beautiful angel. Except I know I'll be forced to return to earth in a few hours because the bloody army owns me, body and soul. I will be on the ferry and back with the company before midnight. It is at times like this that I hate the army. I have cobbers back in Civvy Street who can simply tell their bosses that they cannot come into work because they are sick. Not in the army. There is no such thing as taking leave when you feel like it.'

'We'll enjoy the few hours of your leave that you have left then,' Sally said, reaching over to place her hand on his.

Patrick could smell the sweet scent of her body. He leaned over and kissed her on the lips, and for a moment their touch lingered until Sally gently withdrew. 'Patrick, I don't want you to get the wrong idea. We have only just met, and I don't want you to get hurt.'

Confused, Patrick pulled away. 'I thought you liked me,' he said.

'I do,' Sally replied. 'Being in your company is wonderful, but anything else is doomed. You are a soldier who has no choice of where you will be sent. Nor do I, and my father has plans of opening an office in Hong Kong. I could be sent there any day. We can't be together, not because I don't like you but because of this lousy situation we find ourselves in.'

'Are you saying that you don't want to see me in the future?' Patrick asked, holding his breath at the pain of possible rejection.

'I am not saying that,' Sally replied. 'It's just better we remain friends.'

Her answer crushed Patrick whose desire for her was overriding even his loyalty to the army. In the back of his mind he considered desertion, but he knew that was not a real option. It was ironic that the army had brought him to Malaya to meet the woman of his dreams – only to force them apart.

'I understand,' he said. 'Maybe I should make my way back to the battalion now.'

'We still have a couple of hours left,' Sally said. 'Why not stay with me and enjoy this beautiful place?'

Patrick rose to his feet. He could not stand being near this beautiful woman knowing he could never kiss her again. 'I need to go,' he said bitterly. 'I think the war against the CTs might need me more than you do.'

'Patrick, this is not goodbye,' Sally said. 'We can see each other when you get your next leave.'

'I don't think I can do that,' Patrick said. 'I don't think I can be just a friend to you. It would be too cruel. I'd like to go now please.'

Sally shrugged and packed up the hamper. She walked back to the car and Patrick followed. He could not think of anything else to say and they drove in silence to the ferry terminal.

Patrick stepped out of the MG to join the throng of passengers awaiting transport to the mainland.

'Goodbye, Sally,' he said. 'I hope Hong Kong goes well for you. Maybe we will meet again one day in better times.'

'Patrick,' Sally called as he walked away, but he was lost in the colourful throng of people waiting to board the ferry.

Patrick hardly noticed that he was crossing the strait. All he could do was stare at the small waves splashing the side of the boat and wonder why the pain of losing Sally hurt more than the bullet ripping open his arm. The worst thing about it was that he knew Sally was right. They were from different worlds. He was a simple soldier and she a young woman of wealth and elegance.

Patrick returned to the barracks where he was met by his platoon comrades who had just returned from another patrol deep in the jungle.

Terituba greeted him with a wry smile under the sweat and grime of the day's efforts. 'You bin having a good time laying around the hospital while we bin out in the scrub,' he said and slapped Patrick on the shoulder. Then he saw the sad expression on his friend's face. 'Not so good,' Terituba added.

'Good to be back,' Patrick said lamely. 'How have things been going while I was away?'

Terituba launched into a story about laying an ambush on a CT track, and Patrick listened without hearing. Sally's face was still fresh in his mind. What had his Uncle David once said about his own life? *Lucky in war, unlucky in love.*

*

It was one of those rare but beautiful days in the English countryside when the sun shone brightly in a clear blue sky. Michael Macintosh walked to the crease, trailing his cricket bat behind him. The trials for the school's first eleven were crucial if he was to be seen as more than an upstart colonial kid. Michael had always loved cricket, and back in Sydney had represented his old school as a batsman.

He was acutely aware that in the tiny crowd of people watching was Jane White, the daughter of his hosts in England, Sir Ronald White and his attractive, much younger wife, Lady Georgina White. Jane had been fortunate to inherit her mother's elegant beauty, but the attractive sixteen-year-old was always aloof in Michael's company. This was his opportunity to impress her. He suddenly realised that he was very nervous, not because the spin bowler facing him had a formidable reputation, but because he might be bowled out for a duck in front of Jane.

Michael squared off against the bowler who came in fast and hard. The ball bounced but Michael was able to swing and hit it with all his strength. He was aware of the polite clapping from the pavilion as the ball was driven over the boundary for six. The bowler had turned his back and walked to his run-up start point, shaking his head in disbelief. Michael glanced across at Jane, but she was too far away for him to tell whether she was impressed. He continued to bat and made eighty-six runs before an alert player on the boundary was able to catch him out. As Michael walked off the field his coach said, 'Well done, lad. I hope you can perform as well against Eton.'

Michael reached the pavilion and Jane offered him a glass of freshly squeezed orange juice.

'Jolly good show,' she said with a smile. The way she spoke always amused Michael. He wondered if Britain's upper classes cultivated their own English dialect just to identify with one another.

'Jolly good,' Michael echoed with a grin, mimicking her accent. 'At home we would have said, "Bloody grouse, cobber."'

'You colonials have mangled our beautiful English language with your convict influence,' Jane said with a giggle. 'I know that you had a good education in Australia – where on earth did you learn to use such vulgar language?'

Michael could tell that her attitude to him had thawed in the course of eighty-six runs. She attended an elite ladies' college not far away and it had strong links to his own snobbish boys' college.

'I spent my holidays on a cattle station in central Queensland with some truly rough and tough characters,' he said. 'My cousins taught me how to hunt in the scrub, ride a horse like a stockman and swear like a true colonial.'

'How horrid,' Jane said, pulling a face. 'Did you learn to play polo?'

'No, but I learned how to ride down a scrub bull in the brigalow. I suppose that's a bit like polo.'

'Polo is a gentleman's sport. You must try it sometime. My father has a stable of good ponies.'

Michael sat down next to her and removed the cumbersome lower leg pads. He stole a glance at Jane as she returned her attention to the boy who had replaced him at the crease. She had flawless milk-white skin and grey eyes. She was slim, and her long auburn hair swirled around her shoulders. It was a Saturday morning, and Jane wore a fashionable long skirt.

Jane was leaning forward. 'Isn't that Jason Arrowsmith at the crease?' she asked.

Michael was reluctant to confirm her observation. From the moment he had arrived at his English school, Arrowsmith and his cronies had attempted to belittle him. The boy led a small group whose fathers depended on Arrowsmith Senior for favours in the merchant banking world. Jason was an arrogant, good-looking young man who was also a favourite with the girls from Jane's school.

'Yeah, that's Jason all right,' Michael growled.

Jane turned to him. 'He's doing rather well,' she commented, returning her attention to the young man hitting runs.

'Will you be free this evening?'

'Why do you ask?' Jane asked distractedly.

'I thought that I might ask your father's permission for us to cycle down to the village for fish and chips. I gather they're meant to be very good,' Michael said, almost holding his breath.

'Oh, I am sorry, Michael,' Jane said. 'I'll be attending a party at the Margates' house. Jason invited me to go with him. Possibly some other time.'

Michael immediately felt the wind go from his lungs in his disappointment. Bloody Arrowsmith. Bad enough that he niggled him at school, never mind taking Jane from him.

After the cricket trials were finished, Michael caught a bus to the White country estate with Jane. He was greeted warmly by Jane's mother, while Jane raced upstairs to change for her date with Jason Arrowsmith.

'Did you do well at the trials?' asked Lady Georgina sweetly.

'I think I made the team,' Michael answered.

'Well done, young man,' Lady Georgina said, placing her hand on Michael's arm. 'I shall tell the cook to prepare you a hearty dinner; I expect you're ravenous. It is a pity Sir Ronald is away in London this weekend as I am sure he would have offered you a Scotch to celebrate. Do you play gin rummy?'

'Yes, Lady Georgina,' Michael replied, glancing over her shoulder at Jane who had reappeared in the foyer wearing very red lipstick.

'Jane, ensure that Jason has you home before nine o'clock,' her mother said, dabbing with a delicate handkerchief at Jane's lipstick. 'You know I do not approve of that colour. It makes you look like a loose woman.'

'Mother, this is the 50s. All young women wear bright lipstick,' Jane declared, and Michael thought that the only child of Sir Ronald White could probably get away with anything.

A car horn tooted outside and, when the front door opened, Michael saw a chauffeur-driven Bentley had pulled up in the driveway. He could see Jason Arrowsmith in the back seat. Jane jumped in and the car pulled away just as rain clouds began rolling in on a chilly front.

Michael went back inside with Lady Georgina who produced a pack of playing cards. They played until dinnertime when Lady Georgina retired, and Michael sat down alone at the huge polished teak table to eat a meal of roast beef and Yorkshire pudding. It was delicious and when he had finished he stopped off in the kitchen to thank the cook, an elderly stout lady from the village. Michael noticed that it was already going on ten o'clock and there was no sign of Jane.

Michael was considering going to the living room where the Whites had a television set, when he heard the sound of a car outside. He walked to a window to look down on the Arrowsmith Bentley. He saw the rear passenger door open and Jane step out into the steady downpour of rain. She ran to the front door and the vehicle departed.

Michael went downstairs to greet her. He would make her a hot cup of cocoa once she had changed out of her wet clothes, but when he reached the foyer he was stunned to see that she was crumpled on the floor, sobbing. Michael knelt down beside the stricken girl.

'Jane, what happened?' he asked, placing his hand on her shoulder and feeling her recoil from his touch.

Michael could see that her dress was torn and she had a slight swelling to her face. A cold chill went through him.

'Was it Jason?' he asked, and she nodded between sobs. 'You need to change into dry clothes,' Michael said, helping her to her feet. 'I will make you some cocoa and you can get into bed. I will wake your mother and tell her what has happened.'

'Please, please, do not tell my mother,' Jane begged in a hoarse voice, gripping Michael by the arms. 'I do not want anyone else to know.'

Reluctantly, Michael agreed and led her upstairs to her room. He left her to change. His thoughts were in turmoil as he waited for the kettle to boil on the stovetop.

That bastard, Arrowsmith! He didn't know whether he had done the right thing, agreeing not to tell Lady Georgina. Eventually the kettle boiled and he carried a large mug of steaming cocoa upstairs to Jane's room. The door was open and he could see Jane huddled on top of the bed staring at the wall opposite with a blank expression of shock. Michael gently passed the mug to her and she took it in both hands.

'You do know this should be reported to the village police,' he said quietly.

'No!' Jane replied vehemently. 'My family would not want this to be made public. People would only say I provoked him. I will get over it and everything will turn out for the best. Jason tried to . . .' She paused, not able to say the word. 'But I fought him off.'

Michael felt his anger turning to a cold, dangerous rage. If Jane would not report this, Michael would seek his own style of justice. Deep down in this young man's blood was something that made him more dangerous than most. Although he did not know it, Michael was the product of a man who had fought ruthlessly in war, and a woman who had killed her own father without remorse.

ELEVEN

Michael finished his breakfast in the school's refectory, all the time watching Jason Arrowsmith sitting with his sycophants at a table opposite. Arrowsmith was laughing at his own jokes, and Michael strained to hear what he was saying. Despite the background noise of the other boys in the large hall adorned with heraldry and memorial boards of old boys who had given their lives for king and country, he could hear the gist of what Arrowsmith was saying. It was obvious he was bragging about his 'conquest' of Jane on the weekend and his little group hung on every word.

Michael could feel a strange, cold feeling of violence overwhelming him, and he pushed his chair away from the table to confront the braggart.

'What do you want, Macintosh?' Arrowsmith asked when he looked up to see Michael standing over him at the table.

'I know what you did, you gutless bastard,' Michael said in an icy tone, causing Arrowsmith to blanch. He rose from his chair to confront Michael, picking up a butterknife as he did.

'If you are referring to Jane White, the little slut wanted it,' he said with a smirk. 'Did she run home to Mummy and Daddy to say I forced her?'

'No,' Michael replied, eyeing the blunt knife in the taller boy's hand. 'Worse than that: she told me what really happened.'

'Worse than that?' Arrowsmith frowned. 'You really have a very high opinion of yourself, Macintosh.'

'How about you and I go to the gym to find out all about that high opinion,' Michael said, never taking his eye off the knife Arrowsmith held in his right hand. Michael was aware of the hush descending on the refectory. Jason Arrowsmith had ruled the corridors and dormitories of the school, and his power had never been challenged before.

'Put the knife down now or you will regret it,' Michael said. He could see his confident manner was having an impact on the bigger boy as his smirk turned to a grimace of fear.

Suddenly Arrowsmith swung the knife in a downwards motion, but Michael was ready. Uncle Donald had taught Michael and his cousins the rudiments of unarmed combat. He blocked the bigger boy with his left hand and swiftly gripped the knife arm with his right, snapping it down and forcing Arrowsmith onto his knees. The hush in the room turned to something like a groan. Michael kneeled, gripped Arrowsmith's shirt front and slammed his forehead into his face, feeling his opponent's nose yield under the blow. The knife clattered to the refectory floor. Without hesitating, Michael brought around his right hand in a fist, smashing into Arrowsmith's already broken nose. With a high-pitched scream, Arrowsmith raised both his hands to his battered face and attempted to scuttle backwards away from Michael, whose rage was now red hot. For a second Michael saw Jane's shattered expression, and he slammed his foot into his opponent's crotch as hard as he could. Now Arrowsmith truly screamed in pain.

'Macintosh, stand where you are,' shouted the voice of a housemaster, and Michael complied. He had taken revenge for Jane's assault and was satisfied that it would be some time before Arrowsmith would try to take advantage of another innocent girl.

'You two boys, help Mr Arrowsmith to the infirmary, and you, Macintosh, go to the headmaster's office immediately.'

Michael was well aware of the consequences of his actions. Without a word, he turned and walked from the refectory, while Jason Arrowsmith was half carried, half dragged in the opposite direction. The rage was gone and Michael felt the adrenaline draining from his body. Other than a sore and bloody knuckle, he had no other injuries. His assault had been swift and violent and he would not apologise for that.

*

Sir Ronald White stood in the living room of his country manor in a fury. Before him stood Michael.

'I cannot believe it!' he exploded. 'We offer you our hospitality and this is how you repay us. The headmaster tells me that you offered nothing in your defence for the unprovoked and vicious attack on Jason Arrowsmith. Of course he has no option but to expel you. Arrowsmith belongs to one of the leading families in this country, and I have been informed that his injuries are very serious.

I would not be surprised to hear that the police are involved. You leave me with no choice but to contact your mother and tell her that we will be putting you on the first ship back to Australia. You have no future in a civilised country.'

Michael stood silently as Sir Ronald raged. He had sworn to Jane to keep her secret and he guessed that Arrowsmith would not want to press charges in case the whole sordid story came out. He remembered how Uncle Donald once explained that there was something called frontier justice, and he now understood what that meant.

'Do you have anything to say about the matter?' Sir Ronald asked.

'No, sir,' Michael replied. 'I accept your judgement and will pack.'

'I do not want you to have any contact with my daughter while you await transport back to Sydney,' Sir Ronald ordered, and Michael broke into a broad smile.

'Do you find this funny?' Sir Ronald demanded in an angry voice.

'Sir, I just remembered from my history lessons that the English judges used to sentence convicts to transportation to the colonies. I think I know how they felt.'

'You are not only a criminal but also impudent if you think you can simply assault one of our own. You will never be welcome in our house again. I feel sorry for your parents for having raised such a brute.'

Michael went upstairs to his room. He closed the door and sat on the bed. How strange life could be sometimes, he thought. On Saturday he had been looking at being part of the prestigious school's first eleven and now, a mere forty-eight hours later, he was about to return to Sydney in disgrace. At least at home he would see Nanny

Keevers again. She had been writing to him regularly and, although he had been enjoying living in Britain, he had missed her. She was the only mother he had ever known. He recalled the last time he had seen her. She had tried not to cry as she helped him pack his suitcase, but she'd fallen into deep sobbing. 'Oh, my darling boy, I feel that I will never see you again,' she had said, collapsing onto his bed.

'Don't be silly,' Michael had said. 'I will see you when I come home for Christmas, and I will bring you the best present I can find in England.'

She had reached across to stroke his face. 'Seeing you will be the best present I could have.'

A meal tray was brought to Michael's room by the old cook from the village. She placed it on a side table, and Michael said, 'Mrs Miller, I would like you to know that you are the best cook in England, and I want to thank you for feeding me so well.'

The old lady blushed. 'I've heard about the matter at your school, Master Macintosh,' she said. 'It's the talk of the village. I have not known you for very long, but I would just like to say you are a good young man and must have had a reason for what you did to that other boy.'

'I had a good reason,' Michael said, picking up a soup spoon. 'But it does not matter now.'

After dinner Michael packed a few of his personal things into a large suitcase. He found a copy of *Robbery Under Arms* by Rolf Boldrewood and lay back on his bed to read it for a second time. He knew that it had been made into a film by the British Rank Organisation, starring the Aussie actor Peter Finch.

Eventually it was time to turn off the light and get some sleep. Michael had barely closed his eyes when he heard his door creak open. He came awake quickly and turned to see Jane outlined in the doorway in a long nightdress. She carefully closed the door and crept to Michael's bed, lifted the blankets and slid in beside him.

'I was told you put Jason in hospital,' she whispered. 'You kept your word that you would not tell anyone what happened and now you are being forced to go home. It is not fair.'

'I knew that I would be in real trouble if I confronted that bastard,' Michael said. Jane clung to him and he could feel her naked body beneath her nightdress. 'But it had to be done.'

'Hold me, Michael,' she said and began to cry softly. For moments Michael held her, aware of his burning desire to go further. He kissed her and she responded with her own passion. What happened next was like a dream to him, and a memory he would never forget for the rest of his life. When he awoke in the morning Jane was gone and only the sweet scent of her body lingered on the pillow. Michael was sure he was in love for the first time in his life, but he remembered that very shortly he would be on a ship bound for Australia. Life was not fair.

When he went down to breakfast he was met by Lady Georgina, sitting at the table with her morning cup of tea.

'Is Jane having breakfast with us?' Michael asked hopefully.

'I'm sorry, Michael, but her father has taken her to London,' she said. 'Something happened to my daughter and I wonder if you know anything about that.'

For a moment Michael thought she knew what had happened last night, then he realised what she meant. 'I wish I could tell you, Lady Georgina, but I swore an oath to Jane not to say anything.' Michael picked up a plate and helped himself to bacon rashers, mushrooms and scrambled eggs from a silver dish on the sideboard. 'Maybe some time in the future Jane will talk to you about it.'

'Was it you?' Lady Georgina asked sharply as Michael sat down with his breakfast.

'No, I am not the reason for any distress you may have noticed in Jane,' he replied.

Lady Georgina glared at him. Suddenly her hard gaze softened. 'I suspect that fight you had with Jason Arrowsmith had something to do with my daughter. I have always considered you an honourable young man. Did Jason hurt Jane in some way?'

Michael picked at his bacon with a fork, trying to avoid eye contact. 'You will have to discuss that with Jane,' he said.

'I think I know what has happened,' Lady Georgina sighed. 'Thank you, Michael, for being such a good friend to her. You have been like a big brother to her, and I think my husband should know that.'

Michael felt just a little guilty at the 'big brother' reference when only hours earlier he had made gentle but passionate love to Jane.

That evening, Lady Georgina drove him to the London port in her own sports car to board his ship. It was a cargo ship with a few cabins for passengers. There were no crowds of well-wishers on the dock to farewell those embarking. After his papers had been scrutinised by customs and immigration officials, he was passed to leave. It was then that Michael suddenly felt incredibly alone, despite the fact he was returning to Sydney, Nanny Keevers, and his father.

A fine drizzle of rain fell over the port and a chill was in the air.

A crew member called down from the ship's rail for all to board, and Michael picked up his suitcase.

Suddenly Lady Georgina flung her arms around him, holding him tight.

'Thank you, Michael,' she said. 'I will not forget the sacrifice you made for my daughter.'

Michael disengaged himself and walked to the gang-plank. He made his way to the deck and looked down to see Lady Georgina watching him in the drizzle of the early evening. She waved and he waved back as the ship drifted away from the wharf. Jane looked so much like her mother, he thought as the ship slid further away from the shore. It was time to find his cabin and settle in for the voyage through the Suez Canal and into the Indian Ocean. He wondered what kind of reception he would receive when he got home. Not a pleasant one – not if he knew his mother as well.

So, what was next in his life? Only time would tell. He had travelled to England first-class on a luxury steamship and now he was returning home on a battered and sea-weary cargo ship. The thought that he was being banished for his supposed criminal behaviour was not lost on Michael, who once again smiled at the parallels with Britain's exiled convicts of years earlier.

There were no luxuries aboard the ship and the young man quickly grew bored, until he found out that one of the ship's cooks had come down ill and been put ashore in Aden. Michael approached the dour Scots captain and volunteered to take up cooking duties. The Scotsman stared at him and said that he could have the job, but if he did not come up to scratch he would be tossed overboard. Michael thought he was probably joking but it was hard to tell.

Michael found a battered cookbook in the galley and set out to teach himself how to cook. He proved to be a quick learner, and none of the crew protested at his meals. In fact, they even praised his cooking to the ship's captain. It was hard, sweaty work but Michael revelled in it. He did not care that he was a paying passenger because the work made the days go by quickly.

When the ship eventually reached Sydney, Michael was summoned to the bridge.

'You earned your passage, young fella,' the gruff Scotsman said. 'You will always have a berth on any ship I am skippering,' and he thrust an envelope into Michael's hand. 'I think you have earned your wages for this trip.'

Michael was surprised and, at the same time, humbled by the gesture. He had just earned his first pay packet on a cargo ship that had crossed the Indian Ocean. Before disembarking he went around and shook hands with each of the crew he had befriended: Filipinos, Indians and a couple of Irishmen, who wished him well and extended the same invitation as the captain to join them as their cook.

When Michael stepped off the ship's gangplank with a swagger, he saw his mother and father waiting for him – but no Nanny Keevers. He could see his father's broad smile and noted the scowl on his mother's face. At least half his family was glad to see him home.

TWELVE

'Welcome home, son,' said Charles as he hugged Michael to him.

'Hello, Michael,' his mother said in a chilly voice. 'I hope you have a good explanation for your criminal behaviour.'

'Where is Nanny Keevers?' Michael asked, glancing around the wharf.

'She passed away while you were in England,' his mother replied. 'Charles attended her funeral.'

Michael was too stunned to speak for a moment. 'Why wasn't I told?' he asked when he could catch his breath.

'I'm so sorry, Mike,' said his father. 'I know how much she meant to you.'

'I decided that if you knew, you might want to return home, which would have disrupted your studies,' his mother said. 'As it is, your studies seem to have been disrupted anyway. You do not realise the shame you have brought upon me.'

Michael stared at his mother, trying to comprehend the death of his beloved nanny. 'Oh, I'm sorry that I have brought shame to you, Mother,' he said in a cold voice. 'You have absolutely no idea how important Nanny Keevers was to me.'

'Mike,' his father said in a gentle voice. 'Let's go home so you can rest. We can talk about this later.'

Michael turned to his father who he loved with his heart and soul. The man had been the light of his life under the roof of the Macintosh mansion.

'Yes, Dad,' he said, picking up his suitcase.

On the car trip home, Michael hardly said a word. He was forcing back the tears he felt for the loss of Nanny Keevers. He hated his mother for her indifference to his grief; it was as though she had no human feelings at all.

They reached the house overlooking the harbour and were greeted by a middle-aged woman his mother introduced as their new housekeeper and cook. 'You will find that Gertrude is a much better cook than your old nanny,' Sarah said as she placed her handbag on a side table in the foyer.

Michael pushed past her and stormed up to his room where he threw his suitcase in the corner. He slumped on his bed, burying his head in his hands, and sobbed for the loss of the woman he most loved in the world.

The door opened and his father entered the room quietly. He sat down beside Michael and put his arm around his shoulder.

'I'm so sorry, Mike,' he said gently. 'I wanted to send a telegram, but your mother convinced me that you would cut short your studies. Nanny Keevers died peacefully in her sleep after a bout of pneumonia. I made sure she had a good headstone on her grave; I knew how much that would mean to you.'

'Thanks, Dad,' Michael said, wiping away the tears with the back of his hand. 'I suppose you think I'm some kind of sissy for crying.'

'Son, during the war I saw a lot of brave men cry and they were not sissies. What do you plan to do now that you are home?'

'I'm not going back to school,' Michael said. 'I'm old enough to leave home.'

'But you've done so well academically,' Charles protested. 'You would be foolish not to finish your secondary education and go to uni.'

'I can't explain it, Dad, but I just feel like I want to go out into the world and find something else besides this way of life.' Michael gestured around the room, as though it represented everything he hated about the Macintosh lifestyle.

Charles shook his head. 'I know your mother can be a very cold woman,' he said. 'But deep down I think she loves you. I know she wants you to assume the mantle of the Macintosh companies. Not many young men are given that opportunity. Promise me you won't make any decisions without consulting me first. In the meantime, I thought that you and I could go over to the old Manly beach house for the weekend to do some fishing, and maybe we'll have a cold beer to wash down what we catch. Just don't tell your mother.'

'Sounds good, Dad,' Michael smiled. 'I've never been there before.'

Charles rose from the bed. 'Well, get some rest, unpack and join us for dinner later,' he said with a smile.

Michael watched his father leave the room, his mind in turmoil. He had already made his decision, but he would at least spend the weekend with his father before he left.

★

David Macintosh was now the honourable member of his electorate. His win had been by a large margin against his political opponent, and he had sat in the parliament in Canberra across the floor from Markham's father.

He had had a long day in his office, listening to the people in his electorate and dealing with the flood of memos from his party. He was tired, and dying for a cold beer. As soon as he returned home, he pulled out a long-neck and headed out to the headland where he could simply forget the world, gazing at the serenity of the ocean under a winter sunset.

It was a lonely time without Gail by his side. Why was it that he could not tell her he loved her? The question echoed over and over and the answer was always the same: fear. Fear that she would leave him, like the other women in his life. He knew it was irrational but he could not dismiss it.

'So, the big man of politics is drinking alone.'

David looked up to see Craig Glanville, Gail's son. Craig was now twenty-one years of age, working as a trainee stock and station agent in a business set up by his grandfather, John.

'Pull up a sod of grass and you can drink with me,' David said. Craig sat beside him and looked out at the ocean.

'You know you're a bloody fool,' Craig said, accepting the bottle David passed him. 'You should be with Mum.'

'Your mum has someone else in her life,' David countered.

'And you let that happen,' Craig said, swigging from the bottle and passing it back.

'Your mother made her choice,' David shrugged. 'She is a grown woman and knows her own mind.'

'Well, I know for a fact she'd take you over Hamilton any day.'

David smiled. Stuart Hamilton was wealthy, good-looking and some years younger than David.

'What do you think I should do?' David asked.

'Just go and tell her you love her,' Craig replied. 'Propose to her before Hamilton does.'

David turned and stared at the young man who was like a son to him. 'As easy as that,' he said with a crooked smile.

'I reckon so,' Craig said. 'I know my mum, and I know she still loves you.'

'Well, I will take your advice under consideration,' David said, rising to his feet. 'But tonight I have parliamentary papers to look over, and I have an early start tomorrow.'

Craig swigged the contents of the bottle and walked with David back to the house.

'Don't leave it too long, David,' Craig said as he jumped into his car. 'You never know how long you have in this life.'

*

It was a creepy place, Michael thought as his father opened the front door to the almost crumbling wooden beach house. It smelled musty, and the furniture was from the last century. The caretaker bid them a good weekend and hobbled away to his house nearby.

Michael noticed that the house still had a wood combustion stove with a small pile of timber beside it.

'That stove is the best way to cook the fish we catch,' Charles said, throwing his suitcase on a single bed in a tiny room set off the central kitchen area. 'You can have the double bed in the other room,' he continued as he withdrew a packet of cigarettes.

'This place kind of gives me the creeps,' Michael said. 'It almost feels like being back in the cave on the hill at Glen View.'

Charles glanced at Michael. 'What do you mean?' he asked, taking a drag of his cigarette.

'It's a long story,' Michael said. 'I'll tell you about it one day.'

The two organised dusty crockery and cutlery for their dinner. Charles stoked up the stove and lit the kerosene lantern.

'It's like going back in time here,' Charles reflected as the lantern cast eerie shadows around the room. 'It's as if nothing has changed in the cottage since it was built back in the 1850s. I guess it must have seen many things in its day.'

They ate a meal of tinned meat, tinned beans and spuds baked in their skins. To Michael, who was famished, it tasted delicious.

Charles produced a deck of cards and the two played euchre, with Charles winning most of the hands. They went to bed early with the idea of getting up before sunrise to go down to the beach to fish.

Michael pulled up the blankets of the double bed as the chill of the winter night set in. Almost immediately he fell into a deep sleep until sometime in the early hours of the morning when he jolted awake in a cold sweat of terror. He slowly opened his eyes and attempted to focus in the darkness. He did not know why he felt such spine-chilling fear. There was a movement at the corner of the room and Michael used all his courage to look at it. It was the same Aboriginal man he had seen in the sacred cave! He was an old man holding a long spear and he appeared to be watching him with frightening intensity. There was almost an accusing expression on his dark face. Michael wanted to cry out for help but could not make a sound. He blinked and the apparition disappeared, leaving Michael with a sudden strange thought that it was in this very bed he had been conceived. It was irrational and all Michael could think was that the thought had been prompted by his fear. For the next hour he lay wide awake, wondering if the spectre of the Aboriginal man would reappear. He was still awake when he heard Charles pottering around in the kitchen, lighting the stove.

Michael eased himself from the bed and quickly dressed in the dark. He joined his father in the kitchen where Charles was frying bacon and eggs in a wrought-iron pan. He glanced at Michael. 'You look like you've had very little sleep,' he said. 'Did the ghosts of this old place keep you awake?' he added with a broad smile.

Michael did not answer as he sat down at the table. He knew he could not explain that he had once again seen the spirit of the old man Aunt Jess had told him was Wallarie. But why would he appear so far from the sacred hill? And why would Michael suddenly think he had been conceived here? They were not questions he wished to discuss with anyone.

When Michael and his father returned from a weekend of fishing at the Manly cottage, Michael sat down at the breakfast table with his father.

'Dad, do we still have shares in that shipping company?' Michael asked.

'We do,' Charles replied, poking at his scrambled eggs with a fork. 'Why do you ask?'

'It's just that I liked working on the ship that brought me home, and I was offered a job aboard as a cook.'

'That ship was one of ours,' Charles said. 'But to be a registered seaman you need special papers.'

'I'm sure that you could arrange that for me, seeing as it's one of our ships,' Michael said.

'Your mother would not approve,' Charles said.

'All the better,' Michael said.

Charles put down his fork and looked at his son. Michael was big and strong for his age. He was good-looking and had a confidence beyond his years. He had confided to Charles the real story behind his expulsion from the elite school in England, and Charles had understood – even agreed with his actions.

'What have we got to lose?' Charles finally answered, and Michael broke into a smile.

'Thanks, Dad,' he said, and Charles felt the love in those two words. As the years had passed and Michael had grown up, Charles had realised his son held little resemblance to him. When he looked at Michael, he was reminded very much of David Macintosh. It didn't matter to Charles. He had reared the boy and that made Michael his son.

'I will commence proceedings today to get you the relevant papers. All going well, you will be at sea within a fortnight. I hope you get whatever is troubling you out of your system and return home to settle down. I missed you whilst you were in England, and here you are going away again.'

'It's something I just feel I have to do now,' Michael said. 'I promise to keep in contact and come home to you one day, Dad.'

Two weeks later Charles drove Michael to a commercial wharf on Sydney Harbour where the same cargo ship that had taken him across the Indian Ocean was ready to steam the Pacific for South America. The old Scottish captain greeted Michael warmly, and a few of the original crew welcomed him aboard.

Michael hugged Charles, thanking him for all that he had done to help him secure a passage to see the world from the deck of a Macintosh ship. As his father turned away, Michael saw tears in his eyes.

As the ship departed, Michael waved down at the solitary figure watching from the shore. Although he was sorry to say goodbye to his father, he felt excitement, and a little fear, for his unknown future. He had no idea where his travels would take him, but he hoped that one day the ship would dock in England and he would find Jane White once again.

That evening Charles announced to his wife over the dinner table that he had put Michael aboard a ship steaming for South America, via the Pacific Islands.

For a moment Sarah hardly comprehended what she had been told. But when it sank in she exploded in a fury at her estranged husband, accusing him of being a bad father and putting her only child in harm's way.

Charles weathered the tirade and calmly said, 'I love Michael with all my heart and soul – despite the fact he is David's son. Oh, yes, Miss Keevers told me about your affair with David during the war before she passed away. My only question is, does David know?'

Sarah slumped into a dining room chair and stared at Charles. 'He does, but showed no interest in acknowledging Michael's existence. He even said that you would make a good father to Michael.'

Charles was pleased at David's response; he was an honourable man.

'Then if Michael has some of the natural characteristics of David, he will be able to take care of himself in whatever dangers he may confront.'

★

Rifles had been cleaned, inspected and returned to the armoury. It was time for the platoon to take some leave in Penang after a month of constant patrolling in the jungles of Malaya in search of the elusive Communist terrorists. After showering, changing into clean civilian clothes and being issued leave passes, they jumped onto the truck that would take them to the ferry.

Patrick half-heartedly joined his comrades and sat down next to Terituba. At least with the constant patrolling he had been able to focus on his job as a soldier, but the memories of Sally haunted him in those quiet times. Laughter, ribald jokes and bragging about what would happen when they reached the bright lights of Penang dominated the rowdy conversations, but Patrick remained disengaged from the banter.

'Hey, Pat, what's eating you?' Terituba asked. 'We goin' to get drunk and chase some sheilas, or do we chase the sheilas first and then get drunk?'

'Maybe just get drunk,' Patrick replied.

Terituba did not push the issue. He could see that his friend was hurting and he suspected that it was because of a woman.

They reached the island and the ferry discharged its passengers. Patrick disembarked with Terituba and the throng of Malays, Indians and Chinese going ashore.

'Hey, Pat, you know that good-lookin' sheila over there? She is waving at you,' Terituba said.

Patrick turned his attention to the street opposite the ferry terminal and felt his heart stop. It was Sally and she was standing beside her fancy sports car, smiling at him. 'Sorry, Tracker, but you might have to join the other boys for this leave.'

'Yeah, desert your cobbers for a sheila,' Terituba said with a laugh.

Patrick pushed his way through the crowded ferry terminal to Sally, whose smile was like a wonderful light to him.

'Hello, soldier,' Sally said, flinging her arms around his neck and kissing him on the lips.

'How did you know I would be here?' Patrick asked, dizzy from the kiss.

'I have sources everywhere,' Sally grinned.

'I thought you didn't want to see me again.' Patrick was still stunned by this unexpected turn of events.

'No, you were the one who walked away. And besides, you are a hard man to forget. I missed you.'

That was all Patrick needed to know and he felt as if he was walking on air.

'Hop in,' Sally said. 'This time I am taking you home for a wonderful meal.'

Some of Patrick's platoon comrades who had witnessed the meeting hooted their appreciation for their mate's good luck. Sally cheerfully waved back to them and drove away.

They did not go far before she pulled into the driveway of an elegant colonial mansion with manicured gardens.

'So, this is home,' Patrick said when she stopped at the entrance to the sprawling house.

'For the moment,' Sally said. 'My father has homes in many countries. He is in KL at the moment, so we have the house to ourselves. Do you have any idea how we can fill in your time while you are on leave?'

Patrick grinned, taking Sally's hand and walking with her into the spacious foyer where overhead fans cooled the air and marble floors reflected the tropical light. It was a place of elegance and good taste.

Sally led Patrick up a broad marble staircase to a bedroom. Very few words were needed between them, and when they finally lay back against the silk sheets, Patrick asked one question.

'Why did you change your mind about me?'

Sally rolled over and put her head on his chest. 'A girl can change her mind, can't she? But you are different, and my warning still stands that I am not good for you. Very soon I will be leaving for Hong Kong. I will not be able to see you again for God knows how long. If ever.'

'When we finish our tour we will be sent back to the barracks in Sydney,' Patrick said. 'I could get leave and go to Hong Kong to see you.'

'Let's not think about the future now. Let's just live for the moment,' Sally said, placing her fingers on his lips.

They remained together for the rest of Patrick's forty-eight hour leave pass.

Sally drove him back to the ferry. This time he did not walk away, but he could see a deep sadness in her eyes. He knew that she would probably be out of the country by the time his platoon was granted leave again. It was a real bastard being a soldier when you were not free to be with the woman of your dreams.

THIRTEEN

They were coming across the wire and David Macintosh could not stop them. The enemy wore many uniforms, and the dying soldier beside him had the face of Craig Glanville. Shells rained down and the shrapnel was shredding the bodies of the men he commanded. David moaned, tossed and turned in the bed, alone with his recurring nightmares, when an alien sound cut across the blasts of artillery shells exploding.

David awoke in a lather of sweat and reached for the telephone beside the bed in his Canberra apartment. The cold, dark night was still upon the city, and the luminous face of his watch told him it was 2.30 am. A dread gripped David as he lifted the handpiece. No one called at this godforsaken time unless it was bad news.

'Hello,' David said, shaking off the broken sleep.

'David, this is John Glanville. I am sorry to call you this

time of the morning but I have some very bad news . . . Craig is dead. He was in a car accident on the highway in the hills a few hours ago and died in hospital.' John's voice broke and David could hear his quiet sobbing over the phone as the normally calm man attempted to regain his composure. 'I thought that you should know as Craig loved you like his own father.'

David remembered the dream and felt the tears run down his cheeks.

'I will come home as fast as I can,' he said, and John thanked him before putting down the phone.

Two days later David stood beside the grave of the young man he considered a son. It was a balmy winter's day in northern New South Wales and the cemetery overlooking the ocean was the best piece of real estate in the district. Craig would have been pleased with the spot, David thought, remembering all their times sitting on the headland watching the ocean. Standing opposite him was John Glanville with his arm around Gail's shoulder. Gail held a handkerchief, crying softly for the loss of her only child. There was a large congregation of local people as Craig had been a star in the rugby club and well liked in the district.

When the service was over, David made his way to Gail. He was at a loss for words. What did one say to a grieving mother? David had written many letters to mothers of men killed in his command, but this was different. In times of peace children were supposed to outlive their parents.

'Gail, I will miss him,' he said simply.

Gail looked into David's eyes. 'I know you will,' she said.

The crowd was dispersing, departing for the local community hall where the wake was to be held. David and Gail stood alone beside the open grave.

'Maybe we should go on to the hall now,' David said gently. 'They will be expecting you.'

Gail nodded and, without thinking, David took her hand. She did not resist and the pair walked side by side, under a warm winter sun.

By late afternoon the wake was over and everyone had returned to their homes or workplaces. Gail and David waved goodbye to John and Nancy, both of whom were devastated by the loss of their grandson, and then they were alone again.

They sat at a table at the back of the hall with tepid cups of tea. Gail had wept on and off all day, but for now the tears had ceased streaming down her cheeks. They talked about Craig growing up, and Gail even laughed when David reminded her of the funny things he had done as a teenager.

'You know, Craig came to see me at the farm a few weeks ago and chided me for not proposing to you,' David said.

'Why don't you?' Gail said, and David blinked in surprise.

'I have always loved you and always will,' he said, 'but I am afraid that if I let myself admit how much I love you, something bad will happen to you.'

'Nothing worse can happen than losing my son,' Gail said. 'Or losing you.'

'What about Hamilton?' David asked.

'It's over,' Gail replied. 'He was my attempt to forget you, but it did not work.'

David reached across the table and took both her hands in his own. 'Then I can tell you that I want you in my life until the day I die. As my wife.'

Gail gave a short, harsh laugh. 'A funeral and a marriage proposal on the same day.'

David withdrew his hands. 'I am sorry, my timing is dreadful, but I could not get Craig's words out of my mind. I'm so sorry.'

'Don't be,' Gail said, taking his hands in her own. 'If that was the wish of my wonderful son, then let it be so.'

For a moment David wondered whether he had heard her words correctly. Then he broke into a warm smile.

*

Major Karl Mann left the Malay police outpost and drove to the Australian infantry battalion. A Sten submachine gun lay on the passenger seat, loaded and ready to use in the event of an ambush along the road.

He reached the battalion and parked his car. When he stepped into the battalion HQ he was met by a clerk who recognised him from previous visits.

'Sir, I've just had a signal come through for you,' he said, thrusting out a sheet of paper. 'It's graded urgent.'

Karl accepted the sheet and read the message signed simply 'F'.

'Is the CO around?' he asked the clerk.

'Er, the CO is in a meeting with the adjutant,' the clerk answered.

'Tell the CO that Major Mann would like to speak with him immediately.'

'Yes, sir,' the clerk replied, jumping to his feet and hurrying down a corridor to the CO's office. Karl did not wait but followed the clerk to stand behind him when he knocked.

He ducked his head around the corner. 'Sir, Major Mann is here, and would like to speak to you on an urgent matter.'

'Send him in,' the CO said and Karl walked through, saluted the lieutenant colonel and stood before his desk in a relaxed attention stance. The battalion adjutant, a captain, sat across from Karl in a chair, one leg folded over the other.

'What is it, Major Mann?' the CO asked curtly, annoyed at this officer who seemed to have powerful – but unidentified friends at brigade HQ – and who had been given an authority beyond his rank. The CO suspected that Karl Mann belonged to the shadowy world of British and Australian counterterrorism.

'Sir, I apologise for the intrusion, but a vital message was waiting for me at your HQ when I arrived. It appears that intelligence has pinned Sam Po down to a rendezvous at an identified location not far from here within the next twenty-four hours.' Karl walked over to a map covering the wall of the CO's office, scanning the grids until he found the reference to the hut. 'The location is here – near a kampong – and I require your support immediately.'

Both the CO and adjutant noted the position of the target.

'Adj, what is the current status of our companies?' the CO asked, turning to his adjutant.

'All rifle companies and support companies have been sent on a sweep through the AO. We have one company that has just returned. They are currently in barracks preparing to stand down.'

'Fetch their company commander to me immediately and tell him – with my apologies – that I will require his company to return to active service.'

'Sir,' said Karl, 'if I may suggest, it will not be necessary to stop the stand-down. This kind of mission will only require the use of a section-sized formation. Anything larger may be observed in the location by CT sympathisers. According to our intelligence, we will only be up against two CTs at the most, so a section will be adequate for the job. But I need them immediately.'

'Mr Gauden has one of the best sections in the company,' the adjutant offered. 'I can get him to report to BHQ immediately with Corporal Higgins's section.'

'Good,' said the CO, and the captain departed for the orderly room to instruct the battalion clerk to seek out Lieutenant Gauden and the nominated section.

'What's your plan?' the CO asked Karl.

'It's a little unorthodox,' Karl replied. 'I will require the section to be dressed in native clothing. We will approach the hut as if we were farmers passing on the track nearby. We will only carry pistols and Stens that we can conceal. I will deploy two men in the section to a post not far from the hut with a radio to keep contact with BHQ. The rest of Mr Gauden's platoon can be on standby as a ready reaction force.'

'It seems sound enough,' the CO nodded. 'I will hold you personally responsible if any of my men are killed, Major Mann.'

'I accept the responsibility, sir,' Karl answered. 'But I think this is the best chance we have had to get Sam Po – away from his support across the border.'

'You have some work to do, so I will dismiss you to your duties with my wishes of good hunting,' the CO said.

Karl still had his cap on and saluted the CO before he left the office. Already a confused platoon commander stood in the orderly room, still dressed in his grime-stained jungle greens.

'Ah, Mr Gauden,' Karl said with a grim smile. 'You and your men have been given another crack at Sam Po. I will brief you on the walk back to the barracks.'

The patrol over, Patrick and the rest of the platoon were back in barracks. The rest of the company was making sweeps through the kampongs in the area of operations. Time again for hot showers and cooked food eaten at a table, rather than cold rations under the canopy of the rainforest giants. Patrick was about to shed his jungle greens when someone called, 'Attention!'

Every soldier jumped to his feet. From the corner of his eye, Patrick could see the big major enter the long room, followed by Lieutenant Gauden.

'Stand easy, men. It is with the CO's apologies that some of you will be required to forgo your stand-down. I know Major Mann is no stranger to you, and he will be working with us.'

'It's not a social call then, sir,' a soldier quipped, raising a smile from the major.

'I'm afraid not, soldier,' he replied. 'Mr Gauden will call out the names of the men who I will be briefing at his office in five minutes. All will be revealed then. Your parade, Mr Gauden.'

With that, Major Mann turned and walked out of the barracks. Lieutenant Gauden called out the names of eight men, and neither Patrick nor Terituba was surprised to hear their names on the list. They reported to the platoon commander's office.

'We have received intelligence that Sam Po is supposed to go to a dead-letter drop within this twenty-four hour period,' Major Mann said to the small group of soldiers gathered around in the cramped office. 'The location will be a hut here.' He pointed to a spot on the map spread out on Lieutenant Gauden's desk. 'We will be waiting for him. To execute the operation, you will approach the hut in the garb of local farmers. You will carry only a side-arm or Sten as they are more easily concealed. Each man is to draw his weapon from the armoury, and only two mags of ammo.

I expect the operation will be over in twenty-four hours, and we will return to the barracks.'

Within an hour the section had changed into native clothing and drawn their weapons from the armoury. A truck took them within a mile of the kampong and dropped them off out of view, and the section, led by Major Mann, set off on foot just as the sun was going down over the tops of the distant jungle-covered mountains. Two men left the group to take up a concealed position that had line of sight on the hut, while the others ambled down the narrow track like farmers returning home after a day in the fields.

With great caution they entered the derelict hut and in the gloom saw that it was vacant. A quick search turned up a cache of rice and documents concealed under a straw-weave mat. It was obvious that their prey had not yet reached the hut, and now it was only a matter of waiting.

*

It had been a long and dangerous journey for Sam Po and his comrade, Chin San. But they were only a few hours' march from the native hut at the edge of the kampong. Both men were hungry as their meagre ration of rice had run out two days earlier. At least water had been accessible from small pools after the heavy rains.

'Very soon, Comrade Chin.' Sam encouraged his weaker companion as they continued to move cautiously towards their target and the sun began its journey down behind the mountain tops. Sam knew he was well within the area of operations of the Australian Army and so ambush was a constant fear. To reach the hut meant a small stock of food but, more importantly, a cache of money to purchase more food from local farmers in their own area of operations. There would also be correspondence from the central committee as to future strategies in their guerrilla war. Sam was disappointed that the people had not risen up to support them, and that the revolution to impose a Communist state in Malaya was becoming little more than a dream. Sam had sworn an oath to die for the revolution – unlike the many men now deserting to the government forces who generously rewarded them with cash and land.

Just after sunset Sam saw the hut, but he did not rush in despite his need for food. First, he would sit off the hut in a concealed hide and observe. He had to be sure that his target had not been compromised. His companion would go to the village to make contact with a Communist sympathiser and then report back to Sam. If Sam was satisfied all was safe, they would use the cover of night to enter the hut. It was this kind of caution that had kept him alive for so long.

*

After a couple of hours Chin returned to Sam.

'The comrade has been observing the hut all day and said that all he saw was a group of farmers passing by just on sunset. He has seen no sign of enemy soldiers.'

'Did he know the farmers?' Sam asked.

'He said that he did not know the farmers but he could not see them clearly as it was getting dark.'

Sam mulled over the information. Only a handful of trusted comrades knew of him travelling to this location but news of the farmers disturbed him. Yet when he glanced at Chin he could see how starved he was, and he knew the food was vital. It was a small risk and he would have to take it.

He gave the order to approach the hut, now a dim shape in the light of the rising moon. Sam had his pistol in his hand and his finger on the trigger. Chin was similarly armed and as alert as his leader.

Inside the hut the men had spread themselves out and held their own weapons ready to use. They also held flash-lights, as Major Mann had expected a night contact.

'They're coming,' he whispered. 'Two of them.'

Each man felt the rush of adrenaline and fear. In the next few moments, and in the close confines of the hut, bullets would find targets in soft flesh.

The rickety wooden door creaked open and, for a split second, a figure filled the entrance. The gunfire erupted and Chin hardly knew what hit him as the bullets tore into his body.

The second man turned and began to sprint away. Patrick pushed himself past the door and over the body of the slain CT. He could see the man running in the moon-light and took after him before he could reach a series of rice paddy levees nearby. Patrick stopped for a moment, caught his breath and levelled his pistol to fire off two shots. With more luck than skill, one of his bullets caused the CT to stumble and fall. Patrick began running and, just as he reached the prone figure, the man suddenly sat up and fired three rapid shots at Patrick. He felt one of the rounds clip the lower part of his earlobe and he returned fire, emptying his pistol into the man only a few paces away. The shots found their target, and the CT fell back, dropping his pistol. Both men were out of ammunition but Patrick could see that the CT was alive and critically wounded.

'Are you Sam Po?' Patrick asked, kneeling down beside him.

Though Patrick knew from briefings that the man spoke English, he did not answer; instead, he lay back to stare at the moon on the horizon.

A pistol shot cracked near Patrick's head, startling him, and he saw that the shot had been to the CT's head.

When Patrick turned he saw Major Mann standing behind him, gun by his side. 'I am sure that is Sam Po,' the major said as the rest of the section gathered around, shining their lights on the infamous terrorist.

'Who was this bloke, sir?' Patrick asked, staring at the face of the young man he could see was around his own age.

'He was an interesting character,' said Major Mann. 'When he was young he was a prisoner of the Japs in Changi where he was looked after by an Aussie woman by the name of Diane Duffy – until she died on the last day of the war. Then he disappeared until we first heard of him as the killer of the governor back in 1951 and subsequent leader of one of the most ruthless CT units in northern Malaya.'

Patrick's head was ringing. Diane Duffy! How many women in Changi would have been called Diane Duffy?

'If I may ask you, sir, did this Diane Duffy ever own an air transport business before the war?'

'She did,' the major answered quietly, putting together the pieces from all the files he had read. 'Diane Duffy was your mother, wasn't she? I had no idea there was a connection.'

Patrick nodded, and felt the major's hand on his shoulder.

'I'm sorry, Private Duffy. It's seems almost unbelievable that this man had a connection to your mother.'

Patrick got slowly to his feet and walked back to the hut on his own.

How bloody ironic life was, he thought, that his own mother would be the carer of a future Communist terrorist. But had she survived, maybe Sam Po would never have become a CT in the first place and lived with him in Australia as his adopted brother.

Part Two

Konfrontasi and the Congo

1964

FOURTEEN

Sweat, fear and the heavy weight of the FN self-loading rifle in Michael Macintosh's hands were the reality of his present. The strong and pungent smell of the African Congo was accentuated by the tropical heat that baked the road leading to the township of Kindu on the banks of the Lualaba River. It was a long way from the galley of his cargo ship, upon which he had travelled the globe for six years. But an advertisement whilst he was in Cape Town, South Africa, had brought him to his present reality of belonging to a mercenary force led by the colourful Mike Hoare.

The advertisement had called for fit and able-bodied men to enlist. Military experience was not necessary as the civilians would be given special training once they had been accepted to the force. Michael had returned to his ship, tendered his resignation, packed his few belongings and joined up.

He was not sure why he had chosen the life of a soldier of fortune, but at just over twenty-one years of age, single, and by now bored with his life in the ship's kitchen, he had felt the call to adventure. After passing the entry requirements, Michael had been flown to the Congo aboard a chartered DC3 to join the commandoes being put together by Colonel Hoare. Michael had undergone intensive physical and military training once he joined in a war where the former English soldier wrote the manual on tactics against the brutal Communist-inspired rebels, known to the Western press as Simbas.

Many who had joined with Michael had fallen out when the first shots had been fired. Some had been dismissed because they were deemed not fit enough to be in a disciplined force, while others simply resigned. But Michael was very fit and self-disciplined. In his travels around the world aboard his ship he had continued to study. He had learned an oriental art of unarmed combat ashore in Hong Kong, and already understood weapons handling from his time on Glen View.

As Michael stood awaiting orders from his commando leader, he reflected on a confrontation with the dreaded Simbas, as his column had advanced on the provincial capital, when he had shot and killed many of the rebels as they charged head on, shouting their war cry of *Mai Mulele.*

They were not the first; he had killed many in the days leading up to the assault on the town. Even in his first experience of combat he had been able to overcome his intense fear and put his training into practice. He was thankful that many around him were seasoned soldiers of many nationalities. He had even noticed one seasoned officer wearing the Iron Cross of the Wehrmacht.

They were now only two kilometres from the township and the vehicle column halted and the mercenaries jumped out onto the road. Air cover would be called in to strafe the rebel emplacements with eight .50 calibre machine guns and rockets before the assault by the infantry. Reports had come back from the Cuban pilots flying propeller-driven aircraft that the enemy was reinforcing the southern edge of the town in anticipation of an attack. The Cuban pilots were exiles who opposed Fidel Castro and proved to be very fine flyers.

Like the others of his unit, Michael carried out a thorough check of his weapons. He had honed his bayonet the night before as hand-to-hand combat was not unknown in this war. In the distance they could hear the crump of explosions as the rockets struck, and the continuous sound of assorted small-arms fire.

Sweat rolled down Michael's dirty face, grimed with cordite and the red earth of the Congo.

'Mount up!' the call came, and the mercenaries scrambled aboard their transport for the final dash into the town, while the overhead aircraft circled and dived on the rebels below.

Michael had heard stories of Simba atrocities against the defenceless civilian population of the province. It was said that in Kindu a fourteen-year-old boy had been chosen as executioner in a bid to terrify the population into absolute submission. He would run up and down lines of kneeling men and women, hacking at them with a panga – a version of a machete – lopping off parts of their heads and bodies. When he was exhausted from his efforts of mutilating his victims, he would give the order to shoot them.

The Italians in the unit had a particular interest in the assault of Kindu as, three years earlier, eleven members of the Italian air force attached to the United Nations had landed there and were immediately arrested, hacked to pieces and parts of their bodies eaten in front of the cameras. It was a brutal war in which the so-called rebels were no more than organised bandits whose aims were less political than self-interested, and were expressed in rape, torture, murder, robbery and arson. The Simbas had been told by witchdoctors that they were impervious to bullets. This bolstered their courage when they attacked the out-numbered mercenaries and the legitimate Congolese troops, who often ran away when they learned that the Simbas were coming for them.

Michael had little interest in the politics of Africa, but he did have an interest in the fates of the European and Asian populations currently in the hands of the Simbas. Intelligence had learned that they were to be executed, and the attack might have the effect of rescuing them before the Simbas carried out their threat.

So close was the air support, Michael could hear the empty .50 calibre cartridges hitting the roof of the truck. Adrenaline was surging through his body, and for a moment he found himself thinking about his visit to London a couple of years earlier when his ship had been in port. He had been able to find Sir Ronald White's address in Mayfair and had been greeted by the housekeeper from their country estate where Michael had first met Jane White and fallen in love with her.

The elderly housekeeper remembered Michael and greeted him warmly. However, she was sorry to have to tell him that Sir Ronald and Lady Georgina and their two daughters had moved to New York to live for a few years. 'Two daughters?' Michael had asked, and he thought that the housekeeper seemed a bit uncomfortable when she said Lady Georgina had given birth to a daughter not long after

Michael had been forced to return to Australia. 'Everyone was surprised,' she said. 'But sometimes late-life babies arrive very unexpectedly.' She at least was kind enough to give him a postal address and Michael had written letters to Jane – none of which had received a reply.

Suddenly a row of machine-gun bullets ripped above Michael's head and all thoughts of the past were gone. The killing was about to start again.

★

From the top floor of the office complex, Sally Howard-Smith stood gazing out over Sydney's landscape of rising buildings and tall cranes. Her father's idea of opening an office in the city reflected the growing importance of Australia in global trade, and she had been given the task of setting up and running the office.

She was twenty-seven years old and still a beauty. Her busy working life had not allowed for any steady relationship, although there had been a few affairs with very eligible men. Sally did not feel any pressure to settle down, as so many other young women her age did. Instead, she felt the satisfaction of helping build her father's economic empire, and in her own right she was a very wealthy woman.

'Miss Macintosh will see you now, Miss Howard-Smith,' the voice of the secretary said behind Sally.

Sally followed the secretary through a door into a spacious office with views across the busy harbour. An attractive older woman rose from behind a great, polished teak desk and stepped forward to greet her.

'Miss Howard-Smith, it is a pleasure to meet you in person,' Sarah Macintosh said, taking Sally's hand in a fleeting gesture of greeting. 'Please, is there anything I can have fetched for you . . . tea, coffee?'

'No, thank you,' Sally replied as Sarah Macintosh ushered her to a leather lounge seat before a coffee table spread with coloured brochures advertising the Macintosh Enterprises.

'I was fortunate to meet your father last year at a cocktail party when he was still considering opening an office in Sydney,' Sarah Macintosh said, taking a seat in one of the leather chairs. 'He is an impressive man.'

'More like imposing,' Sally said with a smile. 'I suppose we should get down to business as I know you are a very busy woman, Miss Macintosh. I follow the financial reports and have a relatively good idea of your financial infrastructure.'

'I, too, have read of your father's burgeoning interests in Asia and the Pacific,' Sarah Macintosh countered. Despite the apparent warmth between the two women, they each recognised in the other an inner core of steel.

'I believe that you are prepared to sell your shares in two cargo ships currently operating,' Sally said. 'At the right price my father's company is prepared to make an offer.'

'The *Adelaide Queen* and the *Sydney Star* are the ships in question,' Sarah Macintosh said, removing a cigarette from a gold case and lighting it. She offered one to Sally who politely declined. 'The *Sydney Star* is currently docked here and from last reports the *Adelaide Queen* is somewhere off the coast of West Africa. Both are sister ships, so if you would like an inspection one is almost identical to the other.'

'I have already hired a marine engineer to conduct a survey,' Sally said. 'His report gave the *Sydney Star* a clean bill of health. However, I will not go ahead with the purchase of the *Adelaide Queen* without a similar survey.'

'I fully understand,' Sarah Macintosh said, taking a long draw on her cigarette. 'Nor would I if I were in your shoes. My son is a crew member aboard the *Adelaide Queen*.

According to our schedule, the ship is due here in a couple of months.'

'I am surprised that your son is not here with you as part of your management team,' Sally said.

The older woman rose uncomfortably from the chair and stood before one of the windows. Sally could see that she had hit a raw nerve.

'My son does not wish to be part of the family business,' Sarah Macintosh said with her back to Sally. 'He would rather run away to sea and follow his foolish dream of travelling the world.'

Sally was astute enough to read between the lines and realised that mother and son were most probably estranged. 'I am sorry to hear that, Miss Macintosh,' she said. 'I will contact my father who will make a formal offer on the *Sydney Star* and, all going well, on the *Adelaide Queen* when she returns. I am sure it will be a mutually profitable relationship for both of our companies. I would like to thank you for your time and consideration.'

'I am not being a good host,' Sarah Macintosh said, turning back to Sally. 'I believe that you are on your own in Sydney and single. We have many eligible young men who would love to meet you. Next Sunday afternoon we are having guests over for a tennis party. Would you like to join us?'

'Thank you, I love tennis.'

'Good,' Sarah Macintosh said, extending her hand in a regal fashion.

Sally bid the woman a good afternoon, took the elevator down to the ground floor and stepped out into the hot January sun. She caught a taxi to her Potts Point apartment, which was large and expensive and had a balcony overlooking the harbour. To Sally the apartment was simply a place to sleep and eat. She had known many homes in her life – always expensive – and this was just another one.

Sally could feel the summer heat causing her to perspire, so she stripped off into a fashionable one-piece swimsuit. She poured herself a gin and tonic and turned on the radio to find one of her favourite songs playing – 'Up on the Roof' by the Drifters. She stepped out onto her balcony, stretching out on a deckchair to soak in the remainder of the day's warmth. Sleepy in the late afternoon sun, she had a fleeting memory of the young soldier she had met in Malaya during the Emergency. Patrick Duffy. The recollection of his name flooded her with sweet memories of their lovemaking. No other man had been able to match him in her experience of men, and Sally had come to regret not keeping in touch with him. But she was a practical woman with ambitions, and loving a soldier was not part of her plans. She remembered that his battalion was stationed in Sydney when not on active service overseas.

Just for a moment Sally wondered where he was, before she finished her drink and the song came to an end.

*

Another jungle, another war and the same annoying insects. With a long twig, Sergeant Patrick Duffy cautiously pushed away a giant venomous centipede that had been crawling on his water canteen. He sighed with relief when it used its many legs to disappear into the rotting foliage around him. The insects might be just as perilous, but this war was different. It was virtually a secret war against the Indonesian army on the border of Malaysian Sarawak and Indonesian Kalimantan on the island of Borneo. He looked at the eight exhausted members of his section and knew that he was in the same condition.

Patrick hardly cared for the political rationale that had convinced him to sign on for another three years in the Australian Army. He had been on the verge of completing his original six-year enlistment when his company commander promised him another campaign if he signed on.

As Patrick sat contemplating the wildlife of Borneo, he wondered at his insanity. It was like Malaya all over again – except Malaya was now the independent nation of Malaysia, and its Indonesian neighbour objected to the formation of the new nation, claiming it was British rule hidden behind the cloak of independence, so it had begun armed incursions across the border into Malaysian Borneo.

So here he was in Sarawak on the border with Indonesia fighting a secret war that the media did not report on. After World War II, Indonesian President Sukarno had received political support in the United Nations from Australia against the Dutch reoccupation, and although Sukarno ranted about the British involvement in the present confrontation, he made little mention of Australian and New Zealand involvement in this jungle war of ambush and counter-ambush.

For now, Patrick could rest; it had been arduous crossing into the Indonesian territory of the renamed Kalimantan with an infantry section from his platoon. They had crossed a swamp with leeches and green tree snakes hanging from bushes, and battled with fire ants whose sting could bring tears to the eyes of the toughest soldier. They had come across the footprints of a leopard and startled each time a monkey or orangutan made itself known from the gloom of the heavy rainforest bordering the swamps. The heat was intense and the humidity oppressive in this place on the equator.

As a sergeant, Patrick should have remained at platoon HQ, but the corporal who was to lead the patrol had gone down with heat stroke, and Patrick was able to convince the company second-in-command, Captain Stan Gauden, that he should take his place. The mission was to cross the border and carry out a reconnaissance for signs of Indonesian army camps. Like everything else about the war, the mission was a secret.

Patrick could see his Iban tracker a short distance away chopping up edible plants he had acquired on the patrol. The Iban had once had a fearsome reputation as head-hunters, so Patrick was glad they were on their side in this undeclared war. The brown-skinned warrior wore trousers but no shirt and carried a spear, knife and blowpipe, all good close-quarter weapons. The Iban did not recognise borders as they roamed the jungles. The tracker had picked up signs of Indonesian army boot prints, and Patrick's patrol moved extremely cautiously, avoiding the well-beaten animal tracks; the Australians knew that the Indonesians often laid mines there for those hoping to use the trails as easier means of crossing terrain. It was late afternoon and Patrick was already considering a place to bivouac for the night. There would be no cooking fires and total silence when they made a small shelter against a surprise attack.

The radio they carried was a British model and not very effective, but it provided the only contact they had with the outside world. At designated times they had to report back to BHQ, which was something of a chore, having to set up the radio and attempt to tune in to a frequency.

Patrick hoisted himself to his feet and signalled for the rest of the section to follow him as the Iban tracker set out in front to follow the tracks.

For a moment Patrick thought about some of the more senior NCOs in the battalion who had been transferred to the newly established Australian Army Training Team

Vietnam, operating as advisors to the South Vietnamese forces. Maybe they were having a better time of it, he mused. With a little more seniority he would join them. In the meantime, he moved silently with his patrol and was acutely aware that they could be ambushed. Another country, another war – but the same demanding conditions.

FIFTEEN

It had been another long day at the office for Sarah Macintosh. All that was on her mind when she stepped through the entrance to her home was pouring a gin and tonic and slumping into the big leather armchair in the library. She went to the dining room and saw the familiar sight of her husband sitting at the table. He was ashen-faced, with a letter in his hand. He glanced up at her and she thought he had tears in his eyes.

'What is it?' she asked, taking the gin bottle from the drinks cabinet.

'Michael,' Charles replied. 'He is no longer on the ship. He resigned to enlist with a mercenary force in the Congo. This letter is dated a month ago, and God knows how he is this very moment.'

Sarah felt the blood in her face drain. She had expected him to return to Sydney on their ship and possibly even consider joining her in the Macintosh enterprises. That very day, Sarah had been forced to discuss the future leadership of the companies with her board of directors, who wanted a succession plan in place. She had read about the Congo mercenaries in the papers, which condemned their involvement. Oh, there were shades of David Macintosh in her son.

'Michael has never written to me – always you – so why did you not use your influence to bring him home?' Sarah accused.

'If I had known he was going to do something as stupid as this I would have bloody well flown to Africa to talk him out of it,' Charles snapped. 'It's a dirty little war and I have read that Mike Hoare's mercenary force has already received casualties. When I served as a fighter pilot it was always with the thought that the next generation would not have to face war. Bloody mankind never learns from the past.'

'What are you going to do about the situation?' Sarah asked, still feeling the chill of fear at the possible loss of the heir to all she had achieved. The Macintosh companies were clawing their way back on the prosperity of the last decade. Sarah had been smart enough to take a page from Jessica Duffy's book and followed her investing in mining in the west. The gamble had paid off, and Sarah was forced to grudgingly admit her sister-in-law was a lot smarter than she had initially estimated.

Charles carefully folded the letter, replacing it in the sweat-stained envelope. 'I will do what any father in my position would do,' he said quietly. 'I will go to Canberra and speak with someone who has influence to help me get our son back.'

Sarah was satisfied with Charles's reassurance. He may have proven to be a drunk, but deep within the man she had married was the iron core that had kept him alive in the skies over the Pacific.

It was paramount that Michael return to Sydney to join the extensive Macintosh Enterprises so that everything she had achieved could continue under the family name, as it had ever since the business had been established by her proud Scottish ancestors.

*

The trucks drove in a mad dash towards the heart of the town. Michael fired off two rapid shots at a roadblock. Beside him in the truck the other mercenaries poured out a withering fire, scattering the Simba defenders who ran in panic for the bush nearby. When behind cover they fired sporadically at the convoy.

At the entrance of the town, the convoy halted and the commanders ran to the leader for further instructions for the final assault. Orders were given to seize the ferry, capture the railway station and secure the wharf area. Men were tasked with securing the rear, and the Italians, out for revenge, protested being included in the security detail. The commander understood their need to track down the brutal perpetrators of the slaughter of their countrymen and gave them permission to join the assault force. As he spoke a Ford truck nearby exploded in a fireball, scorching the men in the orders group.

Michael and his comrades dismounted, advancing quickly and using the buildings as cover. When Michael peered around the corner of one building he could see dozens of semi-naked Simbas wearing monkey-skin headdresses, milling about in panic. The sudden attack on Kindu had taken them by surprise and it appeared many were questioning the magic that was supposed to make them immune to bullets.

Michael took careful aim and, with rapid fire, brought down seven of the enemy before his 20 round magazine was empty. He quickly reloaded and took aim into the frenzied mob of rebels. Again, he could see his bullets taking a toll, and he was joined by the others in his commando, reducing the threat.

Michael could see the ferry was a short distance away, drifting down the river with many of the escaping Simbas aboard.

They were easy targets and Michael continued to take aim and fire. He could see the heat from his rifle barrel shimmer under the hot, tropical sun.

The river was running red with their blood when a whistle blew: the signal to cease fire. His commander called on the enemy aboard the ferry to surrender, and they complied.

Behind the small mercenary force followed the Congolese government soldiers, clearing the town, house by house, of any further rebel resistance. It was all over for the moment, and Michael immediately checked his supply of rifle rounds. He could feel the adrenaline draining from his system and saw a fellow mercenary a few feet away, leaning on his rifle and smoking a cigarette. He knew the man relatively well as they had enlisted together and become friends. He was the same age as Michael and hailed from London, where a broken relationship had caused him to leave his job as a motor mechanic and travel to Africa to enlist in Mike Hoare's Wild Geese. The young man also been a territorial soldier and had been trained in the military before enlisting.

'Hey, Frankie, you got a spare fag?' Michael asked, and the red-headed, lean young man tossed a packet of Woodbines to him.

'Thought you didn't smoke,' Frankie said. 'It's bad for your health.'

'Yeah, well, so is this war,' Michael replied, taking a cigarette and tossing back the packet. Michael had a lighter he kept for starting campfires. With a deep puff he inhaled the smoke, feeling its calming effect almost immediately. It was only then that he noticed how his hands trembled uncontrollably. He could feel his legs trembling and glanced around to ensure nobody had noticed his physical state, lest they interpret it as fear.

'We're still alive,' Frankie said, staring across the river running with blood. 'Not so those poor buggers out there in the water.'

Michael found some shade in the lea of a brick wall and slid down with his rifle upright between his legs. Frankie joined him.

'I read that you Aussies have our Beatles touring Down Under,' Frankie said to take their minds off their post-combat jitters. 'I was in Germany when I first heard them performing. Always thought they had a bit of talent.'

'They aren't too bad,' Michael said, taking a draw on his cigarette. 'But I prefer your Pommy group, Gerry and the Pacemakers.'

'Not me,' Frankie said, flicking his butt into the dust of the town. '"You'll Never Walk Alone" reminds me of my girlfriend; she dumped me for our local soccer star. You got a girl?'

Michael thought briefly of the one night he had spent with Jane White, a memory he could never forget, despite the torrid one-night stands when his ship was in port.

'I sort of had a girlfriend when I was a lot younger,' Michael said. 'She was the daughter of a Pommy knight. One of your sirs.'

'Hell, anyone I know?' Frankie laughed.

'Not likely,' Michael grinned. 'You have to have some class, you Pommy bastard.'

Frankie had come to learn that 'bastard' was a word Australians used for someone they very much liked – or hated. He knew with Michael it was an endearment.

'C'mon, you two,' a voice bawled. 'You don't get paid to lounge around.'

Both men eased themselves to their feet.

Michael and Frankie had both been present when the Europeans scheduled to be executed were released. Michael watched as the deliriously happy men and women kissed the cheeks of their saviours. They had only been hours – maybe minutes – from being hacked to death. This was what it was all about, Michael thought as a middle-aged man, babbling in Belgian, kissed him on both cheeks.

They'd hardly had time to enjoy the gratitude of the released prisoners before they were told they would be in the assault group to capture the vital airfield. They advanced in a long skirmish line and the order was given to fix bayonets. Michael slid his carefully honed knife from the scabbard and clicked it into place at the end of his rifle. He had read about bayonet charges conducted in previous wars, and now his stomach was twisted in a mixture of fear and anticipation. This was war at its most basic, when the bodies of friend and foe were locked together and they could see the fear in the other man's eyes and smell his sweat.

Orders were shouted by their commander not to bunch up. A volley from a machine gun, or bomb from a mortar, could easily take out more targets if they were close together. Michael glanced to his right to see Frankie's grim expression.

The tropical night was on them and they could see the lights of the control tower in the distance. Their commander shouted, 'Get in!' and led the charge across the tarmac. Such was the ferocity of the attack that the enemy fled, leaving three of their slower comrades dead on a verandah. The airfield had been taken and the mercenaries had suffered no casualties. Nor had they had to use their bayonets.

Beside him, Frankie uttered his favourite phrase, 'We're still alive.'

But Michael's hands were trembling again and he wondered if his luck was due to run out before the term of his contract.

*

It was rare for Donald Macintosh to travel away from Glen View Station, but he had made an exception to be at his eldest son's acceptance to Sydney University to study engineering. Jessica had a family house in the leafy suburb of Strathfield and today Donald took a train into the city to see his old friend whom he considered a kind of uncle, the solicitor Sean Duffy. Donald was always aware that his battle-damaged face drew curious looks from the people on the streets but he no longer really cared. Time had softened some of the scarring, but not the nightmares he still experienced of fighting in the Pacific campaign.

Donald made his way up the wooden stairs until he reached the first floor and was met by a pleasant young lady. He gave his name and the receptionist called through on her telephone.

Donald did not have to be ushered into the solicitor's office as Sean limped out on his walking stick to greet the man who had been as close as a son to him.

'Don, you old bastard. How the devil are you?' Sean said, embracing his guest.

'Who are you calling old, you old coot?' Donald grinned, disengaging himself from the embrace.

'How long has it been?' Sean asked, stepping back to look at the man who ran a huge cattle property. 'Six, seven years?'

'Six years,' Donald answered. 'The last time I was down in the big smoke was when Jessie and I put Shannon in boarding school. I remember we had a bit of a session.'

'Ah, yes, I vaguely remember you got into a spot of bother with Jessie over that. But she has obviously forgiven your transgression to allow you out again. Come into my office and I promise not to get you into any more trouble.'

Sean's office was cluttered with piles of court briefs wrapped with pink tape, and Donald took a chair at the desk. The two men chattered on about family and reminisced about times past, until Sean turned serious.

'Donald, it's fortuitous that you're here because I think you might be of help with something I have had in my possession the last six years or so. It has haunted me, and just on a hunch I feel you may be able to help.'

'Anything I can do,' Donald replied.

Sean rose from his chair and hobbled to a metal filing cabinet, withdrawing an innocuous-looking cushion. He handed it to Donald without comment and waited for his reaction.

Donald looked at the pillow. 'This looks like one of the pillows we had at the family home. Yes, I remember my father had the special embroidery done in the corner.' Donald turned it over. The bloody outline of the face stared back at him and a chill ran through his body like an icy knife. 'God almighty!' he said in a hushed voice. 'It's like looking at my father . . . How did you come by this?'

'A long story,' Sean said. 'All I can tell you is that it came from a tea chest in Preston's home up the coast. You could say that we borrowed it.'

Donald stared at the face and shuddered. Memories of the hard, stern man flooded him and he wanted the terrible apparition gone from his presence. Donald handed the pillow back to Sean, who replaced it in his metal cabinet.

'When I first saw it I had a nagging feeling that it was of importance,' Sean said, sitting down at his desk. 'Over the years I would take it out, and the more I did, I felt it was tied to old Sir George's death. In my opinion you have confirmed that what is imprinted on that pillow is the death mask of your father. From my experience, the only way it could have got there, is if someone used the pillow to smother a badly injured man.'

'Sarah!' Donald uttered in a hushed voice. 'She was the only one in the house when my father fell down the stairs. That could only mean he was not dead and she finished him off by smothering him. Then she called the police to report the so-called tragic accident.'

'Preston was the investigating officer, and he once worked for your father outside his role as a policeman,' Sean said. 'He then continued working for your sister after your father's death. I would bet London to a brick that Preston was keeping the pillow to blackmail your sister.'

'Oh, dear God,' Donald groaned. 'Murder seems to be a part of our family tradition – going all the way back to Glen View in the 1860s. We really are cursed.'

'Not all the Macintosh descendants,' Sean said gently. 'Your marriage to Jessie was a reconciliation of the two families, and I think old Wallarie has talked to the ancestor spirits on your behalf. Look what you have: a wonderful woman and beautiful family to be proud of.'

'Why do I have an uneasy feeling the spirits of those massacred so long ago on our property will never forgive those of Macintosh blood?' Donald said. 'Who else will Wallarie mark for a violent death?'

'Listen to us,' Sean said. 'All that happened in the past and it's well and truly forgotten today.'

'Not by us,' Donald countered. 'You and I remember.'

'We will be the last,' Sean sighed. 'Wallarie, and what happened to his people a century ago are just part of the unknown history of a bloody frontier. Nobody in our society wants to acknowledge what happened to the Aboriginals of the Queensland frontier. And as for your sister, what she did was just another case of patricide. Not the first and won't be the last.'

When they said goodbye, both men rose and shook hands with iron grips. It was a sad parting, and as Donald made his way down the steps onto the city street, he carried with him a sense of foreboding. Had the curse run its course – or were the vengeful spirits of the dead waiting to strike the blood of the Macintosh clan once again?

SIXTEEN

It was a dreaded Bouncing Betty mine, but it had not activated when Sergeant Patrick Duffy stepped on it. 'Mine!' he yelled. The sweat running down his face from under his bush hat was not all due to the extreme humidity. The anti-personnel mine normally blew into the air around chest height and exploded, showering anyone within a large radius with red-hot shrapnel.

Patrick knew that in Operation CLARET the unspoken order was that any casualties would have to be carried out of Indonesian territory. No helicopter could risk flying in for a medivac, and the chances of surviving a direct blast from a landmine were zero to nil.

'You okay, sarge?' a worried voice asked behind him. Patrick was leading the platoon as their commander had fallen badly ill with a dose of malaria.

'I think I almost pissed my pants, Harry,' Patrick replied,

very gently taking his foot off the buried mine. It had been the click of the mine arming itself that had alerted Patrick to his precarious situation, but there had not been a follow-up explosion. When Bouncing Betty mines went off, it seemed like one explosion when in fact it was two, such was the speed of activation.

'You ought to buy an Opera House lottery ticket when we get home,' someone else said as Patrick walked away with shaky legs. He was pleased to see that his platoon had gone to ground when he had yelled, 'Mine!'

'Okay, no excuse to have a rest,' Patrick growled gently, still experiencing the terror of his near-death experience but not allowing it to affect the men around him. The reconnoitre of Indonesian military movements in Malaysian territory would continue. As Patrick led his men he wondered whether, had he been killed, his death would have been reported as an accident back in friendly territory. His Uncle Sean may have been astute enough to know different, as he had once been a soldier himself and had lost his legs from shrapnel in the Great War. But this was a secret war and those at home hardly knew of its existence, as Australia and Indonesia were not officially in conflict. Even now peace talks were being carried out, but the patrolling continued as a pre-emptive measure to force the Indonesian army back into its own territory.

The platoon found itself facing a murky swamp followed by jungle that had to be cut with machetes, which made everyone feel nervous as the clearing caused noise. The Australian infantry were trained to move silently, using hand signals for just about everything. Leeches and scorpions abounded, and the screeching of monkeys was guaranteed to set off jangled nerves.

Patrick had the responsibility of navigating with maps that were not very accurate. Navigation distance was measured by counting each pace, and the compass kept them moving in the right direction as landmarks were few and far between. Patrick knew he should be looking for a good defensive position before night fell, and prayed that when he did, it would not be infested with fire ants. He had a great appreciation for the role of the junior officer who normally led a platoon and wondered whether his constant rejection of offers from his superiors to attend officer training at Portsea were right. He was doing the job of an officer and knew that he had the respect of the men in his platoon. Maybe he should think about a commission. Terituba had made a lot of friends amongst his fellow soldiers and both he and Patrick saw less of each other now, although they remained as close as brothers. For now, though, his task was to keep a low profile, observe Indonesian troops along the border and get his men back into friendly territory without any casualties.

★

Solicitor Sean Duffy re-read Patrick's latest letter, posted from the theatre of operations in Borneo. He folded the letter and carefully filed it with the many others he had received over the years, ever since David Macintosh had signed up for the last world war. The two boys he had virtually raised had placed themselves in harm's way for what was beginning to feel like his whole lifetime.

He sat in his office and gazed at the pile of court briefs on his desk. Sean was almost seventy years old and had hoped to retire from his legal practice years earlier. He had secretly dreamed that either David or Patrick would study law and join him, but neither man had.

David was now a high flyer in federal parliament, and Patrick a soldier fighting against the Indonesian army.

David had made a point to stay over with Sean whenever his parliamentary work brought him to Sydney, and they had discussed the ramifications of the newly introduced National Service Act conscripting twenty-year-old males into the army. David had expressed his dismay that the act would be amended with a provision to allow conscripts to be sent on active service overseas. The Americans were appealing to the Australian government to send a task force to the new battlefields of South Vietnam. As a politician who had experienced the horrors of three wars, David was reluctant to support the amendment. It was fine for those of his colleagues who had never experienced war first-hand to endorse such an action, but David was still haunted by his memories from the hills of Spain to the craggy mountains of Korea, via the deserts of North Africa and the jungles of New Guinea.

Sean could only hope Patrick would leave the army after his enlistment was up. But the emerging war in Vietnam did not give him much hope, as there was something in their Irish blood that made them warriors.

'Major Duffy.' The voice of his young law clerk snapped him back to the present. 'There is a policeman who wishes to see you. Detective Senior Constable Wren.'

'Show him in, Peggy,' Sean said, and Brendan Wren entered the room.

Sean stood, offering his hand. 'Young Brendan,' he said. 'Good to see you after such a long time.' Brendan Wren was not so young any more. A policeman of almost forty and already thinning hair betraying his years. He had a hard face but gentle eyes.

'Mr Duffy, I have some bad news,' he said, removing his hat.

For a moment Sean felt a chill of fear. Had Patrick been

killed in action? Surely if he had, the army would have sent an officer to tell him.

'What is it?' Sean asked in a choked voice.

'It's Harry Griffiths,' Brendan said, twisting the hat in his hands. 'He has passed away. The boys found him after they had a call from a neighbour concerned that she had not seen him for a couple of days. He was found in his bed and, from what I could see, he died peacefully in his sleep. Probably a heart attack. I knew how close you two were, so after informing his family I came here to tell you.'

Sean slumped back into his chair, attempting to take in the news. Harry Griffiths and he had lost their youth in the trenches of the Western Front and had formed more than a business relationship. Harry was Sean's dearest cobber.

'Thank you, Brendan, for remembering me.'

'Old Harry was a great mate of my dad when they served together on the beat. If there is anything I can do . . .' Brendan extended his hand, and Sean accepted it. When the detective had departed, Sean sat back and stared at the wall, remembering the last escapade they had shared, raiding Preston's beach house. That was years ago now, but the two men had regularly shared company and conversation over a beer at the pub around the corner.

Sean wiped his eyes, reached for his walking stick and hobbled to the receptionist desk. 'Cancel the rest of my appointments, Peggy, and close the office. Have the day off and go to the flicks.'

Peggy was a pretty young woman in her early twenties who wondered why the Major sometimes called her Allison. Maybe he was getting vague in his old age. But she genuinely loved working for the Sydney solicitor who was kind and gentle.

'Thank you, Major,' she replied. 'Are you feeling all right?'

'I'm fine.' Sean smiled weakly. 'I've just been given the news that a dear old mate of mine has now gone from our ranks.'

Soon Sean found himself sitting at the bar in the same place he and Harry had always frequented. The barmaid, a woman in her fifties who had known the two men well, already had a beer poured.

'I heard the sad news about Harry this morning,' she said, placing the glass before the solicitor.

'Another one for Harry, Maggie,' Sean said, reaching into his pocket for a two-shilling piece. Maggie did not question one of her best customers and fetched a second glass of beer, placing it beside Sean's. Sean raised his glass to the empty stool beside him.

'Harry, my old cobber, here's to a life rich in memories.' Sean tilted his glass and drank until it was empty. Maggie knew that before the afternoon was out she would be calling a taxi for the lonely man drinking beer after beer to his old friend.

★

The funeral was held at Rookwood Cemetery and Sean was pleased to see a large and interesting gathering of mourners. Amongst the many friends, Sean saw former retired police officers, boxers, soldiers from the old battalion, and more than one or two colourful characters from Sydney's underworld.

An early spring storm was brewing off the coast and Sean was glad to have brought his umbrella. He nodded to a few familiar faces and made his way over to Harry's son, Daniel, and they stood together beside the grave as the minister droned on about Harry being welcomed into heaven to join the hosts of the righteous.

Even Harry's son flinched at that, and Sean leaned over to whisper in his ear, 'Heaven for Harry is a bar stool in a cool pub, where the beer is always cold and free.'

Daniel grinned and turned to repeat Sean's aside to a woman next to him who looked to be in her late middle age. Sean had never seen her before and was struck by her poise and elegance. She broke into a smile and nodded her agreement to Sean.

When the service was complete, Sean threw a handful of dirt on his old friend's coffin as it was lowered into the ground. Once Daniel had left, most of the mourners drifted away, destined for the nearest pub to raise a glass or two of beer to the memory of their friend, leaving Sean and the woman standing alone by the yawning grave.

A breeze picked up, thunder rolled across the skies now black with the impending storm, and big fat droplets began to fall.

Sean could see that the woman had no umbrella and he immediately offered the use of his. She tried to protest but he insisted, and under the flimsy protection they walked to a shelter a short distance away to wait out the downpour.

'Thank you,' she said when Sean rolled up his umbrella. 'I don't think we have met.'

'Sean Duffy. Were you a friend of Harry?'

'I was a first cousin. I'm Rose Wallace. My memories of Harry are from when I was very young. He was my favourite cousin. Before he went off to the war he would play with me and give me piggyback rides. He was a great teaser and so full of fun. But he came back from the war a different man, and we lost contact. I was told by Daniel that his father had passed away and I just wanted to be here to tell him one last time how much he meant to a snotty-nosed little girl.'

'He was my closest cobber,' Sean said. 'We had one or two good times together.'

'Daniel told me about you two,' Rose said with a glint of mirth in her eyes. 'He said you were both a couple of larrikins. He said he could understand why his father might bend the law, but not a well-known and respected solicitor such as yourself.'

'Oh well, you only live one life, and my life behind a desk and in courts can be a bit boring. Harry was always around to liven things up for us both. Did your husband know Harry?'

'My husband died just after the first war from the effects of mustard gas,' Rose said. 'It was a cruel death, and now I feel fortunate not to have had any children to see him die in such a horrible manner.'

'I was lucky,' Sean said, tapping his artificial legs with his cane. 'I only lost my legs.'

'Oh, I'm sorry,' Rose said. 'I didn't realise. I saw you limping but just thought you had an injury.'

'Years of walking on artificial legs has given me practice,' Sean said. 'Not that I was a famous sprinter before the Great War.'

'Mr Duffy, it seems the rain has eased. Would you like to go for a cup of tea with me at the delightful coffee shop we passed on the way to the cemetery?' Rose asked, touching his arm with a gloved hand. 'My car and chauffeur are just outside the gate. I would love to hear the stories of your escapades with my cousin, and I must confess that I read a lot about you before I even knew you and Harry were friends. You seem to be well known to the newspapers and television.'

She took his arm and they made their way through the gentle drizzle that had followed the storm now rumbling away to the horizon. As Sean walked beside Rose, he wondered at the irony of life. He had come grieving to a funeral and was now walking away from Harry's grave on the arm of a lady he had taken a strong liking to. It was obvious that the feeling was mutual, and suddenly Sean did not feel alone any more.

SEVENTEEN

Exhausted from fighting for the township of Kindu, Michael and Frankie were called to an O group by their commander. Intelligence from a resident escaping the Simbas at the mining town of Kalima reported forty-eight Belgian priests were being held captive and awaiting execution. Michael's commander knew his men needed rest, but his trademark tactic had always been speed and surprise.

During the night he had his force ferried over the river, and by four in the morning they were in place for the strike a hundred kilometres away.

Michael barely glimpsed the sun rise over the African countryside as he sat in the back of one of the transport trucks, dozing with his rifle between his knees. Beside him, Frankie was in a similar state. A couple of hours later Michael was fully awake, rifle ready as the trucks sped into the picturesque mining town that lay between green, forested hills.

The local people fell out of their houses as the trucks entered, giving the Lumumba salute, thinking the white men were Russians. At least the Simbas had realised who the men were and had abandoned a strategic bridge across a roaring torrent. A detachment was dropped off to hold the bridge against any possible counterattack.

Michael saw the flash of a body moving in the grass beside the road and he snapped off a shot, satisfied his bullet had found its mark. His comrades were also firing, leaving dead Simbas spread-eagled along the road. Michael could see the buildings of the mission station and wondered whether they had arrived early enough to save the priests.

The trucks came to a stop and he and Frankie leapt out, rifles ready. A big Simba waving a panga rushed from a verandah at them, and both men fired simultaneously, observing the man's body flung back by the impact of the heavy rifle rounds. Blood immediately oozed from the twin wounds in his chest.

'Go, go!' came the order, and the mercenaries fanned out, firing at any Simba attempting to flee.

Michael crashed through the entrance to the main building and, with others of the assaulting force, made his way to rooms locked with heavy bolts. He could hear the cries of the terrified priests calling to them for their freedom. The bolts were withdrawn and the priests spilled out in their filth-encrusted white soutanes, embracing their saviours.

One of the priests babbled that the civilians in the town were also in a similar situation: prisoners awaiting execution. Orders were quickly issued, and Michael found himself in the streets, going from building to building, releasing the

African workers and their families, who were as grateful for being rescued as the priests.

Michael could not help but feel an overwhelming sense of having done something good – despite the condemnation of the United Nations. He and his comrades were putting their lives on the line, rescuing innocent men, women and children.

The commander chose a triangular piece of ground at the centre of the town, near the post office, to separate prisoners from the local people. He was told that a Belgian miner and his four-year-old daughter residing about ten kilometres away were also being held prisoner by the Simbas.

'You two,' the regimental sergeant major roared, 'get aboard a truck. We have another rescue mission.'

Michael and Frankie scrambled onto the truck and joined the rescue convoy headed for the mining outpost.

Michael noticed uneasily that the track to the house was narrow and surrounded by dense rainforest. There was no chance of turning around if they were ambushed by the retreating rebel force. It was an uphill drive but they reached the summit without incident to find the house backed by equally dense forest. Michael could see a group of Simbas sprinting towards the cover of the rainforest on a steep slope behind the house, but they were too far away to shoot accurately. However, the order was given for the heavy machine guns to spray the forest where the Simbas had disappeared, discouraging them from sniping at the assaulting force. The retreating enemy were called upon to surrender – but none did.

The Belgian miner appeared from his front door and immediately prostrated himself, wailing, 'My daughter, my daughter. She is in the bush. Please, please, stop shooting.' It appeared that she had run off when the firing commenced.

The gunfire ceased and Hoare gave the order for his men to fan out and find the girl. Michael joined the skirmish line beside the regimental sergeant major as they pushed their way into the scrub, fully aware that the enemy could still be there. They called the little girl's name, but Frankie expressed the view to Michael that if the Simbas had seen her first they would have hacked her to death with their razor-sharp pangas. Sadly, both men had witnessed the bodies of children murdered this way in their campaign in the Congo.

It was the RSM who found her first in a clump of long grass. He rushed to the little girl who was sobbing, clutching a ragdoll. He scooped her up in his arms, tears streaming down his rugged face.

Michael slapped Frankie on the back in his joy at the child being found alive and unharmed. 'You miserable Pommy bastard,' he said with a grin, quickly swiping a tear from the corner of his eye. 'See, some stories have a happy ending.'

This day had been one of saving innocent people, and for a moment Michael recalled a short poem by Alfred Edward Housman. Michael loved poetry at school, and as he walked towards the waiting trucks he found himself softly reciting the poem to himself. It was titled, 'Epitaph on an Army of Mercenaries'.

These, in the day when heaven was falling,
The hour when earth's foundations fled,
Followed their mercenary calling,
And took their wages, and are dead.

Their shoulders held the sky suspended;
They stood, and earth's foundations stay;
What God abandoned, these defended,
And saved the sum of things for pay.

'Hey, Aussie, what are you blubbering about?' Frankie asked, seeing the tears streaming down Michael's face. 'We're still alive.'

'Ignorant Pommy bastard, you wouldn't understand,' Michael flashed back without rancour as he slung his rifle over his shoulder and boarded the truck. He knew this day would remain with him for as long as he lived . . . however long that should be in the Congo.

★

It was that time of day when the world seemed at peace with itself. The sun was a huge orange ball over the brigalow plains and a small dust mist drifted at its edge. The temperature was dropping enough to make the coming evening pleasant. Jessica Duffy-Macintosh sat on the verandah of Glen View homestead gazing out across her property. She held a fine china cup of tea and reflected on how peaceful this remote place was compared to the hustle and bustle of the big city and the boardroom meetings she was forced to attend in managing her financial empire.

Jessica watched as her fifteen-year-old son strode across the green lawn now thriving in front of the sprawling house. She smiled at his resemblance to her father. Kim had the dark complexion enhanced by his time working with the ringers mustering cattle. He was tall and broad-shouldered, a characteristic of his forebears, and spoke with a drawl he had picked up working with the European and Aboriginal stockmen.

Over his shoulder was his saddle and on his head was his battered broad-brimmed hat covered in the fine red dust of the plains.

'Hello, Ma. What's for dinner?' he asked with a slow smile when he reached the verandah.

'Nothing – until you wash up,' Jessica answered with her own loving smile. 'Roast beef with pan-made gravy.'

Kim stepped up on the verandah and gave his mother a quick kiss, before disappearing inside the homestead, where she could hear him swapping stories with his father about the cattle they had recovered from the edge of the property.

Donald joined his wife on the verandah, a cold glass of beer in hand. He sat down in one of the cane chairs to watch the sun slowly disappearing behind the scrub.

'Well, I read that you are one of the richest women in Australia,' Donald said. 'Have you thought about retiring and returning permanently to Glen View? There's a vacancy for president in the local Country Women's Association. You could make them the wealthiest branch in Australia.'

'Could you imagine me sitting around having tea and scones, chattering about embroidery?' Jessica said. 'I would go mad. Besides, who in the family will take over the reins of corporate enterprise when I do decide to retreat from the insane world of business? Bryce couldn't leave quick enough to pursue a life at university in Sydney, and from what I can see, Kim is a chip off the old block. All he wants to do is remain at Glen View – or manage another property of ours. As for Shannon . . . well, who knows? At thirteen she has aspirations of becoming an actress. She is certainly pretty enough to do that.'

'I gather my sister has the same problem. I have heard from Charles that Michael had enlisted with Mad Mike Hoare's mercenaries in the Congo. I wonder if he did that to spite his mother.'

'I remember Michael as a shy young boy when he would come to stay with us up here. And now he's a man fighting in some godforsaken war on the other side of the world, just as Patrick and Terituba are.'

'It seems to be a kind of curse on both sides of the family.' Donald sighed and took a sip from his glass of beer. 'The men – and women, when we count your exploits on the frontlines during the last war – seem to gravitate to dangerous occupations like soldiering. I wonder if old Wallarie is still out there looking over us.'

Jessica turned her attention to the place where the old bumbil tree used to stand at the front of the homestead. It was little more than a termite-eaten stump now, but many times Jessica had sat on the verandah wishing for the old man's appearance. But, like the tree, Wallarie was long gone, and all Jessica could think was that he was the spirit she saw in the lightning of the storms over the plains, or the great wedge-tailed eagles soaring on the thermals overhead. Jessica had told her children his story when they were young, but they had little interest in it these days. Even the ancient cave on the hill was a place that held no interest to the new generation. Now it was rock and roll music, transistor radios and television – although Glen View still did not yet have that luxury. So much had been forgotten.

As if reading her thoughts, Donald piped up, 'I got a letter from Bryce's university asking permission to carry out a study of the cave up on the hill. It seems that Bryce mentioned its existence to a person in the anthropology department, and they would like to send out a team to examine the paintings there.'

'There is not much interest in Aboriginal culture,' Jessica said. 'I wonder why they would bother.'

'Funny story,' Donald said. 'It seems a young bloke, although he would not be so young now, by the name of Cyril Walker has a friend in the department. Cyril is a top journo in Sydney these days, and he told his mate about how your father went down fighting for the property.

It must have piqued the interest of the academics. Anyway, do we allow the excursion here?'

'Why not?' Jessica replied. 'Just so long as they understand that no woman can enter the cave.'

'Don't you think that's a little superstitious?' Donald said.

'No,' Jessica replied. 'I am the only one left in the family to protect our traditions. It was the law of my ancestors.'

Donald glanced at his wife and remembered that she carried the blood of the first people to inhabit Glen View before Sir Donald Macintosh, his own ancestor, came to this part of Queensland and slaughtered Jessica's ancestors.

'Have you spoken to your cousin David lately?' Jessica asked, changing the subject.

'I met with him briefly at the Rocky cattle markets last month when he was passing through on a parliamentary fact-finding mission. He didn't have much time to chat, but it was good to see him.'

'I suppose he did not mention this new act they are pushing through parliament to conscript twenty-year-olds for military service,' Jessica said.

'No,' Donald said. 'But I heard from a mate that David is opposed to the bill, which has put him at odds with his own party.'

'I have a bad feeling that this war in Indochina is going to get worse, and that both our sons will get caught up in it.'

'They will have a lottery, to conscript young men, and the chances are that neither boy's birthday will come out of the barrel.'

Jessica turned to her husband. 'But what if they do?' she asked, pain written all over her face.

'Well, Bryce can defer, if he is still at uni,' Donald reassured.

'And Kim, what excuse will he have?'

'We could send him overseas out of reach of conscription,' Donald said.

'What are you talking about, Dad?' Kim said behind them. 'If my number came up, I would go into the army. How could I run away when some of my mates will have to serve? You and Mum did your bit in the last war, and its only right that I do mine.'

'You don't have to prove anything,' Donald said, turning to his son. 'Besides, you wouldn't have to worry about national service for at least another five years. By 1969 the war in Vietnam will be over.'

'You're probably right, Dad,' Kim said. 'I have to admit, I would rather stay here on Glen View with you.'

Donald felt a surge of love for his youngest son who loved this place like he did.

'Daddy, can I have a transistor radio?' Shannon asked, coming onto the verandah and sitting down in his lap. 'All the girls at my school have one.'

Jessica frowned. She knew what the answer would be as her husband had never said no to his beloved daughter. She had Donald wrapped around her little finger.

'I will talk to your mother about that,' Donald said, glancing at Jessica's frown and cringing at the thought that he might have to say no to her.

'Possibly for Christmas,' Jessica compromised.

'But Christmas is forever,' Shannon retorted. 'I need one before I go back to school.'

'I am sure the good sisters at your school have strict rules on the possession and use of radios in the dormitories,' Jessica said and watched as the predictable pout appeared.

'Daddy, please tell Mother that I will be ostracised if I don't have a trannie like all the other girls,' Shannon said.

'"Ostracised",' Jessica repeated. 'I'm pleased to see that the very expensive fees we are paying for your education are showing a result, young lady.'

'Oh, Mother!' Shannon said and jumped off her father's lap to storm back into the house.

'She's just a spoilt baby,' Kim commented, watching his sister disappear into the house. 'Dad, can I have a Winchester .30–30 for Christmas? It'll be good for the feral pigs at the bottom of the property.'

'I'll think about it.' Donald sighed as his son went back inside, leaving him alone with Jessica as the myriad stars began to fill the night sky. 'She's growing up fast,' he said. 'They all are.'

'And if I know you, Donald Macintosh, you will sneak a transistor radio into your daughter's suitcase before she returns to boarding school.' Jessica tried to sound stern but failed, and Donald accepted his beautiful wife knew everything worth knowing about him. His beloved daughter would get her wish – as she always did.

From the depths of the vast plains the cry of the curlews commenced as the moon rose to fade the stars.

What had Jessica's ancestors believed about the eerie wailing of the bush birds at night? They were the spirits of the dead come to earth.

EIGHTEEN

Sergeant Patrick Duffy had been granted leave with his platoon at a beautiful location at the mouth of the Sungai Sarawak. With beaches, tropical seas and majestic rainforest, it was a paradise where the soldiers could temporarily forget the fear and drudgery of their patrols into Indonesian territory.

A cold can of beer in hand, sprawled out in a cane chair in shorts, Patrick leaned back with his eyes closed, thinking only of getting up to fetch another drink. He felt a shadow fall over him and opened his eyes to see Terituba standing there with two cans of beer.

'Saved you a trip to the canteen,' Terituba said, plonking himself in a spare reclining cane chair next to his best friend.

'Corporal, you keep doing that for your platoon sergeant and I will be recommending you for promotion,' Patrick said with a slow smile of contentment.

'I got to get on a sergeant's course first,' Terituba said, taking a long swallow of the refreshing liquid. 'At least in the army they let me have a beer. I can't do that back home. But that Charlie Perkins showin' the whitefella we got rights to vote an' go where we want.'

Patrick thought about his friend's comment. There were laws that prohibited Aboriginal people from drinking alcohol, which did not seem fair. He had seen how the Aboriginal stockmen on Glen View worked as hard as the white men, but by law they were not allowed to have a cold beer at the end of the day.

'I see that Major Mann at the camp today,' Terituba said. 'He is bad news.'

Patrick had not seen the mysterious major since the Malayan campaign when they had trapped and killed Sam Po. The memory of seeing the young man die at his feet still haunted Patrick, given that had his mother lived she would not have abandoned the boy she had cared for in Changi and he might have become like a brother to Patrick.

'Bloody hell, here he comes,' Terituba said, getting up out of his chair, as did Patrick, to stand to attention.

Major Karl Mann was dressed in a starched set of jungle greens. 'Good morning, Sergeant Duffy, Corporal Duffy. Stand easy and go back to what you were doing.'

'Like a cold one, sir?' Terituba asked politely.

'No thanks, corp. I'm still on duty,' Major Mann replied.

'It's been a while since we last saw you, sir,' Patrick said, still standing but reaching for his can of beer. 'What brings you out our way?' he asked, knowing there was latitude for familiarity between a senior officer and NCO who had faced combat together.

'As a matter of fact – you. And some other matters,' said Major Mann. 'I have never forgotten your ability in the field, and so, with my new posting, I thought you deserved a chance to join our newly formed unit – the Australian Army Training Team Vietnam – as an advisor. It would mean a General Service Medal with Vietnam clasp if you do join us. Sadly, Tracker, we only take sergeants and above for the team, but I will be talking to your boss to have you complete your sergeant's course, as I know you two are a team in itself.'

'Thanks, boss,' Terituba answered. 'I got to keep an eye on Sergeant Duffy.'

Major Mann grinned. 'I am sure you do, corp.'

'Patrick, I know you will be going on leave very soon, and you have a month to either accept or reject my offer. I hope you accept as our advisers have to be bloody good at their job, and that requires experience and a good head on your shoulders. You can contact me through BHQ when you decide. I will leave you two in peace to carry on, and say it has been grand catching up with you both.'

With his parting words Major Mann strode away, leaving the two soldiers reflecting on the offer. At least it had also been offered to Terituba on the provision of passing the sergeant's course, which was no simple thing. Terituba had steadily improved his education in the army and achieved high marks in the traditional subjects of English and Mathematics.

When Major Mann was out of sight both men slumped back into their cane chairs.

'Bloody hell,' Patrick said. 'We come to this godforsaken place and the bastard still finds us.'

'I heard you just about get to be your own boss out there in the sticks,' Terituba said. 'No bloody spit an' polish in the barracks, an' they got a place called Saigon where you can get anything you want. Beats what we are doin' now.

Anyway, the bigwigs are holding peace talks an' soon this will all be over. That means we go home. I hate being in a peacetime army, painting rocks and doin' guard duty.'

'You have a good point there,' Patrick said. 'From what I have read it looks like Vietnam could turn into a real shooting war. The Vietnamese kicked the crap out of the French a few years ago, so they know how to fight.'

'You still going to take leave in Singapore?' Terituba asked, taking a swig from his rapidly warming beer. 'I'm going home to Glen View for my leave.'

'I just feel like going back to see the country since it became Malaysia. My enlistment will be up in six months, so if I take up the major's offer I would have to sign on again – and who knows whether I'll get another chance to go to Singapore.'

Both men fell into a silence, reflecting on how Major Karl Mann's unexpected reappearance in their lives might change any plans they'd had before this well-earned leave.

*

Sally Howard-Smith loved the growing vibrancy of Sydney. Television had brought European and American culture to the big island continent so isolated from the rest of the world, and she saw many of the young office girls imitating the fashions of Carnaby Street in London. Dresses were growing shorter and the night life more colourful.

As a result of Sarah Macintosh's hospitality, she had been introduced into Sydney's wealthy social circles. She found the young men stuffy and boring, with their talk of rising in the public service or banking. She had dated a few but found herself unconsciously comparing them to Patrick Duffy, although she had no idea where he was and what he was like now.

Then one day Sarah telephoned to inform her that the *Adelaide Queen* was currently docked in Singapore awaiting inspection before the final contracts were signed for its purchase. Sally telephoned her father in Hong Kong and he suggested she fly to Singapore to make a final inspection in the company of one of their maritime engineers.

Before the end of the week, Sally was sitting in a room in one of Singapore's most luxurious hotels overlooking the sea. She sipped her gin and tonic, gazing out at the mass of big and small ships below as the Asian city reclaimed its place as a crossing point of trade between East and West.

*

Sergeant Patrick Duffy was wearing a casual but smart set of civilian clothes of slacks and silk shirt. Out of his jungle greens he still looked like a professional soldier with his bearing and deep suntan. He had been able to afford the high rates for his accommodation thanks to the small but ever-growing inheritance from his mother's estate, which was being overseen by Sean Duffy. Patrick had decided to live for the day and indulge himself away from the nerve-jangling operations of a jungle fighter.

He, too, had a magnificent view of the water below and stood momentarily at the window, looking across the muddy waters at the sunset. It was time to ride the elevator down to the dining room and order the best seafood meal in town, to be washed down by a magnum of chilled champagne. He stepped into the corridor and walked to the elevator, pushed the button and heard the gentle clang as the doors opened for him to step in.

It was then that he experienced a similar feeling to stepping on that mine, and from the expression on the face of the young woman staring back at him, it was as if she also had the same feeling.

'Sally!' Patrick gasped.

'Patrick!' Sally cried, and for a moment they simply stared at each other until the sound of the door beginning to close snapped Patrick from his shock and he stepped inside.

'Oh my God!' Sally half laughed, half gasped. 'Is it really you?'

'I hope so,' Patrick smiled. 'Because if it's not me I'm in the wrong lift. What in hell are you doing here?'

'I should ask you the same question. Are you still a soldier?'

'I am afraid so. Are you still the lady of the lake?'

Sally remembered their first meeting at the swimming pool so long ago, and when she looked him over she saw that he was even more handsome than she remembered. She suddenly felt a little insecure. Did he still feel that she was beautiful, as he had so often told her when they were in Malaya? She knew it was a silly thought, because so many men since Patrick had told her how beautiful she was.

'I am just about to have dinner,' Patrick said. 'I hope you will accept my invitation to join an old soldier on leave.'

'I was going to dine alone tonight, but your invitation sounds much better. I would be honoured to join you.'

The lift came to a halt at the level of the dining room, and as they stepped out together Patrick felt Sally slip her arm under his. When they sat down at the table laid with the finest crystal and silver, they were silent for a moment, simply drinking in the sight of each other and wondering at the coincidence of being in the exact same place at the exact same time.

Finally Sally broke the poignant silence between them. 'I have to admit that I missed you, Patrick Duffy. It is as if there really is something called fate that has brought us together tonight.'

Patrick reached across the table and took her hand. 'Very soon I am going to wake up in the jungles and swamps of Borneo to find I was having yet another dream of the only woman I ever lost my heart to. I will blink and all this will disappear. Oh, I cannot tell you just how many years you have been in my thoughts. Maybe I should have called you Morgana, the woman who bewitched me forever.'

Sally gazed into Patrick's eyes and could still see the same gentleness, but it was now mixed with a haunted look. He was not the suave but untested type of man she had usually dated, but a tough and solid figure a woman could feel safe with. Then she remembered their passionate lovemaking at her father's villa in Malaya and her face began to flush.

They were hardly aware that the waiter took a long time delivering their first course. They were absorbed in catching up on the events that had shaped their lives, although Patrick said little about his current war in the jungles and swamps of Indonesia.

'And so, here I am in Singapore to look over a cargo ship my father decided to purchase from the Macintosh companies in Sydney,' finished Sally.

'Macintosh?' Patrick said. 'Sarah Macintosh?'

'Yes, do you know of her?'

'She's a distant relative,' Patrick said. 'I kind of grew up with her son, Michael.'

'Another strange twist of fate,' Sally said. 'It could almost make one believe that there is a big wheel in the universe that simply goes around until it reaches the same point again. Like you and I meeting tonight in this place and at this point in time.'

'Whatever it was that brought us together, all I know is that I will never let you go again,' Patrick said.

Sally did not reply but squeezed his hand. She was too practical to think that as long as this man was a soldier she could have a permanent relationship with him. As much as she felt an intense attraction to him, she also knew she could not give up her position with her father's thriving enterprises to follow a soldier around the world or await his return from whatever battlefields were ahead. All she could do was live for this moment.

That night proved all her memories of their passion. It was as if they had been born to love each other. Sally held Patrick in her arms as he slept against her breasts. She gazed through the open curtains of the large window at the twinkling lights of the boats in the harbour. Patrick began to whimper and tremble like a puppy, and she brushed his forehead with her fingers until he began to calm. Sally guessed he was once again in the jungles of his nightmares, and she suddenly understood why he was so different to the other men she had known. He was one of those that earlier cultures had called warriors.

Patrick slowly woke. 'Was I having a nightmare?' he said sleepily. 'Bloody too many of them lately.'

'Go back to sleep and in the morning we'll order breakfast in bed,' Sally said.

Patrick pulled himself into a sitting position, rubbing his eyes to force away the remnants of the dreams of an exploding mine. 'My term of enlistment will be up in a few months. My Uncle Sean wants me to come home and study law. He can article me at his firm, and he wants me to take it over when he finally retires. It would mean a few years before I saw any real money.'

'Money is not a concern to me,' Sally said. 'But you

would have to make that decision for yourself and not because of me.'

'Us,' Patrick said. 'My decision would be made so we could have a future together.'

Sally sighed. 'My heart tells me we were meant to be together, but my head keeps asking *how*? Are you really able to break with the army?'

Patrick turned away to stare out the window at the tropical darkness. His leave would be up in a week and he would have to return to soldiering for a few more short months. *Just one more campaign*, echoed in his mind as he recalled Major Mann's offer. But then he returned his attention to Sally and knew he was looking at the most important thing in his life.

NINETEEN

Michael Macintosh gripped the rifle with sweating hands. Around him in the village he could hear the moans of wounded men, women and children, and the occasional scream of another victim of the Simbas. He stood at the corner of one of the stone houses that had once been the Belgian-Congo residence of the European colonial administrator, now long gone with his family.

Flames from burning thatch roofs added to the oppressive heat of the midday sun. The small force of mercenary soldiers despatched to clear the village had fanned out to suppress any resistance from the dreaded Simbas. Most of the enemy wisely retreated, but a few drunken rebels remained in search of loot and rape. It was obvious that they had uncovered a stash of alcohol, and even inebriated they were dangerous with their Chinese rifles, pangas and spears.

Michael quickly glanced around for his comrades but realised that he was temporarily alone. He could hear crashing around in the house he was to clear, and the terrified screams of a young girl, overridden by the guttural demands of a man in a language Michael did not understand. But he did know from the victim's tone that she was in dire trouble. He heard a sickening crunch, and the girl's screams suddenly stopped.

Michael moved cautiously to the front door and was almost bowled over by a very large and muscular Simba wielding a panga. The sudden meeting of the two enemies took both men by surprise, but the Simba was already raising the razor-sharp panga above his head. Michael reacted immediately, thrusting his bayonet-tipped SLR directly into the man's chest just as the panga came shearing down past Michael's head.

The Simba struggled against the bayonet in his chest, and Michael could smell rotting meat and alcohol on the dying man's breath, so close were they locked together. The man dropped his panga, and Michael twisted the bayonet around in his chest until the Simba's knees buckled and he slumped against Michael, then slithered down to the dry earth, almost pulling the rifle from Michael's hands.

Michael ripped the bayonet from the dead man and stared into the gloom of the hut. He was already hardened to the terrible sights of slaughter he and his companions had witnessed throughout the war against the rebels, but what he saw enraged him. A young woman in her teens lay decapitated beside a baby that had been disembowelled. Already the flies were gathering for a feast, and Michael stepped back, turned and drove the bayonet once more into the back of the corpse at his feet. It was a useless gesture, but the sight of the mutilated young mother and her baby had driven him into a rage. It was time to seek out more of the murdering men who purported to be rebels – and kill them.

'Hey, Aussie!' the voice of Frankie called from down the street. 'Come and have a look at this.'

Michael wiped the blood off his bayonet on the monkey-skin headdress of the Simba at his feet. He strode down the street strewn with discarded papers, and pots and pans to join his comrade, who was standing with his rifle pointed inside a house.

There Michael saw a naked young girl, who he guessed was around fifteen years old, staring back at the two mercenaries. Her eyes were wide and gazing blankly at them. Michael guessed she was in a state of severe shock. Beyond her in the house, Michael could make out a pile of bloody bodies.

'What you say we have a bit of fun with her?' Frankie said. 'She's so far gone she wouldn't know what's happening.' He took a step towards the girl but stopped when he felt the tip of the bayonet against the back of his head.

'Take another step, Frankie, and I will blow your brains out.'

'You don't mean that, Aussie,' Frankie said. 'We're pals. I watch your back and you watch mine. Is some little African floosie worth coming between us?'

'You know the boss's rules. No rape, no pillage.'

Frankie turned to Michael. He had a smile on his face, sure that Michael would not shoot him. 'We don't have any allegiance to these people,' he said. 'We just get paid to kill Congolese rebels. These are not my people – or yours. We're just hired killers.'

'You may be right, but that girl has suffered enough. She is a human being like you and me.'

Michael glanced over Frankie's shoulder and could see the girl had begun to tremble uncontrollably. She was weeping, and sank to her knees with her hands over her eyes.

'Hey, you two, what's going on here?' the voice of their officer called to them from the end of the street. 'Get your arses back to the trucks. We got another village to clear.'

Michael lowered his rifle, and Frankie spat on the ground at his feet.

'I won't forget that you pulled a gun on me today. You'd better be watching your own back from now on because I won't be,' Frankie snarled and then walked away down the street to the waiting trucks.

Michael followed him, replaying the thinly veiled threat in his mind. How had it been that moments earlier they had been brothers in arms and now were deadly enemies? Maybe that was the nature of this occupation, where life was measured only in killing and money.

*

Sergeant Patrick Duffy returned to his unit and was met by Terituba.

'Hey, how did your leave go?' he asked with a broad grin. 'You decided to sign on again and transfer to the training team?'

Patrick unslung his kitbag and dropped it at his feet. He was still in his civvy clothes and knew he would have to change to be on parade within the hour.

'I had time to think things over,' Patrick said, accepting a cigarette from his best friend. 'When my time is up, I'm not re-enlisting. I'm going to take up my Uncle Sean's offer to be his articled clerk.'

For a moment Terituba stood staring open-mouthed at his friend. 'Why would you want to do that when in a coupla of years you could make warrant officer with the company? You could be our CSM.'

Patrick shifted uncomfortably. 'I ran into someone I haven't seen for years, and things happened.'

'It had to be that sheila you met in Malaya,' Terituba said with a scowl. 'So you are letting a sheila break up the best team in the Australian Army?'

'Cobber, it was not an easy decision to make. You and I have served together in two campaigns now, but I have to think about the future. I know that if you re-enlist, you'll go far in the army.'

'Bloody not right,' Terituba said and walked away, leaving Patrick feeling very much alone. They had been together all their lives and now he had chosen to take a path away from his friend. A choice between love and war, and love had won. No doubt Sean would be very happy at his decision to go into law, but that did not ease his disquiet. How was he going to feel when he was safely at home, reading the papers about the war in Vietnam, knowing Terituba was in danger and he was not by his side?

*

The bridge at Kindu had to be held. Michael rested his rifle on sandbags at one end of the bridge, next to a machine-gun crew. He could not see Frankie as he had distanced himself from Michael after the incident with the girl in the village. The sun shimmered in the air in front of him and he quickly picked up the figures emerging from the jungle. A rapid estimation put their number at around two hundred and they were well armed. The order to 'stand to' had been issued to the defenders.

Michael glanced at the loaded magazines at his elbow. He did not feel fear and he wondered if he actually had a soul because he had come to love the danger and adrenaline. Killing had become second nature to him.

'Don't fire until you get the order!' His commander was an experienced soldier who knew that the closer the enemy came, the more accurate the fire from his own defending forces would be.

The Simbas were being led by a man wearing a black burnous with a hood, concealing his face. He was a sinister figure, and the rebels charged towards the small defending force they outnumbered.

Michael set his sights on one of the Simbas carrying a light machine gun and followed him along his foresight. The enemy was coming on in groups, forcing the frontal fire to be split. The target at the end of Michael's rifle sights grew larger and he began squeezing the trigger.

'Fire!' the order came over the hellish screams and taunts of the attacking force, and Michael saw his man stop and fall backwards when he fired. Without hesitating, Michael swung his sights on the enemy combatant slightly to his left and fired; he felt satisfied to see him drop. He was aware that bullets were smashing into his sandbagged emplacement and realised this was not a one-sided affair.

Mortar bombs and heavy machine-gun fire tore into the ranks of oncoming Simbas, ripping away limbs and flinging bodies into the air. Michael kept firing, only stopping to replace another magazine. It was obvious that, between the small-arms fire and supporting weapons, the Simbas had had enough, falling back to leave at least forty-five of their comrades dead on the killing ground before the bridge.

Michael did not need the order to cease firing, as he had run out of targets to fire at. The intense noise of the battle left him with ringing ears and a desperate thirst for water.

He reached down for his canteen and saw that he only had one magazine of twenty rounds left.

Michael swilled down the warm water, wiping his mouth with the back of his hand. He was aware that a shadow fell over him, and when he squinted at the figure he could see it was Frankie.

'We're still alive,' he said before walking away. Michael leaned back against the sandbags and wondered how much longer he would serve with the mercenary force in the Congo. Major Hoare had proved to be a great leader, and Michael knew he would have followed him into hell if he had asked.

A couple of days later the enemy attacked again in greater numbers, led by the mysterious man in black. No matter how much the mercenaries tried to kill him, they failed. He even turned his back on the bridge defenders and walked casually away from them when the attack failed. Afterwards, Frankie strode up to Michael's position and uttered the well-worn phrase, 'We're still alive,' before walking away.

Michael thought about the connection between him and Frankie. Despite the animosity between them now, there remained a bond. Michael thought that bond might be important for what was ahead. The morality of war did not keep you alive, Michael reflected while thinking back to Frankie's actions in the village. It was easy for people safe in their armchairs to judge. They were not exposed to the horror of war as he and Frankie were.

There was an attack to be made on Stanleyville now, and Michael hoped Frankie would continue to tell him, 'We're still alive'. What Michael did not know was that he was about to be involved in one of the biggest – and mostly forgotten – rescue operations of the twentieth century.

Over two thousand European men, women and children were being held hostage in Stanleyville, a large, well set out city with magnificent Belgian architecture in the heart of the Congo. Most of the hostages were being held in the five-storey Victoria Hotel. Amongst the captives were the staff of the American consulate, who had been imprisoned against all international diplomatic rules.

The popular Congolese mayor of the city, Sylvere Bondekwe, had already been dragged to the city centre, stripped naked and had his liver cut out. As he lay in agony dying from his wound, the Simbas distributed the bloody organ to their frenzied followers to eat. The hostages knew of his death and had long given up hope of rescue. And even if the soldiers did come to the city, the hostages knew the Simbas would hack them to death with pangas or, if they were lucky, shoot them.

*

The rains came in the kind of torrent Michael had never seen before in his travels around the globe. Already he had seen days of fighting on the way to Stanleyville where the dripping jungle encroached onto the neglected roads. His comrades had taken casualties and Michael had found himself in hand-to-hand combat when clearing the ambush sites.

He could remember how supercharged his body had been with adrenaline and the way it drained away to leave his body trembling. At one stage he had stepped in to save Frankie, who had been overwhelmed by two panga-wielding Simbas in the thick scrub by the road. Michael had killed both men and grinned down at his old friend with the words, 'We're still alive'. Frankie had reached out with his hand, and in the grasp Michael knew that the incident weeks earlier in the village they had cleared was now forgotten.

The advance had been temporarily halted because of the torrential rain, and both men huddled inside the truck under a tarpaulin that hardly stopped them from being soaked to the skin.

'I'm calling it quits after Stanleyville,' Frankie said, attempting to light a soggy cigarette. 'If I was home I would be in the pub having a pint and a packet of pork crackling. What about you, Aussie?'

'You know,' Michael said, 'it's not the killing that gets to me. It's seeing the innocent victims of this war. Like when we rescued those nuns and priests. They were hardly recognisable as humans after the Simbas got through with them, and seeing those pregnant young nuns . . .' For a moment Michael ceased talking as he recalled one nun wearing little more than scraps of her former habit stumbling to the mercenaries, weeping and wailing, 'God has answered our prayers.' It was not God, thought Michael, but Mike Hoare and his Wild Geese who had come to rescue them.

'I think I might be joining you, Frankie. I have a feeling that after we take Stanleyville the Simbas are going to head off to the bush to hide, and it will mostly be over anyway.'

The morning came in sunshine and so too the advance towards Stanleyville. The long column of vehicles was vulnerable to ambush as they moved north, and each village they passed through meant a firefight with the enemy.

At one village, the enemy allowed the armoured vehicles to pass through before opening fire on the soft-skinned trucks. Immediately the mercenary commando force leapt from their trucks and engaged the Simbas concealed in the long grass either side of the narrow road. It came down to hand-to-hand combat and Michael was in the thick of it, swinging his rifle like a club as a big Simba loomed up in front of him. The heavy butt of the rifle caught the African on the side of the head with a sickening crunch. The Simba fell to the earth, either dead or unconscious. Michael did not have time to ascertain the man's condition, but stepped over him to raise his rifle to shoot at a Simba armed with a light machine gun. As usual, his aim was true and the man stumbled forward, falling to the ground with a round through his chest.

Then, when the road had been cleared, Michael heaved himself into the truck and slumped down beside Frankie.

'You didn't join us,' Michael said, noting his friend was calmly smoking a cigarette.

'Na, I knew you could do all the killing for both of us,' he replied, offering the packet to Michael.

Michael leaned back against the side of the interior of the truck with his rifle between his knees. It was a deadly game now, he reflected, taking turns to add to their body count as they advanced on Stanleyville. He had been briefed that the American hostages were most at risk, as the Communist-backed Africans saw the USA as the real enemy. Every day they had been dragging out helpless Congolese citizens and executing them in front of a giant photograph of Lumumba, the man they considered a martyr. The rescue mission was as much about saving innocent Africans and Europeans from butchery as it was about defeating the murderous rebel army. But time was running out, and each time the convoy was delayed by skirmishes, the less likely it was that the rescuing force would arrive in time.

TWENTY

Sarah Macintosh was looking forward to the arrival of Lady Georgina White and her two daughters, Jane and Victoria. She wished to repay their hospitality to Michael when he was being educated in England – until the unfortunate incident that had him sent home. Sir Ronald was tied up in America on business, but he would join his wife in Australia at a later date.

Sarah would ensure their social calendar was filled with dinners and parties in their honour and she'd connect the family to some of her charitable institutions. Sarah organised for a chauffeur-driven limousine to pick up the three visitors from Kingsford Smith Airport and whisk them to her house on the harbour where they would be staying while in Sydney.

She was just a little nervous, pacing the library until she heard the car drive up to the house. She hurried downstairs to see Lady Georgina alight, followed by Jane and, finally, a pretty young girl of about six years. It was a hot day in late spring and the three wore light cotton dresses. Already Charles was greeting them and issuing orders to the chauffeur to carry their luggage into the house.

'Lady Georgina, Jane, and this young lady must be Victoria,' Sarah said, giving them each a quick kiss on the cheek. 'Welcome to Sydney.'

'It is very warm,' Lady Georgina said, cooling herself with a small fan. 'Such a contrast to New York.'

'You must come inside,' Sarah said. 'I have refreshments ready.'

She led them to the spacious dining room with its French doors opening onto a luxurious garden. Tea was served by the housekeeper on a patio under the shade of a pergola.

Sarah glanced at Jane, who was now in her early twenties, and thought how pretty she was. Then she looked at Victoria sitting demurely at the table, and when Sarah looked into the young girl's face she felt a tremor of shock. It was as if she were looking at herself at the same age; her own eyes looked back at her.

Charles joined the women and his first words only added to Sarah's confusion.

'Young Victoria looks like you, Sarah,' he said lightly and sat down at the garden table without considering his remark as anything but flippancy.

When Sarah looked across at Georgina, she noticed that she had paled at Charles's offhand remark.

'What an odd coincidence,' said Lady Georgina coolly.

Jane shifted uncomfortably. 'I meant to ask, is Michael with you in Sydney?'

'Michael enlisted with the mercenary army in the Congo,' Charles said sadly. 'We do get the occasional letter from him.'

'I am sorry to hear that,' Lady Georgina rallied. 'From what I have read in the newspapers, the men over there are doing a fine job rescuing many Europeans from those savages. I pray that he will stay safe and return to you both. I remember him as a wonderful young man, despite everything that happened.'

'Mother, Mrs Macintosh, if I could be excused,' Jane interrupted. 'I would like to go into the garden and take in the magnificent views of the harbour.' Jane rose unsteadily to her feet and walked away from the table. Sarah could sense Lady Georgina's tension, so she changed the topic of conversation to the weather.

That evening Georgina and Jane were invited to dinner by friends from England, leaving Sarah and Charles alone to care for Victoria. When Victoria had been put to bed, Sarah joined Charles in the living room.

She poured them both a glass of white wine and sat down on a lounge. Charles was watching the end of a new Australian-produced television show called *Homicide*.

'Did you feel that the White family are guarding a family secret?' Sarah asked, sipping her wine.

'What do you mean?' Charles said, switching off the television now the show was over.

'The mention of Michael appeared to cause some distress to Jane,' Sarah frowned. 'And Victoria and Georgina don't look alike. In fact, Victoria looks more like a member of the Macintosh family.'

'What are you insinuating?' Charles asked. 'That somehow Michael is the girl's father?'

Sarah knew it was not uncommon in polite society for the mother of an unwed daughter who fell pregnant to assume the child's maternity. With money, it was easy to be out of the country so such a thing could be pulled off.

Charles shrugged. 'It is possible that Jane reacted to the news of Michael fighting in the Congo because she simply liked him as a friend – and nothing else.'

Sarah swilled her wine around in the crystal goblet. Charles could see from the expression on her face that he had not convinced her. Knowing Sarah as he did, he knew she would not let the matter drop until she had used every avenue to pry into the secret she felt Lady Georgina was concealing. Or at least, dismiss her suspicions.

Charles picked up the television guidebook to see if another programme he enjoyed, the ABC's *Four Corners*, was on.

*

Lady Georgina and her daughter returned to the Macintosh mansion in the early hours of the morning after a pleasant evening wining and dining with friends at a top Sydney restaurant. They made their way to their respective rooms, and Lady Georgina was preparing for bed when there was a light tap at her door.

'Come in,' she said, and Jane entered the room still dressed in her formal clothes.

'Mother, I will not be able to sleep until we have this conversation about Victoria,' she said, standing at the end of the large bed upon which her mother now sat.

'We have been through this many times,' Lady Georgina said in a tired voice. 'If you had taken my advice when she was born and had her adopted in America, we would not be having this discussion.'

'How could I give her up to strangers?' Jane said. 'She is my child and was born in an act of love.'

'You were far too young to comprehend the concept of love,' Georgina said. 'You know full well the stigma of being an unwed mother in our society. Your chances of finding a respectable man to marry would have been greatly diminished. We are the Whites, and it would have brought great shame to your father and I if you had kept the baby in your name.'

'I know you don't understand, but Michael loved me. Pretending Victoria is my sister grows harder each day I live. I had hoped that, when Daddy said we were coming to Sydney, I might have the opportunity to at least speak to Michael and explain things. I don't know what his reaction would have been, but it is something I must find out or the rest of my life will be a lie.'

Lady Georgina rose from the bed and placed her hands on her daughter's shoulders. 'Victoria has already accepted me as her mother. How do you think she would react to learning that her sister is really her mother? Do you think that now is the right time to tell her such a thing?'

For a moment Jane remained silent, reflecting on the dilemma. The pain of each day being with Victoria and pretending to be her sister was emotionally draining. Yet, could she really turn her daughter's life upside down by telling her the truth?

'I think you should return to your room and forget about this,' Lady Georgina said gently. 'You also have to think of Victoria. She is happy and secure with her place in the family.'

Jane nodded and turned to leave. She knew everything her mother said was logical. She had to think about her daughter's welfare. Lady Georgina was a loving mother to Victoria, and Jane had little to offer her as a single mother without an income.

When Jane was in the hallway she saw a light on in the library. She wondered who would be awake at this hour, and when she passed the door she could see Charles sitting at a large desk with a bottle of Scotch. Jane liked Charles and decided to enter the room.

He looked up in surprise. 'Did you have a good evening?' he asked, and Jane sat down in a big leather chair. Only a desk lamp lit the room, and most of the library was in deep shadow.

'It was very nice,' Jane answered. 'But I could do with a drink.'

Charles retrieved a second tumbler and quarter filled it with Scotch. He passed it to Jane with the comment, 'Does your mother allow you to drink?'

'I believe the legal age in Sydney is eighteen. I am old enough,' Jane replied, taking a sip of the alcohol. 'When was the last time you heard from Michael?'

'I had a letter from him last week,' Charles answered. 'He does not write to his mother, but I pass on his news to her. My son and his mother do not get on.'

'Oh, that is sad to hear,' Jane said.

'It's a pity because Michael should be the one to take over from his mother when she eventually steps down running the family companies. Instead, he chose a life roaming the world, and now he's a soldier of fortune in Africa.'

Jane could see that the talk of Michael had distressed Charles. She could also see that he was drunk and tears were forming in his eyes. He gazed down at the desk, gripping the tumbler of Scotch in his hand. 'I don't get much sleep, worrying about the boy,' he said and looked up at Jane whose expression of sympathy was genuine.

'I will tell you a little family secret,' he said. 'I am not my boy's biological father. His real father has never met Michael. But I am the man he calls Dad, and I have always felt like his father.'

Jane sat very still. So, who *was* Michael's father? She dared not ask for fear of upsetting Charles further.

'I'll tell you a secret,' Jane said. 'Victoria is not my sister; she is actually my daughter.'

Charles focused on Jane. 'She's Michael's daughter, isn't she? My wife suspected as much.'

'She is,' Jane replied, knocking back the last of her Scotch. 'I only wish that Michael knew, but I am afraid of how he might react.'

'By God, I think he would be overjoyed – I have . . . a beautiful granddaughter.'

Charles rose unsteadily to his feet to walk over to the large window overlooking the driveway below. 'Are you going to tell my wife?'

'I would rather it remain our secret,' Jane said. 'I suppose we both share things that should remain between the two of us.'

'You're right,' Charles said. 'Secrets not to be shared.'

'Thank you,' Jane said, feeling a burden lift from her shoulders. Her confession had been spontaneous, but she was glad she had made it. At least the man who had raised Michael as a father knew he had a granddaughter.

Jane excused herself, and went to her room where she undressed and slipped under the sheets. The Scotch had gone to her head in a pleasant way, and she began to doze in the darkness when she suddenly had an acute feeling she was not alone. Opening her eyes slowly, she stared into the shadows and stifled a scream, lest it alert the strange figure she was looking at. It was a semi-naked Aboriginal man – she knew that from books she'd read at school – with a long grey beard and scars on his thin chest. He was holding a spear and she could see a sad smile on his face. Then suddenly he was gone.

Jane sat up in bed and looked around frantically. She saw nothing but felt her heart pounding in her breast. It had to be a dream, she told herself. Or the invention of an over-active imagination. But as she drifted into sleep, she thought she could smell the pungent aroma of pipe tobacco wafting in the room. When she reflected on the brief encounter, she felt a chill of dread. It was as if he had come to warn her of something . . . but what?

TWENTY-ONE

Bullets bounced off the steel girders of the bridge as the column of armoured vehicles and trucks rushed across. All were surprised that the rebel army had not put up a determined defence at the township of Wanie Rukula. Even so, the rear-guard defence by the enemy still took two more lives from the assault force of mercenaries. The road ahead was clear and Mike Hoare gave the order to advance at high speed towards Stanleyville.

The word quickly went down the column that Belgian paratroopers had been dropped onto the airfield at Stanleyville two-and-a-half hours earlier.

'Those bloody Belgian paras are good,' Frankie said. 'It might be over by the time we get into Stanleyville.'

Michael glanced along the line of others wearing the mercenary beret. Each man was silent, awaiting what they expected to be a major battle in an urban area.

'Let's hope so,' Michael replied. 'Let's hope they were in time to save the hostages – poor bastards.'

In Stanleyville only hours earlier, rebel-held Radio Stanley had blasted out over the airwaves: *'Ciyuga! Ciyuga! Kill all the white people! Kill all the men, women and children. Kill them all. Have no scruples. Use your knives and your pangas!'*

The previous day the rebel newspaper *Le Martyr* had written, *We shall cut out the hearts of all the American and Belgians and we shall wear them as fetishes. We shall dress ourselves in the skins of the Americans and Belgians.*

Even as the Belgian paratroopers fought their way from the captured airfield into the city, the Simbas rounded up their prisoners and marched them to the street in ranks of three, ordering them to halt and sit down. The hostages could hear the Belgian gunfire coming closer by the minute, but their hope was dampened when they saw a grotesque figure of a man dressed in a monkey-skin cape begin to gesticulate to the guards armed with rifles, machine guns, spears and pangas to commence slaughtering the Europeans and Americans. A shot rang out and the massacre began. Women and children were particularly singled out and shot at point-blank range.

After the first shots many of the prisoners broke and ran for cover in different directions. Some made it, many did not. Many families died together, clutching each other.

The Belgian paras arrived on the site of the massacre to find the bodies of over eighty dead men, women and children.

The mercenary convoy entered the township expecting to fight all the way, but they were met by a solitary Belgian para. They shouted, 'Viva la Paris!' as they passed.

The convoy continued another four kilometres until they reached Lumumba Square at the centre of the town.

There they disembarked from the trucks to await further orders.

While waiting, Michael and the men of his commando formed up in three ranks to be addressed by Mike Hoare, who informed them of how proud he was of each and every one of them. Michael stood tall amongst the ranks with his rifle butt resting by his right boot. Trained and led by this man who stood ten-feet tall in the eyes of his loyal Wild Geese, he felt the pride of a job well done, and only for a moment reflected on those friends he had lost over the months of vicious warfare in the jungles of the Congo.

*

'I had the strangest experience last night,' Jane said at the breakfast table. Only Charles and Sarah were with her as the housekeeper served breakfast.

'Oh, what happened?' Sarah asked, sipping a cup of tea.

'I do not know if I was dreaming, but I am sure I was awake when I suddenly saw an old Aboriginal man standing in the room at the foot of my bed.'

Sarah's cup fell from her fingers, spilling tea across the fine linen tablecloth. 'Wallarie!' she gasped, and immediately stood up and left the dining room.

'Did I say something to upset Sarah?' Jane asked, shocked.

'You have seen the ghost that haunts the Macintosh family,' Charles said with a grim smile. 'Sarah believes that when Wallarie appears under the roof of this house it means someone in the family is going to die a violent death. It is little more than ignorant superstition, but she refuses to see that.'

'He was so real,' Jane said. She paused for a moment, an expression of fear on her face. 'Do you think the old man came to tell me something bad was about to happen to Michael?'

'Surely you don't really think you saw a ghost?' Charles said kindly. 'I think something was said to put the seed in your unconscious and that fed your imagination.'

'It is possible, I suppose,' she conceded. She hoped so because if Sarah was right, it might mean Michael was in danger.

★

Terituba walked the last couple of miles to Glen View in his uniform. His slouch hat provided protection against the blazing sun. He had found that wearing his uniform helped get him lifts from sympathetic motorists as he hitchhiked into the interior of Queensland. It had not helped him get a cold beer – even in uniform and wearing his General Service Medal riband; in fact he had been ejected from a hotel on the coast. Terituba was bitter. He had served his country in two wars, yet the colour of his skin meant he did not have the right to enter a hotel and have a drink.

As he saw the homestead on the horizon and heard the sound of the cattle lowing not far away, he knew he was home. He had not sent a telegram to inform anyone he was on his way. It would be a surprise to his family and cobbers.

Terituba squinted at the haze to see the figure of a man on a horse approaching him at a canter. The mounted man reined his horse to a halt and blinked in surprise.

'Bloody hell! Is that you, Terituba?' the man asked, and the Aboriginal soldier recognised Mitch, the second in charge of Glen View.

'Yeah, cobber, back from the war,' Terituba replied.

'Hop on, digger,' Mitch said. 'I'll take you up to your old man at the house.'

Terituba swung onto the horse behind Mitch and they rode the last mile to the Glen View homestead. There he saw his father sitting with Donald Macintosh on the verandah sipping tea. Both men rose to their feet as Terituba jumped down from the horse, and Billy hobbled down the stairs, supported by a walking stick, to go to his son and hug him.

'You bin away too long,' he said when he released Terituba.

Donald stepped in and shook Terituba's hand with a firm grip. 'Good to see you, son,' he said. 'We are all very proud of your service.'

'Terituba!' The cry from the front door was as explosive as a Mills hand grenade going off, and the three men turned to see Terituba's mother running towards her son, her flour-speckled dress billowing in her rush to reach him.

She grabbed her son and Terituba fought for breath as she hugged him tightly to her. She kissed him all over his face, then finally stepped back to examine him.

'You too skinny,' she said. 'They not feedin' my boy in the army.'

Terituba was not skinny. His fighting years had toughened his body, and every muscle stood out.

'Leave the boy alone, woman,' Billy growled gently.

'I'll get my boy some scones,' Mary said, still taking in this fine-looking young man wearing the uniform of the Australian Army.

'I have a better idea,' Donald said. 'How about I fetch a couple of cold beers to celebrate the return of a digger safely from the jungles of Borneo.'

'Mr Macintosh,' Terituba grinned, 'I haven't had a cold beer since I left Borneo. The bastards here won't let me have one.'

Large bottles of beer were brought to the verandah and the three men sat down in the shade.

'To your safe return to us,' Donald said, raising his glass. 'And that you remain safe in the service of your country.'

The three men took long swigs of the cold liquid, and Terituba took off his slouch hat, placing it on a table nearby.

'You know, Terituba,' Donald said, gazing at the hat, 'you and I have both worn that hat at different times with great pride. How is the army treating you?'

'Good, Mr Macintosh. In the army we don't have white or black skin. We have green skin and my cobbers are my brothers. They stick up for me against whitefellas who call me a dirty Abo.'

Donald understood. 'And how is Patrick? The last news we got from him was that he was thinking about not extending his service.'

'Yeah, he got a girl an' decided that she was more important than the army. He's becoming a civvy after Christmas. Patrick gone down to Sydney on his Christmas leave to stay with his Uncle Sean. Reckons he'll become a lawyer. I think he should stay in the army because he is a bloody good soldier like me. We a team.'

'If you ever wanted to leave the army, you know you have a job and a home here,' Donald suggested.

'Thanks, Mr Macintosh, but we got another war in Vietnam to go to, an' it's going to be bigger than Malaya and Borneo. The army needs me there. We gonna get a lot of nashos an' they will need experienced soldiers who know about jungles an' stuff to help keep them alive.'

The mention of national servicemen going to war caused Donald to feel a pang of fear. His eldest son, Bryce, was coming of age and would be eligible for two years of military service that could take him into a war.

The day passed as Donald and Terituba swapped stories of their army days. Finally it was time for Terituba to go and look up his old friends on the station, leaving Donald pondering this war emerging in what he had once known as Indochina. The Vietnamese had beaten the best of the French army, and now the Americans felt they could do what the French had failed to do. But Donald knew from personal experience that fighting a war in a tropical country of mountains and dense rainforest was not the same as manoeuvring on the plains of Europe in great armoured divisions, supported by air power and artillery. He prayed that Bryce would continue his engineering studies and, if called up, opt to defer his service until the war in Vietnam was over. The problem was there were just not enough tough and experienced soldiers like Terituba to go around when the extra battalions were raised to commit to the war so far north of Glen View.

*

Former Sergeant Patrick Duffy felt out of place back in a world not governed by the strict rules and regulations of the army. At his Uncle Sean's flat in Sydney, he could sleep in till whatever hour he pleased and go where he wanted without a leave pass. It took some getting used to.

The smell of bacon and eggs being cooked in the flat's tiny kitchen wafted over to Patrick, who glanced at the alarm clock at the side of his bed. It was 8 am and Patrick felt guilty for sleeping in, even though it was Saturday morning. Later he would go to the beach to catch a wave or two bodysurfing. Then it would be time to join Sean for a cold beer at the pub, and maybe a barbecue at an old friend's place. The only thing missing from this idyllic life was Sally, who had flown to Hong Kong for a business meeting.

'Hey! You are absent from place of parade,' Sean called as Patrick slipped on a pair of shorts and short-sleeved shirt to join his uncle at the breakfast table. Patrick decided to give shaving a miss and ambled into the kitchen to see his plate of bacon and eggs on the table next to a big glass of freshly squeezed orange juice and a couple of pieces of buttered toast.

Sean sat down at the table, joining the young man he had practically raised after his mother died in Changi prison.

'On Monday we will submit the application to the Solicitors Admission Board for you to be articled to me,' Sean said, shaking copious amounts of salt on his eggs. 'Needless to say I will be paying you more than other articled clerks receive, as you will be looking after the probate and trust accounts while you do your studies. I will pay you what you received as a sergeant in the army.'

'Thanks, Uncle Sean,' Patrick replied, pushing the edge of his toast into the soft centre of an egg. 'I figure I will be a bit older than the average articled clerk.'

'It doesn't matter,' Sean answered. 'In a reasonable time you will be able to take over from me and my practice will be yours. It keeps the Duffy name on the front door.'

Patrick had thought about a career in law. He had been in the top ten per cent of graduating students at school and had established a good network of friends amongst the sons of the rich and powerful. His marks had been so high he could have applied for medicine, but after his experiences as a soldier he had seen more than enough blood and guts.

'There is something else I should mention to you,' Sean said. 'I am getting married in January and I would like you to be my best man.'

Patrick was in the process of swallowing a mouthful of orange juice when Sean casually delivered this statement. Patrick spluttered his juice on the formica tabletop.

'You are doing what?' he gasped, clearing his throat.

Sean grinned at him. 'I thought that might be a surprise,' he said. 'Me, a decrepit old man, getting married.'

Patrick stared across the table at this man he loved as if he was his real father.

'Holy hell!' Patrick said, wiping his mouth. 'Do I know the lady crazy enough to take you on?'

'I doubt it,' Sean replied calmly, cutting his bacon. 'She is a cousin to Harry Griffiths. Actually, I met her at his funeral. One could say that old Harry planned the meeting from beyond the grave.'

'She's not after your money, is she?' Patrick asked bluntly.

Sean laughed. 'She has three times the money I have earned over all the years I have been a solicitor. Her husband was a successful businessman who left her a very rich widow. Poor bastard ended up dying from the effects of gas on the Western Front. You will get to meet Rose next weekend. She is having a fondue dinner party at her Potts Point apartment and you are the honoured guest. She always has a good stock of Penfolds Dalwood claret and pinot riesling on hand. So, old chap, it's goodbye to my beer-swilling days – except when I head down to the pub with you.'

With a broad smile Patrick shook his head. In the army, officers drank claret in their mess. Sergeants drank beer. To complete this new and sophisticated lifestyle, all that was missing was Miss Sally Howard-Smith.

TWENTY-TWO

Sarah and Charles stood in the air terminal with Lady Georgina, Jane and Victoria. It was time for them to return to England to spend time at their country manor.

'I envy you celebrating a white Christmas,' Sarah said. 'Here we always seem to suffer the hottest day of the year, with bushfires burning in the Blue Mountains.'

'You should consider joining us next year,' Lady Georgina said. 'Perhaps your son will be with you and he can take you on a tour of the countryside.'

Charles glanced at Jane, who appeared downcast at the mention of Michael. While Lady Georgina and Sarah chatted about trivial matters awaiting the boarding call, he gently took Jane aside.

'I hope your mother is right about Michael being with us next Christmas,' he said quietly.

'I have been reading about the terrible things happening in Africa,' Jane said. 'I have a recurring nightmare that something awful will happen to Michael, preventing him from ever knowing he has a beautiful daughter.'

Jane glanced at Victoria standing quietly by Lady Georgina's side. She was a holding a stuffed toy koala bear, given to her by Sarah as an early Christmas present and souvenir of her short stay in Australia.

'When she smiles I think I am seeing her father smiling at me,' Jane said sadly.

'One day you and Michael will be together,' Charles said. 'And if he has half a brain, he will see what a wonderful young lady you are. I could not think of a better daughter-in-law.'

Jane hugged Charles impulsively. 'Thank you,' she whispered.

The boarding call came and the White family made their way to the tarmac baking under a hot summer sun. The jet engine Boeing sat waiting for its cargo of passengers. The flight to London would take around thirty-four hours, with eight stops along the way to refuel. Lady Georgina travelled first class, of course, as befitting the wife of a multimillionaire.

They turned and waved to Charles and Sarah who waited until they saw them disappear at the top of the boarding ladder. When they were out of sight, Sarah turned to Charles. 'What were you and Jane talking about?' she asked.

'Nothing much,' Charles shrugged. 'Just family secrets.'

Sarah glared at her husband but she knew she would be wasting her time if she tried to interrogate him. It was time to return to work while Charles returned to their home on the harbour to wile away the hours with a crossword until the evening shows came on television.

But when Sarah returned to her residence that evening Charles had a surprise for her. She had not even reached the cocktail cabinet when he held up a sheet of paper.

'I have an invitation for us to attend the centenary celebration of the establishment of Glen View homestead by Sir David and his wife Lady Enid.'

Sarah turned on Charles. 'I would rather be dead than accept such an insult,' she snapped.

'Maybe Jessie is trying to bury the hatchet,' Charles said, folding the sheet of paper. 'I think I will accept the invitation. Accommodation will be provided and, besides, I have never visited the property. Michael used to come back from up there with glowing reports of life in the bush. Maybe I should find out why before I die.'

'You don't look like you will die for many years yet,' Sarah scoffed, pouring a liberal amount of gin into a crystal tumbler.

'You are wrong on that point,' Charles said, and the tone of his answer startled Sarah.

'What are you talking about?' she questioned angrily.

'My doctor has told me I have cancer and that, at best, I have six months to live,' he said quietly.

For a moment it did not sink in with Sarah that the man she had been married to for almost a quarter of a century would soon die. 'I am sorry to hear that,' she finally replied. 'You have been a good father to my son.'

'And that is about it,' Charles sighed. 'I'm nothing more to you than someone to provide Michael with a father. There was a time you told me you loved me. But that was a long time ago.'

Sarah did not move from the cocktail cabinet to her husband's side. 'Does Michael know?' she asked.

'No,' Charles answered. 'He has enough worries right now just staying alive. You can tell him who his real father is when I am gone. Knowing you, I am sure you will get great pleasure telling Michael he need not mourn for me as I was never his real father anyway.'

'My son will have the opportunity to learn about his real father,' Sarah said. 'But I promise that I will not tell him until you are gone.'

Charles did not bother to reply but turned around and left Sarah alone in the dining room.

It was for the best, Sarah reflected. After all, she had supported Charles all these years and he had done very little in return to help the Macintosh Enterprises. He had always been a burden and now she would be free of him.

*

The case of the Carbolic Smoke Ball company was not very exciting. Patrick scribbled notes as he studied the different aspects of contract law in the university library. How Sean had ever found legal studies interesting was beyond Patrick. He took a deep breath, sighed and closed the law book. He had had enough. It was time to go home and relax with his latest book, *When the Lion Feeds*, by a new author called Wilbur Smith.

Patrick caught a tram and walked the last two blocks to Sean's flat under a hot summer sun. He could see that there was mail in the letterbox and he removed it. As he walked towards the front door, he flipped through the letters until he came to the one he had been hoping to find. It was from Sally in Hong Kong, and Patrick knew what he would be reading before he opened the pages of the Wilbur Smith.

He entered the flat, threw the bills on the kitchen table and went to the fridge to retrieve a cold bottle of beer. With the bottle open and a glass full of the brown liquid before him, he carefully slit open the envelope to retrieve the single page. With a smile he commenced reading, but by the time he had finished the letter the beer was forgotten, and all that remained on his face was a stricken expression. Sally had met another man and fallen in love. She was sorry to inform him so clinically in a letter, but she felt that Patrick might not have left the army if it had not been for her, and that he should have only made his decision based on what he really wanted. She felt bad that he had given up his beloved military life.

He was vaguely aware that Sean had returned home.

'I will grab a glass and join you,' Sean said cheerily, then noticed the dark cloud over Patrick. 'Do you have bad news?'

'Yeah. Sally wrote to say she found another bloke,' Patrick said, picking up the glass of beer and swallowing a great mouthful.

Sean walked over to the table, poured himself a beer and sat down.

'Lucky in war, unlucky in love,' he said, raising his glass as a toast. 'How will that affect your plans to study law?'

With a pained expression, Patrick looked across the table at Sean. 'I truly appreciate all that you have done to get my articles, but I don't think I am cut out for law. If I return to the army now I shouldn't lose much. Maybe I will simply be reinstated at my old rank, and I will chase up Major Mann's offer to join the training team in Vietnam.'

'I could see you were not really happy poring over trust accounts and probate files,' Sean sighed.

Patrick was relieved Sean understood. He knew he would be happier back in a battalion; he had only left the army to be with Sally. Patrick was a born soldier, aware that the father who had been killed before he was born had served in the frontlines of the Great War. It was a family tradition to serve the nation in times of war.

'Will you be travelling with me to Glen View for Christmas?' Sean asked.

'Yeah, Terituba will be home for Christmas, and it will be a chance to catch up with Aunt Jess and Uncle Donald,' Patrick said.

'We will be joined by Charles,' Sean said. 'It will be his first time to the property.'

'Let me guess,' Patrick grinned. 'Sarah Macintosh will be remaining in Sydney for Christmas.'

'It looks like it,' Sean said. 'Just a pity that Michael will not be with us. The kid kind of grew on me. There were times he reminded me of David. At least David and Gail will be staying over at Glen View for Christmas. It will be the first real family gathering we have ever had.'

Patrick poured himself another beer, and when it was gone Sean suggested that they head over to their favourite pub to have a counter meal.

Patrick glanced at the letter, picked it up, folded it and returned it to the envelope. He was broken-hearted but had learned one thing about this woman: once she had made up her mind there was nothing anyone could do to change it. He was not about to beg her; that was not in his nature. The only consolation he had as he left the flat was that she would one day wake up and realise she had made the wrong decision. Patrick was a patient man – if unrealistic. It was true love that made a person blind.

*

Christmas Day at Glen View saw a blazing sun rise over a small tent city around the homestead. Jessica and Donald had spared no expense to make the event spectacular. Cooks had been hired, and off to one side was a small flotilla of caravans to house the extra staff.

Already the delicious aroma of a beast being slowly spit-roasted drifted on the still air. Ice had been flown in, and big buckets kept in the shade contained bottles of beer and soft drink. A keg was also in operation as neighbours from properties far and wide drove – or flew their light aircraft – in to join the centenary celebrations.

Jessica fussed over the cooking in the kitchen, aided by Shannon, while her two boys went looking for other boys to muck around with. Donald, with a beer in his hand, was already outside under a tarpaulin supervising the cooking of the beast. Before lunch, Santa arrived, red-faced and obviously dying of the heat under his costume. He consumed a copious quantity of beer to cool down, but the squealing children did not care as he handed out small presents. A few of the older kids recognised Mitch as Santa and muttered amongst themselves as to whether he should be exposed, but presents and a growl from Santa soon silenced them. Many of the children running wild gravitated to the dam for a swim while a couple of the mothers supervised.

'Charles, it is so good to have you here this year,' Jessica said when she left the kitchen to join him in a quieter spot on the verandah. Jessica had fortified herself with a shandy, and she gazed out at the many people she knew. As usual the men had formed circles to discuss the weather, cattle prices and politics, while the women had retreated to the house to sit around the dining room table, cooling themselves with little hand-held fans.

Near lunchtime Patrick and Sean drove up and were welcomed as family. 'You blokes are shacked up in the workers' quarters,' Donald said, shaking each man's hand vigorously. 'Charles got in first, so he has a room in the house.'

'Bloody RAAF,' Patrick growled cheerfully. 'Always get the best of everything.'

'Yeah, well, the honourable David and Mrs Macintosh got the last room,' Donald grinned.

'Same with bloody politicians – always the best,' Sean added with his own grin. 'I need to catch up with him over a cold beer.'

'He's over there in that circle. He could probably do with being rescued from the mob,' Donald said. 'That's the problem when you're a politician.'

All day people ate and drank. With a lot of noise and laughter and ribbing, the festivities continued in true country style as the sun went down. Country and western music blared from a loud speaker, and weary children found parents' laps to sleep in. As the great red ball descended across the brigalow plains, David, Gail, Sean, Patrick, Charles, Jessica and her three offspring settled on camp stools away from the tents and marquees to sit and take in the serenity of the dying day. They chatted about family matters and anything else that came to mind. It was a peaceful moment in their lives and Patrick was overjoyed to be joined by Terituba who had spent the day with his parents at their quarters.

'I hear you comin' back to the army,' Terituba said, punching his best friend playfully in the arm. 'Best Christmas present I could get. Maybe they make you go through Kapooka again to learn how to be a soldier.'

'I don't think so, and how in hell did you know that?'

'We blackfellas got what you whitefellas call ESP,' Terituba grinned.

'Uncle Sean told you, didn't he?' Patrick said with a laugh. 'Anyway, I got in touch with Victoria Barracks and they told me I could go back with my old rank as I have only been out for a few months.'

'I thought you were goin' to be a bigshot lawyer an' marry your sheila,' Terituba said, taking a bottle of beer proffered by David Macintosh.

'She sent me a Dear John letter,' Patrick said.

'She got that wrong. Your name Patrick – not John.'

'Smart arse,' Patrick responded and raised his bottle to his best friend.

'Where's Donald?' Sean asked, suddenly noticing his absence.

'Oh, he had to run an errand,' Jessica replied mysteriously. 'He should be back in a short time. Just had to pick up someone from the Dunedin property.'

The words were only just out of her mouth when her husband appeared through a fine mist of dust haze, followed by another man.

'Oh, God!' Charles gasped, hardly believing his eyes. 'Michael!'

Behind Donald, Michael Macintosh emerged with a broad smile on his face. Charles was hardly on his feet before he was embraced with a crushing hug from Michael.

'I missed you, Dad,' he said as tears ran down Charles's face. Cries of approval rose up from the rest of the family sitting on their camp chairs.

Charles was reluctant to let go but eventually released Michael to gaze upon his son, soaking in this tall, broad-shouldered young man who had left as a boy. Charles was speechless until he finally uttered, 'This is the greatest gift I could ever have in my life – my son.' Charles glanced across at David who was smiling and Charles nodded his head. It had been David's influence that had brought Michael to him for Christmas from Africa.

Terituba and Patrick slapped Michael on the back and thrust a bottle of beer into his hand.

'Good to see the snotty-nosed kid we had to sort out on his first holiday,' Patrick said, raising his bottle in a toast. 'How did you know about this gathering? The last I heard you were over in the Congo with Mad Mike Hoare.'

'There was nothing mad about Mike Hoare. It was the East Germans who gave him that title, and the left wing Western press decided to use it in an attempt to denigrate a great and brilliant soldier. As it was I had a letter from Uncle David,' Michael said, glancing around at familiar faces, and one he did not recognise. The unfamiliar man rose to his feet and extended his hand.

'I'm your Uncle David,' he said. 'It's good to finally meet you face to face.'

Michael accepted the firm grip, gazing directly into David's eyes. 'I've heard a lot of stories about you,' he said. 'All good.'

'Thank you,' David said. 'You've been fortunate to have such a good dad in your life.' He glanced at Charles and could see his look of gratitude.

'Dad is a truly great bloke,' Michael said, then turned back to Patrick. 'I guess Uncle David used his sources in Canberra to track me down. So here I am.'

It was an evening everyone would always remember, and as the moon rose in the night sky, those gathered could hear the mournful cry of the curlews. It would prove to be the last time they would all be together to share the love of family.

Part Three

Vietnam

1968

TWENTY-THREE

The young man in his late twenties sat alone at a table in the Sydney coffee shop. In the background, The 5th Dimension sang about going up and away in a beautiful balloon. Trooper Michael Macintosh was dressed in civilian clothing of slacks and shirt, but his membership of the elite Special Air Service Regiment could be seen in the hardness of his eyes and the bearing distinctive to professional soldiers.

Michael had enlisted in the Australian Army in 1965 and his application to the SASR had been accepted. The selection course had been much tougher than he had expected but he had succeeded and had already done one tour of Vietnam. At present he was home on a month's service leave before returning to his barracks in Western Australia to be shipped out again.

Michael liked the song playing. It was calming and upbeat. For a brief moment the words took him away from his memories of the long-range reconnaissance patrols deep into Viet Cong territory in Phuoc Tuy Province. There had been so many close calls, and one or two vicious fire-fights. Killing was something that did not cause Michael to lose sleep. He always wondered how he could cope so well. Perhaps it was a family trait.

Before his father, Charles Huntley, had died in 1965 he had told Michael who his biological father was, and also that Michael was the father of Jane White's daughter, Victoria. Both disclosures had shocked Michael, but his tears had been for the man who had loved him for whole his life and was dying before his time.

Michael had flown to London before enlisting in the army and found Jane. As they faced one another in the country manor where Victoria had been conceived, they had been forced to face the fact that time had moved on. Only once did Michael see his daughter, and it almost broke his heart. Her true parentage was tightly locked up, and would stay that way. He knew that was probably for the best. Maybe fighting in the Congo had changed Michael, or perhaps it was that Jane was no longer the girl infatu-ated by the handsome young man from Australia. They had parted as friends and Michael had returned to Sydney.

'Would you like another cup of coffee?' asked the young waitress, snapping Michael from his thoughts.

He looked up at her. She had a slightly sad look but she was very pretty. He guessed she was about eighteen or nineteen.

'Thank you,' he replied. 'I think I will.'

'You must be a soldier,' she said when she returned with his mug of coffee.

'Why would you say that?' Michael asked with a smile that briefly banished the coldness from his eyes.

'My brother was a national serviceman who came back last year. He has the same look as you, and besides, not many young men have their hair cut as short as yours.'

Michael was intrigued by her perceptiveness. 'What look is that?'

'A kind of hard, faraway look. I've heard it called the thousand-yard stare. Although of course nowadays we'd probably say the thousand-metre stare. You have the same look I've seen so many times in my brother's eyes. Jacob has not had an easy time settling back in to civilian life. He drinks too much and gets into fights. Are you still in the army?'

'I am,' Michael said. 'I have a few weeks leave before I do a second tour. Do you work here full-time?'

'No, I'm at uni. I work here to help with the rent on my flat in Glebe.'

'What are you studying?' Michael asked.

'Science,' she said. 'I want to be a chemist one day.'

'I'm Michael,' he said, extending his hand.

'I'm Mila,' she said, taking his hand shyly. 'There's going to be a party tonight. A few of my uni friends will be there.' She scribbled down an address on a scrap of paper. 'I'd like you to come as I'll be there. But I have to warn you that most of the people at the party are part of the anti-war moratorium and a bit younger than you.'

'Are you?' Michael asked, accepting the scrap of paper.

'Yes,' Mila replied. 'I've seen what the war has done to my brother. He was such a warm and loving man before he went to Vietnam. Now he's so changed I hardly know him. If we can stop the war, and conscription, other young men might be saved.'

Michael was silent. He was a professional soldier, and although he did not believe the politicians' domino theory of Asia falling to Communism, from what he had seen of the massive corruption of the South Vietnamese government, he felt that it would have long fallen without the intervention of the USA and her allies in the SEATO alliance. For Michael, war was his occupation.

'I should get back to work,' Mila said, looking over her shoulder. 'I hope you come tonight.'

She walked away and Michael finished his coffee. He rose and nodded to her, then walked out into the late summer sunshine.

*

Only a few suburbs away Jessica Duffy-Macintosh sat opposite the Mother Superior of the exclusive girls' school attended by her seventeen-year-old daughter, Shannon. The room brought back memories of Jessica's early days as a nun and her time on a mission station in the Pacific before the outbreak of the war there. Jessica had come to know Sister Mary well as Jessica had been very generous to Shannon's school, but she still felt uncomfortable in the head nun's presence. She knew Sister Mary was aware that Jessica had renounced her vows many years earlier and, although it was never stated openly, the nun always had an air of disapproval whenever they met.

'It appears that your daughter left in the company of the Price girl,' said Sister Mary. 'We only discovered their absence this morning at chapel.'

'It is not like Shannon to be irresponsible, Sister Mary,' Jessica said. 'I'm sure she will return soon.'

'Mrs Duffy,' the stern nun said, 'I am not sure if you know about the Price girl's background, but her father owns a nightclub in Kings Cross. From what a couple of her friends said, your daughter was keen to sample the bright lights of the Cross. I think there are very good grounds to be worried.'

'That puts things in a different light,' Jessica conceded.

'Tania Price is not a bad girl, but her circumstances have to be considered. They are both very pretty young ladies, and I think we know what the Cross is like with all the American servicemen on leave there.'

'I am fully aware of the dangers, Sister Mary,' Jessica replied. 'I have the resources to have them found.'

'I am sure you do, Mrs Duffy,' said Sister Mary. 'Hopefully they will be found before anything untoward happens.'

Jessica excused herself, walking wearily towards the door of the study festooned with religious icons and a photo of Pope Paul VI. Jessica did not want to admit to Sister Mary that as her daughter was growing into a young woman she was becoming increasingly rebellious and there had been some very heated confrontations between mother and daughter. Jessica knew it was all part of growing up, but she had not experienced this with her two sons.

Worrying about Shannon was bad enough, but Bryce was in Vietnam serving with an artillery regiment. He had gone willingly, as he saw it as his duty to serve his country. He had assured his mother that being in artillery was not as bad as serving as a grunt out in the scrub.

Jessica remembered so vividly the last time she had looked upon her son's face. It had been at the railway station in Sydney just before he and his fellow soldiers were transported north to Townsville and from there to South Vietnam. She had tried to smile but when her eldest son was out of sight she had burst into tears, sobbing on Donald's shoulder as the great diesel-driven engine pulled out of Central Station. Now all she had of him were letters, although lately, thanks to modern technology, he was sending her recorded tape cassettes too.

Jessica shook thoughts of Bryce from her mind and tried to concentrate on the problem at hand. Her first stop would be a city police station where an old friend, Detective Sergeant Brendan Wren, worked. She had met him a few years earlier when she attempted to put pressure on senior police to reopen the Allison Lowe case. Brendan had been identified by Sean as his principal player in getting justice for the murdered young woman, and thus, he was an enemy of Sarah Macintosh in the sense of seeking the truth. Jessica decided that she would visit him and see if he could help in tracking down the two runaways.

★

Michael sat in his mother's spacious office with its view over the harbour. He watched as she lit a cigarette and paced the floor, her hand on her hip in the imperious manner he was familiar with from his youth.

'When are you going to grow up and be a man?' she snapped. 'All this foolish playing at war.'

'It took a bit to get into the regiment, Mother,' Michael said. 'I would not consider myself to be playing at war. It gets very real for us out in the scrub.'

Sarah ceased pacing and turned with an imploring look on her face. 'You know you are the only person I have left in my life since Charles passed away. And you won't even come and stay with me while you're on leave.'

Michael smiled grimly. 'Cut the BS, Mother,' he said. 'All you live for is the family business. I cannot remember one single time in my childhood that you gave me a hug. I cannot ever forgive you for not telling me when Nanny Keevers died. To you she was just another paid employee, but to me she was the only real motherly warmth I knew. I have no doubt that your main concern for my life is that I leave the army when my enlistment is up and join you in running Macintosh Enterprises. I guess your next priority would be for me to marry a girl with a good pedigree and produce grandchildren so you can groom one of them to replace me when my time is up.'

'I do want you to inherit the companies when I stand down,' Sarah conceded, puffing her cigarette in its long ebony holder. 'We have a blood line to continue. You of all people should understand tradition and loyalty.'

'You mistake me for Dad. He was the one who was loyal to you, although I have never understood why. He waited until his deathbed to tell me that your cousin is my biological father. He also told me Victoria White is my daughter.'

Sarah paled. 'My God! I suspected there was something very familiar about Victoria when I first laid eyes on her.'

'Interfering will do no good – Jane's father's name is on the birth certificate, not mine. It must irk you to know that I have actually produced an heir to your precious empire and there is nothing either you or I can do about it.'

Sarah stood, hardly aware cigarette ash was falling on the expensive carpet. 'Couldn't you convince Jane to disclose the truth?' she asked, slumping down on a couch.

'That's not likely,' Michael said. 'In her last letter she said she was engaged to be married and wanted to start a new life.'

'There must be something we can do,' Sarah said. 'I am not going to let the matter rest until there is a resolution.'

Michael rose to his feet. 'Good luck trying,' he said and left, taking the elevator down to the street. It was a Friday and he could feel the festive atmosphere amongst the crowds surging towards the train stations. He was not sure he wanted to go to Mila's party; he was normally a solitary man who found his companionship amongst the brotherhood of soldiers. Still, Mila was very pretty and maybe it was time to see what civilians did on a Friday night in Sydney.

★

Jessica sat patiently in the busy police station on a hard bench near the desk sergeant's station. Eventually Brendan appeared, stepping forward with a warm smile and extended hand.

'Jessica, it has been a long time,' he said as two uniformed police grappled with a big drunken man swearing obscenities. 'Going to be a busy night. It's a full moon. What brings you to a place like this?'

'My daughter, who is only seventeen, ran away from her boarding school this morning in the company of William Price's daughter,' Jessica said and saw a dark shadow cross the police officer's face.

'You mean *the* Billy Price of Kings Cross?'

'The very same.'

'Well, I know one thing that might be a consolation,' Brendan said. 'No sane man with the will to live would lay a hand on Billy Price's daughter – or any of her friends. He is known to adore his daughter, and all she has to do is mention his name up at the Cross and she will be treated with kid gloves.'

'What if some lowlife who has never heard of Price finds the girls?' Jessica asked.

'He'd have to have been living under a log all his life. Every paper in Sydney has at least one article a week about Price,' Brendan said. 'But I will alert all the boys and have the Cross mob keep an eye out for any young girls that don't fit in. I will let you know when I hear something and we'll get them both back safely. How are Donald and the boys?'

'Bryce was called up and is in Vietnam. Kim and Donald are back on Glen View. It was just lucky I was in Sydney for a business conference. I will wait to hear from you before I inform Donald that his precious daughter is roaming the sleazy streets of Kings Cross. Knowing Donald as I do, he would be on the first plane down to Sydney if he knew.'

'Leave it with us, Jessie,' Brendan said. 'I think I can promise that we will find Shannon before the sun rises.'

Jessica caught a taxi back to her Sydney home in the leafy suburb of Strathfield. She knew that she would not catch a wink of sleep until Shannon was found.

TWENTY-FOUR

When Michael's taxi pulled up in front of the Glebe building he could hear the Rolling Stones' 'Paint It Black' blaring out into the street of rundown Victorian terraces. It was a popular rental area for university students, and the scent of marijuana wafted to Michael as he approached the narrow building. Young people, in what Michael had come to learn was hippie dress, spilled out onto the street to admire the row of Harley Davidson motorbikes and chat with the men wearing the colours of a motorcycle gang. This was clearly a party of mixed social groups if bikies were hanging out with students. Most people were already drunk or stoned and hardly gave him a glance as he pushed his way up the old stone steps. A couple were kissing passionately just inside the front door, and the loud music drowned out any normal conversation. He spotted Mila talking to a tall young man a couple of years younger than himself.

'Hello, Mila,' Michael said when he was close enough to almost shout in her ear. She turned and flashed him a smile.

'I thought you might not come,' she said. 'I'm glad you did.'

'Who's your friend?' the tall young man asked belligerently. 'He smells of bacon.'

'I'm not a cop,' Michael said.

The tall young man glared at Michael. 'You don't look like you fit in here, sport.'

Mila took Michael's elbow and steered him away. 'Did you bring something to drink?'

'No, water is fine for me.'

'How are you going to get into the spirit of things?'

'I only came because a pretty lady invited me,' Michael replied with a smile, and Mila blushed.

'Well, let me take you around and introduce you to some of my friends. I won't tell them you're in the army.'

'Just tell them I work for the council in the sanitation department,' Michael said. 'If they start asking questions, I'll explain the difference between sewage and sewerage.'

'Is there a difference?' Mila asked, and burst into laughter. 'You made that up.'

Michael grinned. 'Not about the difference between sewage and sewerage.'

'Forget about my friends. I'll grab my Bacardi and we can go out to the backyard where it's quieter,' Mila said.

Michael liked her suggestion as the music was almost as deafening as standing next to an M2A2 105 millimetre howitzer when it fired off an artillery shell. She took his hand, guiding him through the mass of bodies in the tiny house, to the kitchen where she recovered a bottle with her name written on it. Then they broke through to the backyard which was a little less noisy and occupied by people smoking joints. Mila found an old lounge with the stuffing oozing out of tears in its fabric; it was at least something to sit on. Then she poured rum into a plastic cup.

They were hardly settled when Michael noticed two girls dressed in the shortest miniskirts he had seen. He frowned: they were clearly very much underage for this party. The two girls were standing together sharing a joint, and their presence was attracting unsavoury attention from two large bikies wearing their club colours. One of the girls turned her face in Michael's direction and for a moment he stared, trying to place her in his memory.

'Shannon!' he said aloud, and the girl looked up, startled. Michael rose from the lounge chair and walked over to her. 'Shannon Duffy. What are you doing here?' He could see both shock and guilt written all over her face.

'Michael!' she gasped, looking like a stunned animal caught in the headlights of a car. 'Did my mother send you to take me back to school?'

'I'm pretty sure your mother doesn't know you're here,' Michael said.

'Who's your friend?' the other girl asked, taking a long draw of the joint.

'He's my cousin,' Shannon answered. 'Please, Michael, don't tell my mum you saw Tania and me here.'

'You can tell her yourself,' Michael said. 'I'm taking both you girls home now.'

He took Shannon by the elbow, intending to guide her from the house and hail a taxi. The second girl did not budge but instead attempted to grab Michael's arm.

'If you don't let go of Shannon I will tell my old man that you molested her,' Tania said. 'My old man is Billy Price and he'll fix you.'

'Does your father know you're at this party?' Michael

asked and saw the girl shrink away. 'You can join Shannon in the taxi.'

'Hey, man, leave the kids alone,' said one of the bikies.

Michael turned to him and saw that the man and his companion were as large as he was, but there was something in Michael's eyes that spoke of extreme violence when he growled, 'If I were you, I would stay out of family business.'

Michael sensed that his confrontation with Shannon had caused unwanted attention in the small backyard. He was vastly outnumbered, and knew what he must do. One of the bikies stepped forward. He was big and mean-looking, but he also carried a pot belly. Michael did not hesitate. Years of martial arts training, coupled with hand-to-hand combat as an SAS soldier, had honed him into a lethal fighting machine. He waited until the bikie was almost on him, then used all his force in a lightning-fast blow, smashing the heel of his hand into the man's nose. The bikie fell back in utter surprise, spraying blood across those close by, then slumped to the ground with his hands to his face, moaning his pain and shock.

The second bikie lunged forward, swinging a blow that Michael blocked with his left arm while, at the same time, delivering a savage thrust with the fingers of his right hand into his opponent's eyes. The big man screamed his shock and staggered back, clutching his face. Shannon had stood watching open-mouthed but now she attempted to leave and Michael grabbed her by the arm.

The crowd in the small yard parted to allow this terrifying man through. Mila followed, and so too did the second girl who had boasted that her father would fix Michael.

By now a buzz had rippled through the party and already someone was calling for an ambulance. Calling the police was not an option, considering the heavy use of Indian hemp.

'Mila, where are you going?' asked the belligerent young man Michael had first encountered, grabbing her by the arm.

'Let me go, Justin,' she said, attempting to shake off his grip.

'Let her go,' Michael snarled.

'Or what, tough guy?'

That was a stupid question. Justin did not even see the punch coming as Michael drove his fist into the man's stomach, buckling him instantly. Michael continued with the three girls in tow through the crowd, now scattering for safety from the violent maniac in their midst.

Out on the street Michael hailed a passing taxi cab and bundled the two girls into the back. He smiled grimly at Mila as she climbed in after them, then he took a seat beside the driver.

'You first, young lady,' Michael said, turning to the daughter of the infamous crime lord of Kings Cross.

Tania sheepishly provided the address of her father's nightclub. There was something in Michael's eyes that warned her disobedience was not an option. When they arrived, Michael escorted Tania inside. The place was full of American servicemen on R and R leave from Vietnam.

A man stepped from the shadows, accompanied by two brawny bouncers. 'What are you doing with my daughter?' he asked threateningly.

'I think you should ask your daughter that, Mr Price,' Michael said.

Billy Price glared at his daughter, then looked up at Michael. 'Do I know you?'

'I think you might know my mother, Sarah Macintosh,' Michael said and saw the look of surprise on Price's face. He had seen this man with his mother when he was a child.

'I must apologise but I have another delivery to make tonight.' Before Price could respond, Michael strode away, leaving a very forlorn daughter to face the wrath of a worried father.

When Michael climbed back into the taxi he glanced at Shannon and Mila in the back seat.

'You did not tell me that you fought as a mercenary in the Congo and that you're an SAS soldier,' Mila said almost accusingly.

'How did you learn that?' Michael asked, and saw the guilty look on Shannon's face.

'Shannon has a very high opinion of you,' Mila said. 'Why didn't you tell me who you were and are now?'

'A couple of good reasons,' Michael answered. 'The first being I have only just met you, and secondly, what does it matter?'

They drove in silence until the taxi reached Jessica's Strathfield residence. Michael paid the fare, and the three walked up the pathway to the modest but attractive house with its stained-glass windows. The lights were on inside and Michael rang the doorbell. It opened to reveal Jessica still in her day clothes. For a moment she tried to focus on Michael standing under the porch light, and then she saw her daughter standing behind him.

Jessica stepped out and embraced Shannon, smothering her with kisses.

'I thought you might be worried about her, Aunt Jess,' Michael said.

'Michael!' Jessica exclaimed. 'How is it that you found Shannon?'

'I was not aware that she was lost, but she was at a place where she should not have been.' He turned to Mila. 'This is a friend of mine, Mila, who helped me extract Shannon.'

Jessica stepped back to examine her daughter wearing

far too much make-up and a skirt that hardly concealed her panties. Her face clouded. 'Go to your room, young lady. You and I will talk later. You are fortunate that your father does not know of your escapade.'

Shannon did not protest, and went meekly to her room.

'Come inside and I'll make a pot of tea,' Jessica said. 'You can tell me how you came across my delinquent daughter.'

Michael and Mila followed Jessica inside into the kitchen where she sat them down at the table. Michael explained how he had stumbled across Shannon and Tania. He left out the part about hospitalising three men in the process of his extraction.

'The last I heard you had joined the army and gone to Vietnam with the SASR. I guess you're now on leave.'

'I also heard that Bryce is doing his stint in Vietnam as a nasho,' Michael said, taking a lamington from the tray Jessica placed on the table.

Mila remained silent until Jessica turned to her and asked, 'Have you known Michael very long?'

'We've just met, Mrs Duffy,' Mila said. 'But in the brief time I have known Michael he has proved to be a very interesting man.'

'More than you know,' Jessica smiled. 'If he had any sense he would not be in the army but helping his mother run her companies. I say that even though she is one of my major competitors.'

Mila glanced quizzically at Michael who was blithely sipping from his cup of tea.

'My Aunt Jess means the Macintosh Enterprises,' he said. 'My mother is Sarah Macintosh.'

Mila's eyes widened. 'I've read about your mother in the *Women's Weekly*. She's supposed to be the richest woman in Australia.'

'Second richest,' Michael grinned. 'Aunt Jess here is the richest.'

Mila glanced at Jessica sitting at the end of the table. The modest home did not reek of wealth, and Michael's statement caught her off balance. 'Jessica Duffy! I've also read about you. Your life story is fascinating. You're a war hero.'

'Thank you for the kind words, but the war was a long time ago, and I think Michael's mother and I are on an equal footing with our business concerns. My sister-in-law might do even better if she had Michael by her side.'

'That will not happen, Aunt Jess,' Michael said, finishing his tea and lamington. 'I suppose I should get Mila home as it is getting late. May I call a taxi?'

Within minutes the cab was at the front door, and Jessica gave them both a warm hug. 'Thank you, Michael,' she said. 'You are always welcome under my roof – and so are your friends.'

'Thanks, Aunt Jessie. I might be back before I am shipped out again.'

On the taxi ride to her Glebe flat, Mila said very little, but she slipped her hand into Michael's.

When they arrived Mila, without a word, led Michael by the hand in to her flat and closed the door behind them.

*

The sun rose on a hot Saturday morning and Michael pulled himself into a sitting position, gazing at the sleeping face of the girl he hardly knew. She was just as beautiful asleep as she was awake, he thought. Very gently, he extracted himself from the bed and quickly dressed without waking her. He exited the flat, and when Mila finally awoke she could see that he was gone, but the bed was sprinkled with red rose petals and the delicious aroma of food wafted in the air. She sat up, covering her breasts modestly with the sheet, as he walked into the bedroom carrying a tray containing two mugs of coffee and a plate of hot croissants.

'I thought perhaps you had gone forever,' Mila said. 'The rose petals are beautiful. Thank you.'

Michael sat down on the bed, placing the tray between them. 'I still have some leave before I have to go back, and I could not think of anything better than spending it with you,' he said. 'I think it is time that I learned a little more about you, then maybe we can go to the beach.'

Suddenly there was a loud knock. Michael slid from the bed and cautiously opened the front door to find two burly uniformed police officers standing on the steps.

'Do you live here?' one of them asked bluntly.

'No,' Michael replied. 'What's this about?'

'Does Mila Welsh live here?'

'I do,' Mila answered behind Michael. She had grabbed a dressing-gown and stood clutching it around her.

'Were you at a party last night in Glebe with this gentleman?' the police officer asked.

'I was.'

'What do you know about the serious assault of Mr Justin Wainwright at the party?' the police officer continued.

'If that is the man I hit assisting Miss Welsh, then I am guilty,' Michael answered in an angry voice.

'You put him in hospital with a ruptured spleen, and funnily enough, we found two bikies admitted from the same party, both suffering severe injuries. You will have to come with us to the station for further questioning. What is your name?'

'Michael Macintosh. I am a member of the armed services.'

Michael had a sinking feeling that his Saturday morning was going to turn out very badly indeed.

TWENTY-FIVE

The cells stank of human excrement and stale alcohol. The din from drunken inmates echoed around the watch house, and Michael sat in a corner of a cell he shared with the drunks gathered up off the streets of Sydney. Saturday night was approaching and he had been informed by the charging sergeant that he would appear before the magistrates court on Monday morning, charged with assault causing grievous bodily harm. Michael had said nothing in his defence, and only enquired as to the fate of Miss Mila Welsh, who had also been brought to the station for questioning. He was informed that she had provided a statement and had been free to return home.

'Macintosh,' a voice boomed. 'You are to come with me.'

Michael stood and followed the uniformed policeman down a corridor and into a small, dingy room. When Michael entered, he saw his mother sitting at a table, the inevitable cigarette in its holder in her hand. Her expression reflected a mixture of maternal concern and annoyance. Michael was surprised to see the concern; he had never seen it in her before.

'Why didn't you call me when the police brought you here?' she asked.

Michael shrugged. 'I suppose because I got myself into the mess. How did you know I was here?'

'I received a phone call from a Miss Mila Welsh informing me you had been arrested on a serious assault charge, and I immediately came here. I was told of your bail conditions and the police said I can apply for your temporary release when you go before the court on Monday.'

'I doubt that I will have the cash to pay for bail,' Michael said, 'let alone employ a good lawyer.'

'Money is not the problem,' Sarah said. 'It is the person you assaulted that is the problem. He is the son of a well-known Sydney family and he has had his spleen removed. The family is insisting that you face the full force of the law.'

'I honestly did not intend to injure him,' Michael said.

'Be that as it may, the fact is you are in serious trouble and could be facing a prison term. I will be hiring the best defence our money can buy.'

'Well, I doubt any lawyer will be able to successfully plead my case,' Michael sighed. The worst thing about any conviction would be his dishonourable discharge, first from the SASR, and then the army.

'I would not despair yet,' Sarah said. 'Do not underestimate the reach of my contacts in this city. Just behave and I will see you on Monday in court. If there is anything you need, just ask.'

Michael stared at his mother, smartly dressed and out of place in the inner-city police station, as she turned to walk past the uniformed policeman standing in the doorway. As he was escorted back to the large cell he shared with the drunks, he wondered what his mother meant by the reach of her contacts.

★

'William, it has been many years,' Sarah said, standing in the empty nightclub that smelled of spilled beer and cigarette smoke. A cleaner was taking down chairs from tables.

Billy Price ushered Sarah to a table and indicated to his barman to bring them coffee.

'I have to admit, as much of a bitch as you are, I have missed you,' Billy said. 'I have already heard your young fella has got himself into a spot of bother. He didn't deserve that, considering how he got my Tania out of a sticky situation. Is there anything I can do? I feel I owe your lad one for sticking his neck out for my girl.'

'There is,' Sarah said. 'But time is of utmost importance because Michael is due to appear in court on Monday morning.'

Billy Price looked hard at Sarah. They had been lovers during the war but had eventually drifted apart. Billy had married one of his very attractive barmaids and settled down to a seemingly respectable domestic life. But it was only a front, as he was considered one of the most dangerous gangsters in Sydney's criminal underground. His power reached into the pockets of corrupt politicians, police and even judges and magistrates. 'What did you have in mind?' he asked with a half-smile.

'I thought that you might have a quiet word with Justin Wainwright; see if you can persuade him to withdraw his statement.'

'I can do that,' Billy replied. 'Do you know where this Wainwright fella lives?'

'He has a flat in Glebe he shares with another student,' Sarah said. 'I have the address here.' She passed the under-world figure a scrap of paper. 'I believe he is still in hospital for the moment, recovering from an operation.'

Billy took the paper, glanced at it and turned to the barman. 'Go and tell Blitzer and Jack I need them to come around to the club now.'

'Yes, boss.'

Billy returned his attention back to Sarah. 'Consider it a done deal,' he said. 'I heard that you are a widow now.'

'William, times have changed, and my true love is my business – you know that.'

'It always has been,' Billy sighed.

Sarah rose and left the nightclub, stepping out into the streets of Kings Cross. A few hungover American servicemen with young girls on their arms wandered in search of a cafe for breakfast. Sarah signalled to her driver waiting at the kerb to pick her up. She had done all she could. Now her son's fate was in the hands of her old lover.

★

Monday morning arrived and Michael had not been able to shave or wash before he was escorted to the magistrates court adjoining the police station. He was held in a room off the courthouse, and a man in a smart suit sought him out from the other prisoners awaiting their appearance.

'Mr Macintosh, I am the solicitor who has been hired by your mother to represent you at this hearing. My name is John Hertz,' he said, shaking Michael's hand. 'I have been informed of certain matters, so you will not have to speak at all unless you are addressed by the beak.'

'Okay,' Michael said, just a little confused at the brevity of his defence. The solicitor disappeared, and after an hour Michael heard his name called three times, as was the legal tradition.

He stepped into the courtroom, glancing around and seeing his mother sitting on a bench in the public section. She smiled and nodded to him. The solicitor waved for Michael to join him at a table, and the police prosecutor stood to address the case to the magistrate. Michael remained seated as the prosecutor and magistrate engaged in legal talk. But what Michael did understand was that the aggrieved party had submitted a statement to say that he had made a mistake and that Michael Macintosh was not his assailant. However, the prosecutor argued a witness statement from a Miss Mila Welsh contradicted the victim's misidentification.

'Stand up, Mr Duffy,' the magistrate said. 'I believe that you have recently returned from a tour of duty in Vietnam with our SASR, is that correct?'

'Yes, Your Worship,' Michael replied.

The magistrate frowned, and Michael sensed that he was not out of trouble.

'I must ask you a very important question, Mr Macintosh. Did you in any way intimidate any witness who might have brought evidence against you?'

'I swear on the honour of my regiment that I did not in any way attempt to influence the witness, Your Worship.' Michael was telling the truth, but he had a sneaking suspicion his mother was somehow behind Wainwright withdrawing his statement.

The magistrate looked down at the paper file on his bench and was silent for a moment. Then he looked up at Michael standing before him. 'I have two conflicting statements, and I must view Miss Welsh's version of events as potentially being tainted by your association with her.'

'Your Worship . . .' the police prosecutor protested but was silenced by the magistrate raising his hand.

'Sergeant, I will finish my address, if you please,' he said. 'I feel that it will not serve justice to proceed with this matter as Mr Macintosh is returning to Vietnam in the near future. I feel that is enough to justify dismissing this case, since the victim of this matter does not wish to give evidence against Mr Macintosh. Now, I think we should have a break for morning tea.'

The court constable ordered all to rise as the magistrate left his bench.

'Does that mean I am free to go?' Michael asked his solicitor, who rose from his chair, briefcase in hand.

'And there will be no black mark on your record,' the solicitor said, slapping Michael on the back just as his mother approached with a broad smile. Michael gave her an enquiring look.

'I knew that they would not convict you,' she said, patting him affectionately on the cheek with her gloved hand.

'Miss Macintosh,' the solicitor said, 'thank you for the prior information. It certainly helped me out with the shortest GBH I have ever defended in court. I must hurry back to the office, so I will congratulate you, Mr Macintosh, on being able to walk out of here, thanks to your mother.'

He scooped up his paper-stuffed briefcase and hurried away.

'What did you do?' Michael asked.

'Nothing that you need know about,' she replied with another pat on the cheek. 'I would ask you to join me for lunch, but I think you need to return to your accommodation, shave and take a shower. You have my phone number.'

When Michael stepped out of the courthouse he saw Mila standing forlornly at the bottom of the sweeping stone steps. She ran to him.

'Oh, Michael, I am so sorry,' she said, embracing him. 'I told the police that you were protecting me, and your solicitor said that I might be called to refute my statement, but it obviously did not come to that. I am so sorry I caused so much trouble.'

'You did the right thing,' Michael replied. 'I never dreamed that I would be walking out of here today, except on bail. The magistrate has dismissed the charge against me. Now, I think I will go to my uncle's flat, have a shave, a shower and a cold beer. Would you like to go out to dinner with someone who has just been released from police custody?'

'I would love to,' Mila replied without hesitation. 'And I promise I won't invite you to any more parties.'

Michael smiled. He kissed Mila goodbye and then caught a taxi to Sean's flat, had his shave, shower and cold beer. But he knew there was something else he must do and caught another taxi to the offices of the Macintosh Enterprises near Circular Quay.

He was ushered into his mother's office where he found her briefing one of her managers. Her face lit up when she saw her son.

'I thought I should come and thank you for getting me off the charge,' he said when the manager departed.

'It is the least a mother can do,' Sarah said. 'I know that you and I have never had a close relationship, but I have realised that all I have achieved will mean nothing if you are not involved in the future of the Macintosh Enterprises. I have always harboured the idea that your real father, David Macintosh, is the embodiment of our ancestor, Michael Duffy, but now I think it is you.'

'Charles will always be my real father to me,' Michael said. 'It is obvious that David Macintosh spurned me from the very beginning.'

'He was not in a position to accept you as his son,' Sarah said. 'There was a war on, and he did not think he would survive.'

'Charles was flying spitfires over Darwin, and his chances of survival were pretty slim, but he took me on as his own son, giving me the love of a father,' Michael said.

'That is all in the past,' Sarah said with a dismissive wave of her hand. 'Your enlistment will be over next year and I hope you will consider returning home. You have done enough for your country. It must occur to you from time to time to settle down to a peaceful life with a wife and children. I am not referring to this Mila Welsh girl, of course. She is the daughter of immigrant parents. I assume she is simply a passing distraction.'

Michael looked sharply at his mother, feeling his anger rising. 'I don't know at this stage what Mila is to me, but it is not any matter that concerns you, Mother.'

'You must meet a young woman from your own station in life – not the daughter of refugees.'

'You haven't changed a bit,' Michael said, shaking his head. 'Still only interested in the precious family name. But despite everything, you are the only mother I will ever have and I am stuck with that. When my time is up in the army, I will take up your offer of a position here.'

Sarah's face lit up with a happiness Michael had never really seen before. She crossed the room to him.

'Thank you, Michael,' she said and held out her hand to welcome him to the Macintosh Enterprises. So much for the warm embrace of a mother.

Michael left the office wondering why he had made such an unexpected decision. Maybe meeting Mila had changed his outlook on life. In her company he found a strange and gentle peace, despite the turbulence of their first few days together. Maybe it was time to come home and seek out a new life.

TWENTY-SIX

The heat was starting to go out of the air in the early autumn of 1968 in Australia's political capital, Canberra. But not in the chamber of the lower house, where the honourable David Macintosh could hardly believe his ears as Angus Markham addressed both sides of the house. Angus Markham had virtually inherited the Sydney seat when his father resigned from politics. It was a safe seat for Markham's party and he had not had to work hard to persuade the electorate to vote for him.

'I would like to ask the member from our rural north if it is true that he is the father of an illegitimate child, who is now a grown man our honourable member has refused to acknowledge.'

A hush fell over the chamber and David sat red-faced, wondering how he could reply to the accusation. How in hell had Angus Markham discovered Michael?

David rose, standing silent for a moment. All eyes from both sides of the house were on him, including those of the leader of his party, the Prime Minister.

'That is a personal matter and I do not think it is of concern to the running of this great nation of ours. I do not deny I fathered a son during the war, but the matter is only of concern to the boy's mother and me.'

David resumed his seat, still stunned by the revelation deliberately aimed to attack his character.

'Have you ever been man enough to contact your son?' Markham continued, and David was relieved to hear the speaker of the house intercede. Markham persisted, pointing out that all members should be above reproach, and the rumblings of 'Hear, hear' rose from the members of the opposition.

David could feel his anger rising. Here was a man who had deserted his men in the heat of battle when they needed him most. Now he was using his parliamentary privilege to besmirch David's character and no doubt the accusation would be headlines in tomorrow's papers. Gail knew about Michael, of course, but in his conservative rural electorate the news would no doubt cast him in a bad light, as Markham intended.

The speaker banged his gavel, insisting that Markham desist from any further slur against David's character. Markham sat down with a smirk on his face and was patted on the back by fellow members of his party sitting beside him. David was aware that many eyes were still on him and guessed that he would be receiving a call from his party leader after the house closed for the day.

Sure enough, when the house rose, he felt a tap on his shoulder and made his way to the Prime Minister's office. It felt like being back in school again and being summoned by the headmaster.

David knocked and went in. The Prime Minister was sitting behind his desk, and the deputy stood by the window. David closed the door behind him.

'Why didn't you tell us about your illegitimate son?' the deputy asked.

'Because it is of no concern to you. It has no bearing on how I represent my electorate,' David replied.

'Every bloody thing about your personal life is of concern to us,' the Prime Minister said. 'You have been a solid member of the party – despite your personal views on our involvement in Vietnam – and this matter will no doubt be headline news in the morning.'

'My son is due to return to Vietnam, and despite what Markham said in there I have followed his whole life from the sidelines. He is my flesh and blood, but even if I had no son I would still have grave concerns about backing the Yanks in a war we can't win. As you know I was on a fact-finding tour to South Vietnam last year, and my military experience tells me that our American cousins are trying to fight a counterinsurgency with conventional tactics. It won't work. Since the battle of Long Tan we have stamped our mark indelibly on Phuoc Tuy Province, and I am satisfied our boys are doing an excellent job. But it is only one of many provinces in the country. From my discussions with Westmoreland's staff, I get the impression they are not interested in our experience of winning a counterinsurgency war against the Communist Chinese in Malaya.'

'We are getting off the subject,' said the Prime Minister, rubbing his face in frustration. 'You know news of your son will get back to your electorate.'

'I know that,' David said. 'It will be big news – until something else comes along and then it will be forgotten.'

'Let us hope so,' the deputy said with a sigh. 'I think you should return to your electorate for a while and avoid the Canberra press.'

David knew that he was now persona non grata with his party, and he left the Prime Minister's office under a dark cloud.

He walked to the car park and heard a voice behind him yell, 'Hey, Macintosh, have you ever spoken to your bastard son?'

David swung around to see Markham in the company of two of his fellow party members. The sun was setting over the nation's capital, and years of rage welled up in David at the man he should have reported for cowardice. He could hear Markham sniggering to his two companions. David strode with a limp across the car park towards him. The smirk on Markham's face evaporated when David drew close and Markham could see the deadly anger in his eyes.

Markham took a couple of steps back. 'I wouldn't do anything rash,' he said uncertainly. 'I have two witnesses if you attempt to assault me.'

'That bastard – as you refer to him – is currently serving in the Australian Army and is about to return to Vietnam for a second tour of duty. It takes extreme courage to volunteer for that, courage you failed to demonstrate back in New Guinea when you ran away and left your platoon leaderless. I should have had you court-martialled then, and I have regretted not doing so ever since.'

David turned on his heel to walk away and felt the crashing sting of an object to the back of his head. He swivelled to see the briefcase drop to the ground. Without hesitating, David swung a right hook to Markham's face.

Markham staggered back, squealing his protest and holding his hand up to a bleeding nose. 'You saw that!'

he screamed in a high-pitched voice to his companions. 'Macintosh struck me without any provocation. Call the police.'

David stepped back with a grim smile. 'You were lucky, Markham. I am a bit out of condition these days, because my punch should have floored you.'

Markham's companions stood transfixed as David walked away to his car. He was angry with himself. He had always kept himself fit, exercising on a daily basis, but in the last couple of years he had eased off his tough physical training regime. He obviously needed to get back to it.

The incident in the carpark was hardly worth a second thought to David, until the next day when the police knocked on the door of his Canberra flat. They informed him that he would be questioned on a matter of assault occasioning actual bodily harm to one Angus Markham, member of parliament.

David went with the two plainclothes officers to a nearby police station and answered all their questions. He did not leave anything out, and was left alone in the inter-view room while the investigating officers went away to discuss the evidence they had gathered. Eventually the two officers returned with grim expressions.

'Mr Macintosh, I am afraid you will be summonsed to attend court. Two independent witnesses have corroborated Mr Markham's account of what happened and we are bound to carry out the law.'

David sighed. He knew the two fellow party members had lied and said the assault was unprovoked. He was as good as sunk. David was allowed to leave, and the next day awoke to see the headlines: *COWARDLY ATTACK ON WAR HERO POLITICIAN IN THE PARLIAMENT CARPARK.*

'Bloody hell!' David swore to himself. They were even calling Markham a war hero! The article went on to say that Mr Macintosh had been enraged by Markham's revelation that he had fathered a child out of wedlock and he had attacked Mr Markham without provocation. David groaned at the exaggerated report intended to titillate readers rather than report the facts. The telephone began to ring off the hook, and David decided to take leave to be with Gail. He drove away from his flat to the popping of many newspaper cameras and the staring eye of a television camera capturing the flight of the political thug for the evening news across Australia.

*

Sean Duffy read the papers and watched on the evening news as David pushed his way through the mob of journalists outside his Canberra flat. Sean was furious and launched himself from the big leather armchair with its magnificent view through the great glass doors to the mansion's balcony overlooking Sydney Harbour.

'Bastards!' he swore at the top of his voice. It was time to return to his old office and prepare a brief for the best barrister he knew. If David was to attend court to defend himself, he would need Sean in his corner.

'Did you call out to me?' Rose asked, carrying an expensive silver tray with a pot of tea and cups on it into the sunroom. Marriage had been good for both of them and their love grew deeper with every waking day.

'No, I was just venting my anger against those vultures in the press,' Sean said, accepting the cup Rose passed to him and sitting back down.

'It's about David, isn't it?' Rose said, settling onto a couch. 'It's been all over the papers and TV, and I know how much he means to you.'

'David is as close as I will ever have to a son, and a father does not desert his son.'

'So it appears I will be a widow again while you take on David's case,' Rose smiled.

Sean put down his cup and stood, gripping his walking cane. He walked to his wife and kissed her gently on the cheek. 'Thank you for being so understanding,' he said.

'You have always been a man of action,' Rose said. 'I have been concerned that retirement might kill you with boredom. If anyone is capable of getting David off, it will be you.'

Although Sean did not have the facts before him, he wondered whether he still had the skills of the reputed best criminal solicitor in Sydney, and whether he would manage without his old friend, Harry Griffiths, beside him. No matter his concerns, he knew that this would be the most important case he had ever handled in his many years of law practice.

*

The ocean was still warm, and David Macintosh was able to swim for a good kilometre before returning to the beach below his old house. The macadamias still grew in their orderly lines but, now unattended, most of the nuts just fell on the ground. He and Gail had purchased a nice house in town within walking distance of his office in the main street. Sometimes, though, David had a need to be alone, and Gail understood. He would return to the old house and sit on the edge of the cliff that overlooked the tiny beach below.

It was funny, David thought as he stood amongst the big waves rolling in, how things had changed since he had first starting coming to this beach. In the distance he could see three young men with long blond hair riding surfboards, catching the late-afternoon waves.

Salty water ran off his body as he waded through the hissing surf at the edge of the beach. He walked towards his towel and noticed a man sitting beside it. The sun was in David's eyes, so it was only when he was a few feet away that he recognised Michael Macintosh – his son.

'I see that the press is giving you a hard time over me,' Michael said.

David shrugged and sank to his knees on the sand. 'How did you know I was here?'

'Your wife told me,' Michael said. 'I have a little leave left, so I thought it was time to meet with you. My dad told me on his deathbed that you agreed your real identity would remain a secret while he was still alive. He also told me that it was you who was able to track me down in Africa and organise my discharge so I could travel back to Australia to be with him. So, that time back at Glen View for Christmas I thought I was shaking the hand of my mother's cousin – not my father.'

David gave his son an appraising look. Michael looked very much like he had at that age. There could be no mistaking that they were father and son.

'I suppose you've come here to tell me what a real bastard I was for not recognising you when you were born,' David said, and noticed the flicker of hurt in his son's face.

'To be honest, I am not sure why I wanted to see you,' Michael said. 'Maybe out of curiosity, or maybe because I have read what the papers are saying about you and I figured you might need a bit of fire support.'

'I am not going to apologise for not recognising you as my son when I was first told by your mother,' David said. 'It is kind of complicated when it comes to matters concerning your mother.'

'Because I know my mother for what she is,' Michael said, 'I can understand how complicated it is. I was lucky to have such a great dad in Charles, that it doesn't matter you were not around. I guess, at best, I see you more in the light of an uncle in my life. You know what is scary, though?' Michael continued. 'How similar our choices in life have been. You chose to fight as a mercenary in the Spanish Civil War and I chose the Congo. You returned to fight for Australia in the army during World War II, and now I am a soldier in the same army, serving in Vietnam. I can see I have taken after you in looks, and maybe even in some mannerisms. What's that old saying – you can't pick your parents, only your friends.'

'Maybe you and I could be friends,' David said, and Michael gazed at him for a long moment before answering.

'I think we could be friends,' he agreed. 'For the moment you are a stranger to me, but we seem to have a lot in common. Certainly our fists have got us both into trouble recently.'

'Let's head up to the shack then and continue this chat over a cold beer,' David said.

Both men walked up a sandy track to the little house, where David retrieved the cold bottles of beer. They went to the edge of the cliff to watch night descend on the east coast of Australia.

They sat side by side drinking, and before long they found themselves laughing as they swapped stories of their military life in faraway places. David confessed that he was opposed to the war, partly because he knew Michael was in the thick of it and partly because he thought it was unwinnable. He was virtually alone in his opinion and his views were not for public knowledge.

That night David opened cans of bully beef and baked beans. They ate and continued drinking until the early hours of the morning, when they both fell asleep on camp stretchers in the shack, listening to the sound of the waves crashing on the shore.

The following day Michael was due to catch the train back to Sydney and David drove him to the railway station. Both men stood on the platform awaiting the train's arrival. The rural station was deserted and peaceful, with pot plants of ferns hanging along the platform awning. The sound of rainbow lorikeets squawking in the rainforest trees on the opposite side of the platform was the only noise in the calm air.

'If you need a character witness at your court hearing, you can always call me,' Michael said. 'Just send a message to SAS Hill, Nui Dat, Phuoc Tuy Province, South Vietnam.'

'I went to Nui Dat last year on a fact-finding tour,' David said. 'When I made discreet enquiries I was told that you were out in the bush on an op. After the Tet Offensive I believe our task force will be deployed between the retreating enemy from Saigon and the Ho Chi Minh trail. I have a bad feeling about that, so be bloody careful when you go back in.'

The sound of the train broke any further discussion on the war. Michael hefted his kitbag and David was reminded of the times he had stood waiting for a train to take him to war. Michael turned to face his father and was suddenly aware that he was in his embrace.

'Take care, son,' David said. 'I am very proud of you. I always have been.'

Michael pulled away, seeing the shine of tears in his father's eyes. This Michael had not expected.

'Just remember to contact me if you need that character reference,' Michael said, attempting to put on a cheerful face as the train pulled into the station.

Without another word, Michael walked to the doorway of the carriage and boarded without looking back at the man who, a mere twenty-four hours earlier, had been a stranger to him. He did not want David to see the tears in his own eyes as there was no certainty they would ever see each other again.

The train pulled away and Michael could see the solitary figure of David Macintosh standing almost to attention on the empty platform.

TWENTY-SEVEN

The towering scale model of the multistorey building rose up between lesser buildings on the wooden board at the centre of Jessica Duffy's boardroom. Around it milled potential investors and members of Jessica's project team. Jessica stood by a great plate-glass window, gazing at the Sydney skyline. She could see the vacant block of land that had been cleared at great cost for the building's construction.

Jessica held a glass of vintage champagne in one hand and reflected on how her father's dream had progressed from captured diamonds in the Great War to a financial empire spanning many industries. With good financial guidance, Jessica had rolled over profits into even bigger ventures and her companies had gone public on the stock market. She was reputed to be one of the richest women in Australia, and already she was looking towards Asia for future investment opportunities.

The thought of Asia overwhelmed her. Bryce was currently in Vietnam and she was counting the days until his return. Her son had assured her that, as a gunner, he was not exactly in the frontlines of combat, as his role was to provide fire support to the foot-slogging grunts out in the scrub; but the recent Tet Offensive across South Vietnam had made Jessica afraid for his safety. She knew a lot about combat; she had been awarded decorations from both the Australian and American governments for her service in the Pacific War. She also knew that fire-support bases were a prime target of the enemy. After all, many of the big battles the Americans fought in this war were over the North Vietnamese Army destroying isolated fire-support bases.

'Mrs Duffy.' Jessica turned from her panoramic view of Sydney's CBD to see her chief project manager standing behind her.

'Yes, Mr Apps, you look worried,' she said.

'The quantity surveyors have brought something to my attention,' he said quietly. 'There has been a rather large blow-out in construction costs. You may have to consider taking on a partnership in this project.'

'How much of an overrun in costs?' Jessica asked.

The project manager gave the figure and Jessica was stunned. How could that have happened?

'There is one other company I think could come in on the deal,' he said. 'The Macintosh Enterprises. They have parallel infrastructure to get the building up on time and within budget. From my knowledge, they are the only ones who have the capital we need. We will be ruined if we attempt to go it alone.'

Sarah Macintosh, Jessica mused. An alliance with the enemy. But there was a rumour circulating that when Michael's enlistment was up he would be introduced into the management of Sarah's companies. Jessica liked Michael and he was definitely not his mother's son. He could be a peacemaker between the two well-known family enterprises.

'We'll keep this matter to ourselves for the moment,' Jessica said. 'I will take immediate steps to find a partner.'

The project manager looked relieved. He knew Jessica Duffy was a woman who was able to fix difficult situations. She had proven so in the past, and the businesses had flourished under her leadership.

He walked away and Jessica contemplated how she would set up a meeting with her arch rival and bitter enemy. The last time they had been face to face was when Jessica had married Sarah's brother, Donald, just after the war. That had been almost a quarter of a century ago. Jessica knew Sarah would never step inside the Duffy enterprise offices, so their meeting would have to be on neutral ground.

*

The sun was rising over Sydney, emerging from the Tasman Sea to spread across the harbour and into the suburbs. Michael lay on his back. Mila's arm was across his chest, and she was still sleeping. When they had finally drifted into sleep, Michael had entered the world of nightmares. Mila had gently stirred him from the hellish nocturnal world of phantom figures dying or trying to kill him. He had been whimpering and trembling, but with her soothing words he eventually fell asleep in her arms, and now the warm rays filtering through a tattered curtain in Mila's flat brought him back from his nightmarish dreams.

'What time is it?' Mila asked sleepily as she woke.

'Six-thirty,' Michael replied, glancing at his wristwatch. 'I have to get ready to catch my flight.'

Mila was now wide awake. Michael was talking about his civilian flight to the war in Vietnam. The wonderful time they had spent together was over, and she knew it might be a year before she was reunited with him. It had been a short but intense affair. Only a woman who loved a soldier knew that every second together was precious. She tried hard not to cry. In these last moments with Michael, she wanted everything to feel normal – as if he was doing little more than going to work in an office and would return that night.

She slid from the bed and padded naked across the floor to the small kitchen. Michael admired her body from the bed.

'What are you doing?' he called.

'I'm making you breakfast,' Mila answered, clattering a frypan onto the little gas stove. But that was as far as she could go before bursting into great sobs of distress. Michael slipped from the bed to go to her, placing his arms around her body.

'Hey, I'll be back before you know it,' he said lamely. She turned and placed her head against his chest. Michael could feel her tears.

'What if something happens to you?' she said.

'Simbas couldn't kill me, nor will Charlie – or any of the other noggie friends he has.' He tried to sound convincing, but he knew the North Vietnamese Army and the Viet Cong were a tough, brave and intelligent enemy who had been fighting all their lives, as opposed to the Congolese rebels who were little more than psychopathic killers.

'I wish you didn't have to go,' Mila said, clinging to him with all her strength. 'You have done enough for the army. You have already done a tour, and there must be others who can go instead of you.'

'The regiment is a bit short on men,' Michael said. 'They need me.'

'So do I,' Mila said defiantly. 'This country doesn't care about you. Fellow students call you baby killers and spit on you when you come home from the war. Surely your mother could talk to the right people to get you out.'

'Even if my mother could pull strings, I would not leave until my enlistment is up,' Michael said. 'I can't let my mates down. If I did, I would have to live with the guilt for the rest of my life.'

Mila's tears flowed and Michael held her gently. 'I will come home,' he said. 'But now I have to go. I'll write every chance I get and hope you'll do the same.' He kissed her on the forehead and stepped away.

Outside on the street, Michael looked at the civilians going about their daily lives. He knew most of them did not give a damn about the sacrifices being made by young Australians so far away. He turned and looked back and saw Mila, dressed in a filmy dressing gown, watching him walk down the street. Michael waved but dared not look back again because, if he did, he knew he might seriously consider her proposition for him not to return to the war.

*

It was a perfect autumn day in Sydney, and Jessica had her driver drop her off at the little seafood restaurant in Watsons Bay where Sarah had agreed to meet her. She noticed that there was a Bentley already parked, and a driver stood beside the car smoking a cigarette.

Jessica had dressed for the occasion. She wore a tailored suit that spoke a no-nonsense approach to business. When she stepped inside the restaurant she saw Sarah sitting at a table for two by a window with a view. Other people sat and chatted over plates of oysters, crab and fish. Jessica walked across to Sarah – who did not stand to greet her – and sat down.

'Jessica.'

'Sarah.'

The greetings were cool but polite.

'It has been a long time,' Sarah said, reaching for a cigarette to place in her long ebony holder.

'The wedding, back in '46,' Jessica said. 'I was fortunate to have caught up with your son recently. He is a wonderful young man.'

Both women appraised each other over the table. Jessica could see that Sarah had not lost her beauty, and she hoped that people were right when they said she too had shaped up well for the passing years.

'You have no doubt received the correspondence about our tower project?' Jessica asked, glancing at the menu.

'I took the liberty of ordering a chardonnay,' Sarah said, not answering the question.

The chilled wine was delivered, glasses poured and food orders taken.

'Well, what do we toast?' Sarah asked. 'The profits your project will bring to the Macintosh and Duffy families?'

'No,' Jessica said, raising her wineglass. 'We drink to the safe return of our sons from the war.' Jessica could see that the toast hit a nerve with Sarah. It was Jessica's subtle way of reminding her foe that they were mothers and shared a common bond in sons facing death on a daily basis.

'Yes, to the safe return of our sons,' Sarah agreed, and raised her glass.

'The figures you quoted are very large,' Sarah said, settling down to the subject she loved most in the world. 'But the Macintosh companies are prepared to cover it.'

Jessica looked surprised. Sarah had agreed so quickly. Jessica had thought this would be a long drawn-out meeting, and she would need to work hard to persuade Sarah to enter into the project.

'So, are you saying that we will enter into a partnership on the project?' Jessica said.

'We will need to thrash out a few more details, but yes, we can support you on a fifty–fifty basis.'

Only for a moment did Jessica consider the matter. This was an arrangement that would bring big profits to both sides.

'I can have the contracts drawn up and you can go over them with your financial advisors,' Sarah said.

The meals arrived and both women picked at their delicious trays of seafood.

'I know matters have been strained – to say the least – between you and I,' Sarah said. 'But the past is history, and we should consider more amicable relations in the future.'

Jessica was taken by surprise by Sarah's statement. 'Did you arrange to have my father murdered?' she asked bluntly and could see the shock on Sarah's face.

'I had nothing to do with your father's death,' Sarah replied indignantly. 'What happened on Glen View was out of my hands. I rue the day I ever hired that horrible man to legally remove your father from the property.'

'It was not legal, and my father died fighting for his land,' Jessica said. 'But if you swear on the name of your family that you had nothing to do with my father's death, I will accept your word. I know how much you value the Macintosh name.'

'I swear on my family name that I was as shocked at your father's death as anyone.'

Jessica stared into Sarah's eyes. She appeared to be telling the truth, but Jessica did not trust her completely. 'I can only accept your word,' she said. 'You are right when you said we must put the past behind us. The past is little more than a ghost. It is the future that we must look to.'

Sarah raised her glass. 'I think we can now propose a toast to the future prosperity of both family enterprises,' she said, and Jessica agreed.

'Now I must apologise, but I have pressing matters back at the office,' Sarah said, indicating to the waiter to bring the bill for the meal. She paid him and departed the restaurant.

Jessica sat alone at the table, trying to sort through her mixed feelings about the meeting. It had been one of those moments in her life she was not sure should have happened. But this was a big enterprise requiring millions of dollars, and the project needed assistance if it was to go ahead.

*

Sarah Macintosh went to her office, sat down at her desk and gazed out at the city skyline. She smiled. Out there was a great piece of vacant land intended for development. But the land would be the burial ground of the Duffy financial empire. How easy it had been to lull the woman into a trap. From the moment the proposal outlining the building of the great office block had crossed her desk, Sarah had schemed to turn the temporary partnership into a means to bring Jessica Duffy to her knees. She would bankrupt Jessica and watch her come crawling, begging for mercy.

Many years had passed, but revenge against her enemies was never far from Sarah's mind. When David had married that other woman, Sarah had waited to destroy him for his perceived betrayal. It had been she who had leaked the matter of their son to Markham, and now she would have her revenge against Jessica Duffy for being part of the family that took Glen View away from its rightful owners: the Macintosh family.

'Miss Macintosh, can I get you a cup of tea?' her secretary asked, peering around the door.

'Oh no,' Sarah smiled. 'I would like you to bring me the best bottle of champagne from the boardroom liquor cabinet and cancel my appointments for the day. I will be having a private celebration for the rise and rise of the Macintosh empire.'

TWENTY-EIGHT

Facing up to Gail's father-in-law at his home was more daunting than the possibility of having to stand up in court and answer the charges of assault. But John Glanville had been David's mentor and very good friend from the beginning. The old man sat with his feet up on a stool and a beer in his hand.

'You can probably guess that I have had phone calls from the party,' John said.

'They want me to resign,' David said.

'Sadly, yes,' John sighed. 'The adverse publicity is damaging. It is bad enough that the press makes our PM's face a subject of scorn in their political cartoons. John got his scarred face when his fighter plane was shot down defending Singapore. At least I know that you have a friend in the PM, because you both fought for this country in its most dire time of need. Now the press is calling Markham a war hero when we both know that is not true.'

'You know the press,' David said, staring into his glass of beer. 'They have no interest in the truth – just stories that will sell papers, with the age-old excuse that they're in the public interest. Bloody public interest – read that as newspaper profits.'

'Sadly, Mr and Mrs Smith – who think that the press tell only the truth – will believe what they read. You may have to consider standing down.'

'Yeah, I have already thought about resigning,' David said. 'At least Sean Duffy has come out of retirement to organise my defence. If anyone can win my case it will be Sean.'

'I hope so,' John said. 'The way things are, the opposition will be putting pressure on the courts to have you locked up and the key thrown away.'

'It really irks me that Markham's party can put him up as a war hero and paint me as some kind of cowardly bully.'

'That is the nature of the political beast,' John said. 'But you have seen a lot of dangerous times in the past, and politics is no different.'

'I have discussed the matter with Gail and made my decision. I will tender my letter of resignation to the PM. I guess I'm going to have to learn more about macadamia farming.'

'Your resignation will be a noble gesture,' John said. 'It's just a bloody shame that it has come to this.'

David rose from his chair. 'Gail asked me to invite you and Nancy over for dinner tomorrow night.'

John thanked him and David left. He walked to his car and felt as though a weight had lifted from his shoulders. The fact that he opposed Australian troops in Vietnam had made him a lone voice in his party, and it had been harder and harder to support military involvement for the sake of the party line. Now, if only he could walk out of court a free man he would be able to return to Gail and his beloved northern home. He just hoped Sean would be able to weave his legal magic and get him off the assault charge.

★

Gunner Bryce Duffy-Macintosh gazed out across the scrub. The deployment of his battery of 105 millimetre howitzers from Nui Dat to Bien Hoa was intended as fire support for the two battalions of infantry being deployed to provide interdiction of North Vietnamese Army units moving to and from Saigon in a mini Tet Offensive, three months after their disastrous first attempt across the provinces of South Vietnam. The flat scrub-covered land they were deployed to reminded Bryce of Glen View. Even the sweltering heat reminded him of home, but unlike Glen View, this heat was humid. He stood, leaning on a shovel, stripped to his waist, as a small bulldozer pushed up earth to form bunds: small walls built to help give the big guns protection from direct fire. They did not, however, protect against mortar rounds.

It was late afternoon and Bryce had the task of digging out shell scrapes to position their M60 belt-fed machine guns further forward as a means of better defence.

He reached for the water canteen on his web belt and took a long swig of the warm, brackish water. From the air, when they had been ferried in by chopper, he had seen with a farmer's eye that the area they occupied was gently undulating with no hills in immediate proximity. There were views of rice paddies, open grassy land, bamboo clusters and a creek bisecting the larger task force AO, given the name of Surfers. But mostly Bryce could see a landscape of low, tough scrub about the height of a man.

'You're on the gun tonight,' a bombardier said when he passed Bryce. 'So make sure you dig as deep as you can.'

Bryce acknowledged the order from the artillery corporal. He had a bad feeling about this deployment. Someone said that the Yanks on their flank were taking heavy casualties against fresh, well-armed and well-trained North Vietnamese regulars coming in off the Ho Chi Minh trail. But someone else said that their AO was relatively free of enemy troops. Bryce hoped so because all he wanted to do was finish his national service, go home, drink as much cold beer as he could and eat the biggest Glen View steaks the cooks on the property could serve up to him.

*

Only a couple of kilometres away, Sergeant Major Patrick Duffy felt very uneasy as he stood in the scrub. Next to him was the company commander with map and compass. Both men had served in Malaya together, then Borneo and now Vietnam. Major Stan Gauden wiped the sweat from his forehead and checked his map again.

'According to what I know,' he said, 'the Kiwi arty and our own battery are too far apart. We will have wide gaps to defend between them. This whole thing is a shambles.'

'I get the same feeling about our deployment,' Patrick said. 'Call it an old soldier's instinct, but I get the feeling that the nogs are watching us, and that there are a lot more of them out there than intelligence has told us.'

Major Stan Gauden turned to the soldier he trusted above all in the battalion.

'Pat, we're low down the military food chain, so who would listen to the hunch of a couple of old diggers?'

'This is going to be different,' Patrick said. 'The battalion is more used to patrolling, ambushing, and cordon and search operations. I get the feeling that the nogs are going to try and wipe us out, and if I am right, they will be able to because they have superior numbers. I think we are about to engage in a set piece battle, like our Yank brothers have been doing for years.'

The infantry major nodded his head in agreement. It was time to organise his company into a defensive role. The guns of the artillery were the primary weapons to defend, as their fire-power could be devastating to an enemy in such open country.

★

Trooper Michael Macintosh laid out his cleaned M16 rifle on his camp stretcher. He had watched from SAS Hill as the infantry and arty units were moved to Bien Hoa Province from the taskforce HQ at Nui Dat. He knew why, and also knew that he and his special force comrades would be tasked to assist with intelligence gathering. They would be required to move into the province to collect information on NVA and VC units: numbers, weapons and locations. The intelligence they collected was beyond value for military commanders; it could mean the difference between winning and losing in a war where forest and jungle concealed the movement of large formations.

'Hey, Macca, you have mail,' the HQ clerk said, walking between the SASR soldiers sitting around on beds or cleaning weapons. 'You blokes hear the joke about a North Vietnamese noggie who had orders to take a mortar bomb down the Ho Chi Minh trail?'

'No, Smithy,' replied one of the soldiers.

'Well, he spends weeks going down the track under B-52 bombs, rain and all the other crap, to finally find the noggie mortar crew. They take the bomb off him and drop it down the tube. Then one of the crew turns to him and says, "We want you to go back up to Hanoi and get another one."'

'So, what's funny?' the special forces soldier asked.

'The noggie quit and deserted.'

No one laughed and Michael reflected on a certain amount of truth in the story. The people they were fighting were as tough and resourceful as any soldiers in the world.

Michael took the letter and instantly recognised the handwriting on the envelope posted from Australia. He sat down on an empty ammo box to read it. He smiled as her loving words flowed through the pages to him, and for a moment he was not in a war zone but in a tiny flat and a particularly comfortable bed occupied by a beautiful and passionate young woman he had come to love.

'Okay, fellas, we have a briefing in ten minutes,' Michael's sergeant said, popping his head around the flap of the tent. 'Looks like the boys over in Bien Hoa might be in for a rough time.'

Michael slipped the letter into its envelope, placing it with the others in a metal ammo box he used to contain his few valuables. Roll on 1969, he thought as he headed for the briefing. He had had enough of war, and the thought of returning to Mila was almost overpowering.

The SAS sergeant's statement had been an understatement. Forces of enemy soldiers vastly outnumbering the Australians were already assembling to unleash hell on the defenders still digging in. Gunner Bryce Duffy-Macintosh was about to learn that being in artillery was not the safest job in the army after all.

★

Sergeant Terituba Duffy swatted one of the many irritating, crawling insects from the back of his neck. The tall grass concealed his platoon but held in the high humidity of this tropical country. He smiled wryly at the memory of other places he had campaigned – always bloody extreme heat and humidity. Even when the torrential rains fell, it did not ease the heat and humidity. Always thirst dogged the soldiers. No matter how many extra water bottles they carried, it was never enough.

The platoon commander was only a few metres away, and Terituba knew that he must keep an eye on the young, inexperienced national serviceman who had graduated from the officer training school of Scheyville. Terituba was pleased to see that the young officer was smart enough to listen to his advice and felt that he would turn into a good leader of men. The two-week company patrol in search of the elusive enemy was into its fifth day and nothing had been found.

Terituba pushed aside the tall grass with the barrel of his SLR, and suddenly the lead scout of the platoon a few metres from him signalled a halt. Terituba slowly lowered himself to the musty earth on one knee, keeping the scout in sight. The explosive blast of a landmine to his front hurled Terituba backwards. He was vaguely aware that it had lifted him off the ground and he was lying on his back in the long grass.

'Get a dust-off!' a voice yelled above the loud screams of the soldier wounded by the landmine.

Terituba recognised the voice of the leading section's corporal and thought that it was strange the man was leaning over him, staring at him with a shocked expression.

'Sarge, stay still. Don't try to move,' he said, and Terituba now felt the pain overtake his body. He could see a lot of blood on the corporal's hands, and it dawned on Terituba that it was his blood. It was squirting from a ruptured artery in his neck and a strange peace was overwhelming him. He closed his eyes and could hear a desperate voice saying, 'Get a hand over the neck to stop the bleeding.'

'The chopper is on its way,' someone said, and then the darkness came to Sergeant Terituba Duffy. He could see a dim figure and knew it was Wallarie, waiting to meet him.

Terituba did not hear the next few words from the corporal.

'Boss, I think he's gone.'

★

Sean Duffy paced the living room of the Potts Point mansion. He knew the case was next to hopeless. David would be convicted on the word of the witnesses. The committal hearing was set down for less than a week and, right now, he needed a miracle. The press were pushing the fact that David had viciously attacked a war hero, and one thing Sean knew was that Markham was no war hero. A desperate thought entered Sean's mind. The Prime Minister was a real war hero for his RAAF service as a fighter pilot in the battle for the skies of Singapore. He had to contact the PM's office in Canberra and request his help.

Sean picked up the phone and dialled David's office in Canberra. He was not there, but his personal assistant took the call. Sean explained who he was and what he needed. David's personal assistant was a young lady who idolised her boss, and without hesitating she said she would do as Sean asked. There was one man who could help, and Sean prayed he was still alive and could be located.

★

The telephone call she received from her project manager in Sydney caused Jessica to experience a sudden rush of pure fear. She had only just returned to her Strathfield house and hardly had time to walk in the house before the phone started ringing in the hallway.

Jessica placed the phone back on the receiver and was met by Shannon.

'What is it, Mum?' she asked, seeing the stricken expression on Jessica's face. 'Has someone died?'

Jessica turned to her daughter. 'Just a small matter. I have to return to the office to sort it out.' Shannon was not fooled. She could tell that something was terribly wrong.

Jessica rang for a taxi and within the hour stood in her office with the project manager.

'The company that was to assist us with the funding for the project has gone bankrupt, and the investors learned before we did,' he said. 'They are wanting to sue us for breach of contract. We are running out of options.'

Jessica walked over to the large glass window to gaze out at the vacant lot of land in a row of newly rising buildings. The vacant block was now like a tooth had been removed, leaving the wound ulcerated.

'Sarah!' Jessica snarled. 'She's behind this.'

'Do you mean Sarah Macintosh?' the project manager asked. 'It was definitely a Macintosh company that went down. But I cannot see how any person of her reputation would allow that to happen.'

Jessica turned to the project manager. 'You do not know the lengths to which my sister-in-law will go to destroy me. Even at the cost to her own reputation. Set up a meeting with her. We have to get this matter sorted before word gets out to our shareholders.'

'I will get on to it immediately,' he said.

Jessica bid him goodnight and slumped down in her comfortable leather chair behind her desk. The sun was setting over Sydney and a cold shiver ran through her. Jessica had gambled on the project, but that was the nature of business. She cursed herself for entering into a deal with her arch enemy. She had thought the ace card was the money that would be made for both of them, but she had underestimated Sarah Macintosh's overriding need for revenge.

Jessica returned home but did not sleep well. The following morning, the sound of the newspaper boy's bike and the thump of the paper on the porch brought her out of a restless state of half-sleep.

Jessica rose from her bed, slipped on a dressing gown and went into the kitchen. Shannon was already at the table with the paper and a glass of orange juice. Ever since the escapade with Tania, for which they were lucky not to be expelled, Shannon had been the model daughter.

Jessica greeted her daughter with a kiss and a hug.

'I brought the paper in,' Shannon said.

'Thank you, darling,' Jessica said, sitting down.

She flipped open the newspaper, and when she reached page four she gasped.

'What's wrong, Mum?' This was the second time in less that twelve hours Shannon had seen the stricken expression on her mother's face.

Jessica stared at the bold print: *DUFFY ENTERPRISES ON THE SLIDE TO POSSIBLE LIQUIDATION.* Jessica had no doubt who was behind the rumour.

*

The meeting was arranged for that afternoon, and Sarah had insisted it be held in her boardroom. Jessica had little choice, knowing that the confrontation would take place on Sarah's battlefield. Sarah had informed Jessica that the meeting would involve only the two of them. Even that decision smelled of malice to Jessica.

Jessica arrived at the Macintosh offices and was ushered directly to the boardroom, where she saw Sarah sitting at the head of the table. Jessica took a seat at the opposite end of the long table, not wanting to be near her despised sister-in-law.

'Well, Sarah, how did you succeed in destroying an enterprise that would have made us both a lot richer?'

'Good afternoon to you too.' Sarah smirked. 'I am not sure what you are insinuating.'

'You know bloody well what I am talking about. Your company that was supposed to help fund the project went belly up.'

'That was terribly unfortunate,' Sarah replied with a sigh. 'But you know the risks we take on a daily basis in business. I suppose I should have taken legal steps in our contract to indemnify against such an unforeseen situation. But, as your lawyers will tell you, I forgot.'

Jessica stared at Sarah and wondered if she had the slightest hint of a soul. 'What do you want?' she asked.

'What I like about you, dear sister-in-law, is your ability to get to the point. I am sure by now you know your share-holders are selling off their stock. I suppose it is a normal reaction to this morning's report in the papers.'

'I wonder who fed the media the news about my share in the project being at risk,' Jessica said, thinking how much she would like to strangle the smirk off the woman at the end of the table. After all, Jessica had killed in war and this was a financial battle.

'I will bail you out if you sign over Glen View to me. I am sure you will get back on your feet again. After all, what is a piece of dusty land in Queensland worth, compared to the future of your vast financial investments? It is nothing, and I am sure you could move my brother to another one of your properties so that he can run around with his ringers. Oh, I forgot, you sold all your other cattle stations to fund the project in Sydney.'

Jessica stared for a short time at her opponent, and then slowly broke into a smile. 'You lost your beloved David to another woman, and now I am going to deny you the other thing you most want – Glen View. I think I might consider retiring from business and return to my property to be with those who love me. I have always found so much peace sitting on the verandah, gazing across the red earth of my ancestors. You will never have what you most desire.' Jessica rose from the chair.

'You are a bloody fool, Jessica,' Sarah yelled. 'Within a week you will see all that you have worked for crumble around you – unless I step in to help. Is some obscure cattle station worth that?'

'It is to me – and to your brother,' Jessica replied. 'Do your worst, and I hope one day you rot in hell. Remember, the spirits of my Aboriginal ancestors look over my family.'

Jessica left the boardroom feeling as if a huge weight had been lifted from her shoulders. She had no doubt that Sarah could take away all that she had worked for, but, to Jessica, family was far more important than all the money she had. Her father had given his life to defend that obscure, dusty patch of brigalow scrub on the plains of Queensland, and she was not going to let it go. Jessica broke into a broad smile as she made her way out onto the street. Yes, Sarah might be able to destroy her financially, but Glen View would remain in her family forever.

TWENTY-NINE

Gunner Bryce Duffy-Macintosh was forcing himself to stay awake behind the M60 belt-fed machine gun. His number two beside him was having the same problem. The hard physical work of the previous hours and the sapping heat had taken its toll. Behind him the big 105 milli-metre howitzers were bedded down behind earthen walls. Beside him lay an M79 grenade launcher. The shotgun-like weapon could fire what appeared to be a giant bullet with an explosive head.

Bryce knew he would not get much sleep tonight, as he also had to do radio piquet. He lay in almost total darkness, taking in the sounds of the tropical night. He could hear the distant whistle of high-flying jets on their way to seek out targets; at a lower level was the distinctive whop-whop of helicopter blades, and the constant twinkling of flares lighting up some distant patch of jungle.

The rumour from the old hands was that they expected an attack in the night. How many would assault and when was not known. Even this knowledge was not enough to ward off the overpowering desire to sleep. But as Bryce dozed, he could hear the bursts of small-arms fire, rocket-propelled grenades and mortar bombs exploding. He knew the sounds of the firefight were coming from within the area of operations, but they eventually died away.

Then it began to rain, which was welcomed by many diggers who collected the clean water, using their tent shelters to do so. A good supply of drinking water was something every frontline soldier in Vietnam valued because their canteens could not keep up with their thirst.

The rain continued till around midnight, by which time Bryce was soaked through to the skin. Being wet, either from sweat or tropical downpours, was something soldiers lived with, along with the accompanying skin diseases. It was then that Bryce heard and saw a green machine-gun tracer flying low overhead. He remembered that the enemy used green tracers, whereas Australian tracers were red, and he felt a knot of fear in his stomach. He gripped the machine gun into his shoulder and slid his finger to the trigger. But the firing stopped, and Bryce thought it was probably a probing action by the enemy.

Bryce relaxed a little but could not dismiss the foreboding he felt. He was frightened but there was nothing he could do about it. The overpowering instinct not to let his mates down helped settle his nerves, but he could still feel the creeping fear.

In the very early hours of the morning he and the others in his machine-gun crew saw shadowy figures crossing a dirt track to their front.

'What do we do?' Bryce's offsider whispered.

A call was put in to the arty command post over the field telephone, and the answer came back that the figures had to be the enemy. Bryce noticed that the figures had moved into position where the burst of enemy fire had come from earlier. An eerie silence fell on the immediate location, and Bryce was once again gripping the pistol grip of the M60. All in the battery defensive positions could hear the rustling out to their front and knew it came from large numbers of enemy soldiers moving about in their AO. But permission to fire was denied as it was not certain where all the friendly forces were that confused night. They waited, and in the distance they could hear intermittent small-arms fire coming from the general direction of the infantry battalion locations.

'Hey, Duff, you are to return to your gun,' the voice of his bombardier commanded in the darkness. 'We have a fire mission to support the grunts.'

Bryce was pleased to return to his crew manning their 105. He felt less exposed behind the earthwork bunds.

*

Two kilometres away, Sergeant Major Patrick Duffy heard the incoming rocket and small-arms fire on his company. He could also hear one of the platoon's machine guns returning fire. What he did not know was that one of the company's platoons had taken devastating casualties from the NVA's assault. Rocket-propelled grenades had exploded in the tree-tops, showering red-hot shrapnel and timber splinters down on the soldiers in their open shell scrapes. Now Patrick could hear the distant screams of his wounded men.

But the artillery had been called in to drop high explosives on the estimated locations of the enemy. From Patrick's long experience he calculated the enemy must have had a good idea of the dispositions of the platoons. At the company HQ he watched as the wounded were brought in, and he knew that this was just the beginning. It had all the hall-marks of an intelligent and tough enemy manoeuvring into position for a much larger assault in their AO.

The activity seemed to quieten down. There was a good reason for that. The NVA's primary target was the big artillery guns of Bryce's battery. They were fully aware of how important it was to destroy them before turning their attention to mopping up the infantry. It was a basic tactical move that would have been made by the Australians in the same position.

At least it gave time to the infantry to call a dust-off, the flying in of medivac choppers to take out the wounded. The courage of the chopper crews was evident when they risked using lights to come into the prepared landing zone. This made them easy targets for any enemy with an RPG or even a small arms fire.

A calm had descended on FSB Coral. Grunts and drop shorts rested, some smoking at their guns or in the forward machine-gun positions.

Bryce sat with his back to the bund and reflected on what had just happened. He thought that with any luck the enemy was not in big enough numbers to take them on. It was wishful thinking as a large force of highly trained, fresh and well-equipped NVA continued to move stealthily towards the guns of his battery. He also did not know that infantry HQ was aware of the enemy movement, but in the dark it was impossible to locate the specific positions of the enemy. It was a waiting game.

It was the exposed infantry mortar platoon around four in the morning who were first aware of the enemy. They could hear the voices of what one experienced soldier said amounted to at least four hundred men gathering for an attack.

Bryce saw a green flare and then a red flare burst in the sky almost over the battery of guns. He immediately rose and scrambled to join the gun crew. Out to their front an enemy mass, who had crawled up to the outer defences of the gun position, rose as one only metres away, but dropped back to the ground when a barrage of their own mortars and rockets came crashing down on the Australian gun positions so close by.

Bryce scrambled to the top of the bund and saw waves of enemy moving forward. He flicked off the safety and commenced firing his 20 round magazine into the massed formation. He saw enemy soldiers drop as the deadly heavy-calibre rounds found their mark. Beside him, someone else was firing their pistol, and behind him his crew were almost in a state of shock.

Bryce could see that within seconds he would be overwhelmed by the attacking enemy, and he slid down to the base of the bund. Already the NVA were on the opposite side, hurling grenades to clear the Aussie gunners and occasionally reaching over the top to fire their AK-47s down on the gunners below. The gun sergeant realised that they could not hold off against such large numbers, disabled his gun and yelled to his gun crew to get out while they could. Bryce did not need to be told. All he wanted to do was survive.

Bryce had fallen back amidst a scene of exploding NVA rockets, mortar bombs and the continuous babble of the enemy. He got to a gun crew who were loading splintex shells into the breech with the barrel lowered to horizontal. No artillery tables were needed to calculate fall of shot, as the gunners simply looked over the barrel at the NVA pouring towards them. The splintex antipersonnel artillery shell was like a giant shotgun blast. Each shell contained 7200 small, metal darts invented to tear into massed ranks of advancing enemy, and was devastating. Nearby one of the battery's guns had been damaged by a rocket blast and its ammunition was being moved to the operational gun.

The lanyard was yanked and Bryce saw one enemy soldier with an AK-47 directly in front. When the big gun barrel recoiled, the enemy soldier was virtually vaporised by the blast. As quick as the breech was slammed open another splintex round was shoved in. Over his shoulder Bryce recognised a member of the infantry mortar team join them. It was a bad sign; they must have also been overrun. At first the gun sergeant thought his half-second delay on the explosive round had not worked and he immediately changed the fuse to instant detonation. Unknown to the Australian gunners, the half-second rounds had exploded amongst the second wave of NVA forming up to reinforce the first and had decimated them, disrupting their attempt to overwhelm their enemy.

One of the ammunition supply dumps behind the gun was hit by an RPG, and the high explosive artillery rounds began to burn. Despite the danger, four gunners remained in their positions to guard the battery command post nearby. At least the burning ammo dump provided a reference point for helicopters circling overhead in the dark. Ground-to-air communication soon had the gunships differentiating between friend and foe and they added their deadly fire-power in support of the beleaguered gunners. Rockets and machine-gun rounds from the air support tore into the NVA soldiers caught in the open, and this was taking pressure off the desperate gunners. All around the besieged artillery fire-support base the infantry were engaged in their own battles to survive.

The drone of the C47 overhead was a welcome sound. The aircraft was very much like the venerable DC3 and was armed with mini-guns and flares. Within a moment the noise of its multi-barrelled machine guns could be heard as one continuous roar – like a sheet of cloth being ripped down the middle. The propeller-driven gunships were known to the Aussies as 'Puff the Magic Dragon' or simply 'Puff'. They also went by the names of 'Snoopy' and 'Spooky'. The long hose-like trails of their tracer came down from the sky, sowing four hundred bullets into a ten-metre circle. It was sure death for any NVA within that radius – and the circle would keep moving, seeking out any other enemy caught in the open.

Bryce was hardly aware of time passing. All he focused on was fusing and handing the heavy rounds to the gun crew he was supporting. There was no let-up in the tenacity of the NVA soldiers pushing forward their attack on the battery position. Despite the heavy concentration of fire on the guns, the artillerymen carried out their duties unflinchingly, firing missions in support of the infantry. Even now, three of the battery's six guns were dedicated to answering calls of support from the battalions fighting desperately outside the fire-support base. It was a night of deafening explosions and flares drifting in the tropical air.

*

Sergeant Major Patrick Duffy watched the battle being fought over the location he knew marked Bryce's artillery battery.

'Looks like the poor bastards from the arty are copping

it,' Major Stan Gauden said to Patrick as they watched from the company command post.

Patrick thought about Bryce and prayed that he would survive what he could see was a possible elimination of the artillery unit. He had a sudden image of Bryce as a young boy on Glen View. Bryce would always insist on going bush with Patrick and Terituba, and they would be annoyed by the younger boy's company. Bryce was no longer an annoying younger boy, but a young man who should have been home working as an engineer, making lots of money and chasing girls. Patrick thought about Jessica and continued to pray that she not have to be told her son had been killed in action. If ever Wallarie was needed to protect a Duffy, it was now.

'I have a feeling we will be in for it soon enough,' Stan said, gazing at the firework-like display of deadly weapons.

'If what is going on over there,' Patrick said, 'is any indication of the scale of operations, we have stumbled into a main force of NVA. A bit more than the intel guys estimated. If they brass the FSB they will come after us, knowing our fire support will be considerably reduced.'

Stan nodded. For so long now the infantry had relied on the knowledge that when they were in trouble the artillery would be there for them. The major returned to the CP, leaving Patrick gazing out into the Vietnamese night. He knew that when the sun rose the enemy would withdraw in order to avoid being caught out in the open, and they would be an easy target for the prowling ground support aircraft of the American air force. He looked to the east but still could not see the first rays of a rising sun. It was the longest night of his life.

★

Bryce could feel the sun on his skin. His senses were hardly working as he slumped, exhausted, onto the red earth of the gun position, amongst the discarded piles of 105-millimetre brass cases. He was aware of jet engines screaming through the thick haze of cordite smoke but also that the sounds of battle were fading. The enemy were falling back to concealed positions, like vampires avoiding the sun. He wondered how he had been able to function during the previous hours of hell, and how he had been able to control his fear and keep going. Bryce glanced across at his SLR only a few feet away and remembered his training. Before he rested he must first clean his rifle. He reached for it with hands that shook so badly he wondered if cleaning his rifle was actually possible. None of the exhausted soldiers on the battleground knew that this was just the beginning of a month-long battle.

*

David Macintosh met Sean Duffy at the old man's favourite pub in Sydney. Sean already had a cold beer on the table in front of him.

'Sit down, Dave. I've already ordered you a beer,' Sean said.

David sat down. It was early morning and only a handful of diehards stood at the bar for their first drink of the day. But David immediately noticed another, half-glass of beer also on the table.

'Do we have company?'

'Ah, yes,' Sean answered evasively. 'He has just headed off to the gents.'

When his beer arrived, David took a long sip and wiped away the froth from his mouth with the back of his hand. 'May as well have as many beers as I can before they lock me up,' he said with a wry smile.

'It's not going to court,' Sean said. 'Markham and his witnesses have pulled out of giving evidence. It is only a formality for me to travel to Canberra to ask for the matter to be dismissed.'

David was stunned by the revelation. 'How in bloody hell did you do it?' he asked. 'Markham was hellbent on having me convicted.'

Sean broke into a broad smile and leaned back in his chair. 'You have a lot more friends than you would ever know, David Macintosh. The Prime Minister is one. I was able to contact his office and request assistance finding someone who I thought might prove to be a good witness in our cause. Using the resources of the government, we were able to track down our man and . . . Ah, here he is,' Sean said, looking over David's shoulder.

'Hello, boss,' the man said to David with a warm smile. 'Long time no see.'

David stared at the man standing in front of him and suddenly he was in the jungle of northern New Guinea, discussing a serious matter with a platoon sergeant.

'Bloody hell! Sergeant Harris!'

Harris reached out his hand and David gripped it. 'Damn! It has been a few years,' he said as Harris sat down to retrieve his beer.

'I read about how that bastard Markham was out to get you, and how the papers were saying he was a war hero. I kind of figured that if you punched him out, it had to be natural justice for how he almost got us all killed that day. Then Mr Duffy tracked me down. I live up in Brisbane these days selling real estate. It seems that he was able to find me through my TPI pension record. Anyway, Mr Duffy had a talk to Markham's legal eagle with me present. His solicitor must have contacted Markham about what I would say in a public court, and there you go – no case to answer.'

'I informed Markham's legal rep that Sergeant Harris was also going on television to talk about how Markham lost it under your command and should have been court-martialled for cowardice. It seems Markham's party did not want that kind of public exposure. I believe Markham is going to make a public announcement, that in the spirit of bipartisan co-operation he would rather the matter be dropped. It will make him look magnanimous, but who cares.'

David raised his glass. 'To the best bloody lawyer in the country, my Uncle Sean Duffy. And to those of the battalion who are not with us today.'

Sean and Harris raised their glasses, and they would continue to do so for some time that day. All needed taxis to get home, and David stayed the night with Sean at his old flat. In the morning he prepared to return north to Gail and his new life outside politics. He had no regrets resigning, even when the Prime Minister personally asked him to reconsider, speaking as one former warrior to another.

THIRTY

What a day! Sarah Macintosh had called a special meeting of her board to make the announcement. The room was packed, and the board members were surprised to see champagne glasses set before them. Sarah stood at the top of the table, while junior managers went down the table pouring the bubbly wine into each glass.

'Gentlemen,' Sarah said, and a hush fell on the room. 'No doubt you have read the newspapers, or seen reports on television, about the sudden demise of our opposition. It seems the Duffy companies are crashing. I think it is safe to say that Macintosh organisation is the last man standing . . .'

'Last woman,' one of the board members piped up, and a ripple of subdued laughter echoed in the room.

'Last woman standing,' Sarah smiled, and the room broke into applause and chants of 'Hear, hear!'

'So, gentlemen, raise your glasses to—' For a moment Sarah ceased speaking, and everyone in the room could see how pale she had become. She appeared to be staring at the back of the room and one or two board members turned to see what had caused her sudden change of mood. They saw nothing but the wall adorned with portraits of Macintosh men, dating back to Sir Donald.

But Sarah could see something.

Wallarie stood as an old man watching her. His face was a dark cloud. Then he disappeared as suddenly as he had appeared.

'Miss Macintosh, are you feeling unwell?'

The question snapped Sarah out of her trance.

'No, no,' she hurried to reassure, but her hand trembled, spilling some of her champagne. She sat down, and one of the members rose.

'To the boss, and the ever-upward progress of the Macintosh enterprises.'

All rose, turning to Sarah, and toasted the queen of the financial empire.

Sarah hardly heard their praise. It was as if Wallarie had appeared to deliver bad news. At first she was afraid, and then she grew angry. She had finally defeated Jessica Duffy and secured an heir to her empire. Her son would finish his tour and return to Australia. He would marry a young woman of good breeding and produce the next generation to rule over the family empire. If only her father could see how successful she was. Ah, but she had murdered her own father, she remembered without any remorse. Nothing and no one, not even her father, could be allowed to stand in the way of her dynasty. She had won. So why did she feel Wallarie had come to tell her something different?

★

Jessica Duffy sat at the kitchen table of Glen View homestead with her husband, Donald.

'So, this is about all we own now,' Jessica sighed. 'I am sorry I lost everything. Please forgive me.'

Donald grasped her hands in his own. 'There is absolutely nothing to apologise for,' he said. 'We still have the property, and now I will have you with me. Running the Duffy companies took you away from me for so long, I am almost glad the business is lost. Maybe my sister has done us a favour. I love you, Jessie. I always have, and now you have the opportunity to take over the local CWA branch.'

Jessica laughed. 'There is nothing more important in my life than you and the children,' she said. 'I pray every day that God will keep Bryce safe and bring him back to us.'

Donald had listened to a sketchy radio report concerning a fierce fight over a fire-support base called Coral. All the report said was that a number of soldiers had been killed and wounded. Then the radio news went on to give greater coverage to the demonstrations against the war in the capital cities. Donald reassured himself that if anything had happened to his son he would have known by now, and he did not mention the war news to his wife lest she worry even more. Even so, he was concerned. He had fought at Tarakan, where he had witnessed the horrors exploding shells and small-arms fire could wreak upon the human body. He was not a religious man but he said a small prayer for his son's safety. To be on the safe side, he also asked Wallarie for his protection. Jessica's Aboriginal ancestry had well and truly rubbed off on him.

*

Trooper Michael Macintosh sat very still; so still that he could almost hear his own heart beating. He stared through the thick undergrowth of the old rubber plantation at the young Vietnamese soldier urinating into the bush opposite him. The enemy was barely three metres away, and for the moment unaware how close he was to an M16 pointing directly at him.

Michael was with his team of four on a reconnaissance mission to locate the NVA HQ, and they had moved stealthily into the area after a helicopter had dropped them kilometres away. During the night they had been alerted to the sound of a large force moving through their area and had been driven to go to ground.

But the NVA did not discover the Australian patrol, and the four SAS soldiers had remained very still in their hide. They had taken turns sleeping back to back and were heavily camouflaged.

At dawn the enemy had stirred in their bivouac and appeared to be readying to move on. No doubt they were headed for an assembly point to join the nightly attacks on the Australian brigade in AO Surfers. All had been going well until one NVA soldier, with an AK-47 slung on his shoulder, had walked across to their hide to relieve himself.

Michael stared at the young soldier through the foliage and their eyes met. For a moment Michael could see the confused look on the young man's face, as if he was trying to interpret what he was looking at. He grabbed at his weapon and Michael was forced to fire at almost point-blank range. The soldier fell back with a strangled scream as two shots of high-velocity 5.56 rounds tore into his chest. Michael instantly went to his 40-millimetre grenade launcher situated under the rifle barrel, and fired a high-explosive round at the NVA soldiers already rushing towards his position. The grenade landed amongst a bunched group, flinging them aside as the shrapnel tore into their bodies.

'Gotta get out of here!' the section leader yelled, leaping to his feet and sprinting in the opposite direction, with Michael and the other two troopers following. Small-arms fire cracked around them as the radio man in the section desperately put in a call for a hot extraction. As highly trained special forces soldiers, they took turns stopping and returning fire at the enemy pursuing them through the dense scrub and rows of old rubber trees. The leap-frog action caused the NVA to fall back to a relatively safe distance but did not stop their pursuit.

Michael felt something sting the side of his neck and thought it must have been one of the ever-annoying fire ants that lived in the trees. He flung his hand up, found it covered in blood and realised he had been grazed by a bullet. His lungs felt like they were on fire as he used all his fitness to keep ahead of the pursuers. So far all four of the team were still alive as they hurtled towards a predesignated helicopter landing zone. But to their horror they saw figures flitting through the early morning shadows of the trees ahead of them. Michael guessed that it must be another enemy company, alerted to the presence of four SAS soldiers in the area. They were cut off from their Landing Zone. Michael could hear the radioman talking to the pilot of the Huey coming in to rescue them. They had only one hope, and that was to make a right turn and head for the thicker cover of the copse of rainforest trees to their north. They did so, forcing the enemy to follow them into the cover and concealment of the denser undergrowth. For a moment they were safe as the enemy thrashed about, seeking their location.

When they reached cover, they quickly took up defensive firing positions. Michael reloaded his grenade launcher, while the radio man continued his communication with the pilot of the chopper they could now hear somewhere over-head through the thick foliage. They were instructed by the Huey pilot that the extraction would be by a cable lowered through the tree canopy.

The section leader threw a smoke grenade a short distance away.

'I see groovy grape,' came the answer from the chopper pilot, and the purple colour of the smoke was confirmed by the patrol leader.

The experienced pilot brought his chopper overhead and, within a very short time, the extraction line crashed through the trees only ten metres from the team. But the smoke drifting on the humid air indicated their position to the enemy, and the helicopter was receiving small-arms fire from the ground. Seconds counted, and the first two of the SASR troopers were winched up into the belly of the chopper, while Michael and the section commander provided covering fire. It was just as Michael and the section commander grasped the lowered cable that the enemy burst through the undergrowth onto their position.

Michael released his grip on the cable to fire his grenade launcher into the mass of enemy screaming in their perceived victory, and immediately switched to full automatic on his M16, spraying the oncoming figures. He saw some fall, but the incoming fire was intense. His section leader was yelling at him to hitch up to the cable, but just then a bullet smashed into Michael's hip, spinning him around to fall to the earth.

'Get out!' he screamed at his section leader, who was holding the line. 'I'm done for.'

The section leader let go of the cable to move towards Michael, but the incoming AK-47 fire was kicking up earth at his feet and splattering Michael with twigs and branches from the scrub around him. Michael made a desperate waving action with his rifle, and the section leader could clearly see that he would not be able to help. He turned, gripped the line and was hoisted through the trees.

Michael quickly changed rifle magazines and rolled onto his stomach, screaming at the pain from his shattered hip when he did so. Directly to his front was an NVA soldier with a bayonet-tipped rifle, and Michael raised his own weapon to fire a short burst into him. Then the firing pin clicked on empty.

He could hear the chopper flying away, small-arms fire from the ground following it. Then Michael could no longer hear the sound of the chopper and a strange silence fell on the scrub as the rifle fire died away. Michael knew that he was alone and completely surrounded by the enemy, who were acting a little more cautiously in their approach on the sole special forces soldier in the tiny clearing. A pretty red-base Jezebel butterfly flitted above his head, oblivious to the danger.

Michael heard the plop of something near his position and looked over to see the NVA grenade just before it went off, throwing him onto the ground. The shrapnel had riddled his body but had not killed him outright. Blood dripped into his eyes from a head wound, and he tried feebly to wipe it away. But his hand was shattered, and he laid his cheek upon the earth. A bullet from an AK-47 slammed into his back, and the heir to the Macintosh millions was killed so far from home as the butterfly alighted on his bloody face.

★

Hardly anyone took notice of the pretty young woman standing outside Sydney Town Hall, watching the crowd of anti-war protestors assembling with their placards. It was a festive atmosphere and even the uniformed police appointed to manage the milling demonstrators appeared at ease.

No one noticed the tears in her eyes as she watched from the footpath. Only hours earlier she had read that Trooper Michael Macintosh of the Special Air Service Regiment was missing in action. Her brother, Jacob, had visited her at the coffee shop and handed her the morning paper. He had known about his sister being head over heels in love with an SASR soldier currently on service in South Vietnam.

'Poor bastard's been brassed,' Jacob muttered. 'Sorry, sis.' Her brother had served as a radio operator with an infantry rifle company and he had come home a different person. But at least he had come home.

Jacob had told her that missing in action for a SASR soldier held out little hope of him surviving. The enemy were known to torture any prisoners to death rather than take them captive. One method of execution was slitting the victim's belly and pulling out their entrails on a stick. Jacob reckoned that Michael would be better off dead than to have been taken alive.

Mila had taken off her apron, excused herself from work at the coffee shop and caught a train to Town Hall Station, where she knew a moratorium protest was due to assemble. She watched the crowd gather. They were mainly students from her own university, and she recognised a few of them. She saw some faces filled with rage and wondered if they really considered the sacrifice being made by young men their own age. She thought bitterly that some of these same protestors, safe on the streets of Sydney, would graduate their courses and go on to dominate Australian politics and industry, while the young men returning were being spat on and scorned by these same ranting people. None of her friends had ever had to bear the grief of losing someone to the war.

'Hey, Mila, come and join us,' a voice called from across the street. 'It's going to be a groovy day.'

Mila wiped her eyes, turned her back on the crowd and walked away. She would go home to her little flat and stare at the walls, remembering that she had written a letter to post this day. A very special letter to tell Michael she was pregnant. She had feared that he might not welcome her news, but that was a moot point now. All she knew was that she would give birth to their child and never let it go. And she would not tell Michael's mother, who had made it plain to Michael that Mila was not welcome in the family. Well, Sarah Macintosh would never know that her son was the father of a child. Only her own loving parents would know the truth.

★

Donald Macintosh saw Michael Macintosh's name in the list of dead, missing and wounded, and felt a deep sadness. The media was giving poor coverage of what he had worked out was a major battle being fought by the Australians in Bien Hoa Province. He read that the vicious conflict was taking Australian lives on an almost daily basis. Centurion tanks had joined the battle, and he knew from experience that what was happening was a full-scale brigade operation. All arms and the air forces were involved to stem off the over-whelming numbers of enemy making contact every day with the Australians in the field. There had been no letters from Bryce in weeks.

It was late afternoon and Jessica joined her husband on the verandah. She sat down beside him and stared at the horizon. Donald knew what she was looking for in the distance, and she was not disappointed. The mail delivery truck threw up dust as it trailed its way towards Glen View. Jessica leapt up from her chair, hurrying to meet the mailman at the front gate. Donald watched as he handed his wife a pile of letters and small parcels. He waved to Donald, who waved back and left on his long route to the next property.

Jessica walked back to the house, flipping through the mail, and when her face lit up Donald knew she had found that one very precious letter. She waved it in the air.

'It's from Bryce,' she yelled.

Sitting down again beside Donald, she opened the letter with a trembling hand.

'Read it out loud,' Donald said, and Jessica put on her spectacles. Her son apologised for not writing for a while because he had been a bit busy. He said very little about the events at his fire-support base but reassured them he did not have much more time before his service was up and he could return home.

'I told you Bryce would be okay,' Donald said. 'He has your stubborn will to survive, and probably has Wallarie looking out for him. I read some bad news today, though. Young Michael Macintosh is listed as missing in action.'

'Oh no!' Jessica cried. 'I can still remember when he first came here as a little boy, so quiet and shy. Your sister will be devastated.'

'My sister has no feelings for anyone but herself, but I think losing Michael will have an impact on her. I will write a condolence letter. Not that there are any words that can give solace to someone who has just lost a son.'

Jessica carefully folded the letter from Bryce and gazed at the setting sun. She had lost the fortune she had for years struggled to build, but she still had her son and the land that they walked on. Life was short, and Sarah's millions could not bring back her one and only heir. Despite their differences, Jessica felt a terrible sadness for her sister-in-law. No mother should bear the pain of losing a child.

Jessica and Donald sat in reflective silence as the sun disappeared from the sky and the cries of the curlews drifted out across the brigalow scrub.

THIRTY-ONE

Sarah Macintosh rose at dawn in the empty mansion. The housekeeper had been granted a couple of days' leave, so Sarah decided that she would have breakfast at a stylish cafe not far from her office before she went to work. She ordered her chauffeur to pick her up early as she had a very busy day ahead with her managers, organising to consolidate their victory over the sudden crash of the Duffy companies. Sarah smiled sadly at her reflection in the long bedroom mirror. She could see that she was still a very attractive woman, and she contemplated how she might find a new lover to share her bed.

Beneath the bedroom window she heard the crunch of tyres on the long gravel driveway and was annoyed that her driver had arrived earlier than instructed. She would go downstairs and chide the man, but when she opened the door she found a grim-faced police officer and an army officer wearing the uniform of a military chaplain. Sarah was confused.

'Mrs Sarah Macintosh?' the policeman asked.

'Yes.'

'May we come inside?' the chaplain asked.

Sarah opened the door to the two men and turned to them in the hallway with a quizzical expression.

It was the policeman who spoke. 'I am afraid that I have sad news concerning your son, Trooper Michael Macintosh. He has been reported missing in action in an incident occurring a couple of days ago in the Republic of South Vietnam. Is there anyone we can call at this moment to be with you?'

Sarah stood stricken. How could Michael be missing? He was only weeks away from leaving the army and joining her in the family enterprises. It was he who would take the Macintosh name into the next century. All hope of gaining his daughter, Victoria, to be groomed was well and truly dead without the co-operation of the White family. Her only option was for her son to return.

'No,' she finally replied, and the two men excused themselves, leaving her standing in the hallway in a state of emotional turmoil.

Sarah suddenly realised how very much alone she was. Her dreams of her son continuing the dynasty were gone forever, and all the money and power she possessed meant nought at this moment in her life. She could hear the police car driving down the driveway and stared into the empty hall.

'The curse,' she whispered, staggering towards the stairway where she had once murdered her father to gain power.

What was left? The question echoed without an answer.

Slowly, Sarah climbed the stairs to go to the library.

What was left?

★

When the driver arrived at the Macintosh mansion, there was no answer to his knock on the front door. He waited patiently for an hour, occasionally attempting to raise his boss, but still she did not appear. Finally he drove to the Macintosh offices and reported the matter to her senior staff, who were waiting for her in the boardroom.

'I read in the papers this morning that young Michael was reported as missing in action in Vietnam,' one of the senior managers said. 'I think someone should go and see if she is all right.'

The other managers agreed, and two of them organised to drive to Sarah's house on the harbour. They knocked on the door but did not get a reply. In their concern, they called the police, who arrived and made a forced entry. The two police officers entered, calling her name without a response. One went upstairs, glancing into the dimly lit library.

'Hey, Rod,' he called down the stairs. 'I think you had better get up here. I think I've found Miss Macintosh.' He was joined by his colleague, and both men stood in the doorway, staring at the body of a woman hanging from a stout curtain rod. Her face was almost black, and her swollen tongue protruded from her mouth. It was obvious that she was dead.

'Bloody horrible way to die,' Rod said. 'Slowly choking to death.'

'Bloody hell!' the other policemen swore. 'Did you see that?'

'See what?'

'I could have sworn I saw a blackfella standing in the corner watching us,' the shaken constable replied. 'I must have been spooked by the dead woman.'

*

Sergeant Major Patrick Duffy crawled towards the forward platoon under 122 millimetre enemy rockets flying overhead in an NVA attack on his company position. The fiery trails of a small-arms tracer lit the night sky as he crawled forward. A frantic radio call from the platoon commander to company headquarters had informed them that ammunition was running low, and Patrick had taken it upon himself to crawl along the dusty earth, dragging a case of rifle ammunition to the shallow forward pits of the men defending the perimeter. He knew the platoon sergeant, who would normally have arranged for resupply, and felt that he would be too busy just trying to stay alive in the confusion of the battle.

Dirt splattered his face when a bullet hit the ground inches from him. Patrick paused, spitting out earth he had swallowed when the bullet hit. It was a week and a half since the enemy first launched attacks against the Australians at FSB Coral, and in that time all the units in the AO had been under constant attack. Casualties were mounting, but Patrick knew that the NVA were losing a lot more of their soldiers. It had come down to a war of attrition: seeing which side would be the last one standing.

He could see the silhouette of a bush hat only metres away and knew he was close to his own company platoon. It was then that he felt the impact of a bullet slam into his collarbone. He did not see the ricochet of the tracer AK-47 bullet but could immediately feel phosphorous burning in his chest. He did not remember screaming, but he must have as he lay on his stomach under the incoming enemy rounds. Patrick let his grip on the ammunition case go and was vaguely aware a shadowy soldier had grabbed it.

'You okay, sir?' the soldier asked him, crouching down.

'Shot.' Patrick gasped in pain as another soldier joined them in the dark.

'The CSM has been wounded,' he heard the first soldier say. 'Dunno where though.'

'Chest,' Patrick groaned. 'Went through the top of my shoulder, left side.'

'Get the medic when you get the ammo to the boss,' the second soldier said. 'I'll keep an eye on the CSM.'

Within minutes Patrick was aware of someone's fingers probing his shoulder. 'Looks like a round has hit the CSM. We have to get a dust-off for him as soon as possible. I think the bullet is in his chest.'

Patrick was dragged back to the company HQ, where Major Stan Gauden was one of the first to see him.

'Bloody hell, Pat, what were you doing out there?'

'The boys needed ammo,' Patrick said through gritted teeth. 'I wasn't doing much so I thought I might help.'

'Get a dust-off organised now,' Major Gauden said, turning to his radio operator. 'He is not walking wounded.'

By now the medic who had accompanied the rescue party back to company HQ had cut away Patrick's shirt and the small purple jagged hole could be clearly seen at the top of his collarbone. There was no blood, as the red-hot bullet had cauterised the entrance in its deadly path.

In the early hours of the morning, the medivac chopper flew Patrick and two other wounded soldiers out. As he lay on the floor of the chopper, Patrick realised that he was wavering between life and death, but a strange voice in his head told him that he would not die. This was not his destiny. Patrick had the thought that it was a man's voice, before he slipped into a blissful state of unconsciousness.

*

The surgeons in Australia considered their patient to be extremely lucky to still be alive. His condition had been stabilised as much as possible en route from the field hospitals in Vietnam to the highly qualified surgeons in Australia who were able to open him up and remove the bullet, but they still wondered whether their patient would live. But Patrick did, and after a few weeks he was almost back on his feet.

He had expected his first visitor in Concord Hospital to be Sean Duffy, but he'd received a message that Sean and Rose were off on a cruise. Sean had sent him a telegram saying he had signed over the deeds of the Sydney flat to him and would return as soon as he could. So in fact his first visitor was David Macintosh. Patrick was very pleased to see the man he had idolised when he was growing up.

'I heard you copped a bullet in Vietnam,' David said, sitting down on a chair beside Patrick's bed. 'Good to see you made it through.'

'I heard about Michael. I'm sorry.'

David looked away at the mention of his son's death. He had used his influence amongst his old comrades in government to have the combat incident passed on to him. When David read the report, he knew from his experience as a soldier that his son would not have survived the contact. Missing in action simply meant that the army had not recovered his body. Sarah was also dead, by her own hand. It seemed the age-old story of a curse on his family could almost be believed. The Macintosh dynasty was drawing to a close, with only David and Donald still standing.

'As soon as you're out of here, Pat, we'll head over to Sean's old drinking hole and raise a glass to fallen comrades,' David said.

'That sounds like a plan,' Patrick replied. 'You know something funny,' he continued. 'While I was being choppered out of the AO, I could have sworn I heard old Wallarie telling me I wasn't going to die. I was pumped with a lot of morphine at the time, so maybe I was hallucinating.'

'Wallarie has a soft spot for the Duffy mob,' David answered with a bitter laugh. 'But I suspect he has never forgiven us Macintoshes for what we did to his people all those years ago on Glen View. That is, if you believe in superstitious blackfella curses.'

★

A small but heavy parcel arrived at Glen View and Donald took it into the kitchen to unwrap the brown paper. Jessica stood beside him as Donald laid a solid brass plaque on the table.

'I think Billy and Mary will be pleased with this,' Donald said, reading the inscribed lettering. It recorded the passing of Sergeant Terituba Duffy, killed in South Vietnam, 1968, and would be affixed to a small cairn on top of the sacred hill of Wallarie's people.

'He took our family name,' Jessica said. 'It was the least we could do for such a wonderful man.'

A car had driven up outside, beeping its horn, and Donald glanced at his wife.

'Are you expecting visitors?' he asked, and Jessica shook her head. They both went to the verandah to see a young man wearing an army uniform and slouch hat step from behind the wheel of the car.

It was Jessica who exploded in a demonstration of pure emotion. 'Bryce!' she screamed as she ran down the steps. 'Why didn't you tell us you were coming home?' she chided between tears of joy as she embraced her son.

'I had to get my discharge out of the way and pick up this beauty with the money I saved. I just felt like driving home to you all as a surprise. Hello, Dad.'

Donald was down the stairs and hugging his eldest son as hard as he could. He stepped back to admire the young man wearing his ribands of service on his chest. 'It is so good to have you back, son,' he said. 'I read about the battle for Balmoral and Coral.'

'Yeah, it was a bit tough for a while,' Bryce said, just as his younger brother rode in from mustering cattle.

'Yer back, ya bastard!' Kim said, flinging himself from his horse to embrace his big brother. 'You still in the army?'

'No, I got my discharge, and this will be the last day I wear an army uniform,' Bryce grinned. 'An officer warned me that if I did not sign up again I might end up digging ditches in Civvy Street. But I told him that at least I wouldn't have to sleep in them.'

It was a scene of joyous reunion that had been repeated many times for many years of Australia's short European history. Each generation prayed the next would not experience war – but their prayers were never answered.

*

When Patrick walked away from the solicitor's office after signing off on the title deed to Sean's flat, he took in the city around him. Christmas was around the corner and there was a festive air that was so different to what he had known only months earlier in the battle for the fire-support bases of Balmoral and Coral. Somehow he did not mind being medically discharged from the army, and every day his health was improving. However, his defence force pension was not enough for him to retire on, as he had not completed the twenty years needed to be granted full benefits. Patrick knew he would need to find a job.

He opened up Sean's flat, picked up the afternoon paper, and sat down in Sean's favourite old recliner. This alien world of being a civilian took some getting used to. The popular music had taken on a whole new sound, and young Australians a rebellious attitude to all the old traditions of his generation. He had to admit there was something wonderfully fresh in the culture, but he knew he did not fit in.

Patrick flipped through the newspaper to the employment section. One small advertisement caught his eye immediately. It was seeking men with military experience for security jobs. A Sydney office would interview applicants for the Singapore-based company. He called the number and made an appointment to be interviewed the next day.

When Patrick arrived at the multistorey building in the city's central business district, he found the name of the company on the wall in the foyer and took an elevator to the eighth floor. Inside the reception area, three other men sat waiting. A pretty blonde receptionist beamed a welcoming smile as Patrick presented his name, along with a resume folder of his military service. She told him to have a seat, and Patrick took up an empty chair beside a man around his own age. The man leaned across and introduced himself as a former SASR member, and Patrick felt his hopes take a hit. Surely the recruiters would be more impressed with the application from the former special forces soldier.

'Mr Duffy, you may go in,' the receptionist said eventually, and Patrick wondered why he was so nervous. He took a deep breath and stepped into the room. There were three people sitting at a table facing him: two men in suits and one well-dressed woman. Behind them was a large glass window with a panoramic view of the city's skyline.

For a moment Patrick held his breath as his eyes fell on the woman. She glanced up from her notes and their eyes met. Patrick could see the utter shock on the woman's face.

'Patrick!' she exclaimed, causing the two older men to look at her.

'Miss Howard-Smith,' Patrick exhaled.

Sally pushed herself from behind the long table and walked to Patrick. For seconds they simply stared at each other.

'How the devil did you know we were recruiting?' she asked.

Patrick broke into a warm smile. 'I didn't know it was your company,' he said. 'I saw the ad in a paper yesterday, but I suspect there is a force beyond our understanding that actually guided me here.'

Patrick could see in Sally's eyes that she was glad to see him. She turned to the other two members of the panel and said, 'Mr Duffy will fill the vacancy. He does not need to answer any of our questions as I am already aware of his service record. As a matter of fact, I can say that Mr Duffy proved his competence when I first met him in Malaya in 1958. Gentlemen, you may take a tea break for now.'

'You know I got shot again,' Patrick grinned when the two men had left.

'But you are well enough now,' she said, with just a trace of worry in her expression. 'And if you are wondering, I am no longer married. It did not work out.'

'I never married,' Patrick said. 'I was always hoping that the magical lady of the lake would one day reappear above the water and see me on the shore.'

Sally took Patrick's hand, tears in her eyes. 'God, I missed you, Patrick Duffy,' she said. 'Your memory has always haunted me, no matter how much I tried to forget you. I have to face the possibility that we were always fated to be together.'

No words were needed as Patrick drew Sally to him and the kiss sealed their feelings.

EPILOGUE

The Birth of a New Century

My name is Wallarie, and this is my place of Dreaming. I was once a warrior of the Nerambura clan of the Darambal people, and for many years I have told you the story of two whitefella clans. Their story continues, but I will not be able to tell it to you because I am going to join my people amongst the stars. The Old People have told me it is time to leave your world. They say I have interfered enough.

I suppose you want to know what happened to the Macintoshes and Duffys. It was sad that Michael died because he was a good man with a bad mother but the Ancestor spirits said he could not be spared because of his blood. Mila gave birth to twins – a boy she called Michael, and a girl she called Monique. Mila finished her studies and became a pharmacist. When Michael was eighteen he left school to join the army. He served with the SASR in the Gulf

War, and when he came back his mother finally told him of his real father who had served with the SAS in Vietnam and been killed. Mila's son had always been restless, and when he learned about his father and his membership of the regiment, and served in the First Gulf War he began to understand his heritage.

Monique went on to study accountancy and became a top economist in the banking system. Michael would have been very proud of his children.

Michael's own father, David Macintosh is gone. He went for a swim below his old house on the beach and disappeared. They look for his body but never find it. That was back in your whitefella year of 1987. Gail, his missus, she now in a retirement home where they look after her.

You want a happy ending. Patrick Duffy a happy ending. He and Sally got married and had two girls. Patrick and Sally are very old now, and live in a big house in Sydney, where their grandchildren come to visit.

The sun is going down on my traditional lands. It is almost Christmas time in your year of 2000, and I can see Jessica leaning on a walking stick, holding the hand of her great-granddaughter. They are amongst old weather-worn stones that mark the graves of many of her ancestors – and those of the Macintosh clan. It has been so long since I rode the plains with my white brother, Tom Duffy, as what you whitefellas call bushrangers. Today so much has changed, but before I go to my ancestors I will tell you a funny story of how some things never change.

When Sarah hanged herself, the Macintosh companies were inherited by David and Donald. They agreed to sell out and both men donated their share to charities. They agreed there was too much bad history with the Macintosh family fortune. The old family house on the harbour mysteriously caught fire and burned to the ground one night. The vacant land is now a small park dedicated to the soldiers of all wars who did not return. That was David and Donald's idea. Now people sit on a bench and reflect on the Australian men and women of the armed forces who made the ultimate sacrifice for their country.

I will tell you a funny story. Back in 1964, Jessica allowed some people called anthropologists to visit the sacred hill for studies on my people. She warned the young anthropologist woman not to enter the cave, because it was forbidden to women. Only men could go in. The young woman listened but did not follow the rules. She went to that hill and entered the cave. That night a terrible storm rose up over the hill and a bolt of lightning hit her tent, killing her instantly. The storm went just as quickly – and so did the anthropologists. I told you it was a funny story, but I see you don't think so.

They have all forgotten me now – except Jessie. So I will go to my ancestors in the night sky.

*

Jessica held her great-granddaughter's hand as the little girl with the raven hair, olive skin and deep brown eyes prattled on about her friends at school and how she would like some ice cream. Mondo had spent the afternoon playing near where the old bumbil tree used to stand, which was now a shaded area under a pergola covered in grapevines. Jessica had watched her from the verandah, and had seen her chattering away to her imaginary friend, although privately Jessica thought that, at seven years of age, she was too old for make-believe companions.

Jessica was in her early eighties, yet age had not bent her back. The walking stick was to help her with a painful hip, but otherwise she was in excellent health. She walked with the little girl back to the verandah of the Glen View homestead, and the young cook, a Czech backpacker, brought a bowl of ice cream for Mondo.

Jessica watched with a smile as her favourite great-granddaughter ate the ice cream. Mondo's grandmother, Shannon, had dropped out of society after school, joining a hippie commune in northern New South Wales. There, she fell pregnant to a young man who promptly deserted her. She named her daughter Rhea, and Rhea grew into a responsible young woman who studied medicine, and graduated at the top of her class. She married a fellow doctor and had her own daughter, Mondo. Rhea said she had once had a strange dream in which she was talking to an Aboriginal woman who had been born on Glen View many years earlier. She said her name was Mondo. Rhea always laughed about the name because it came from a dream. Jessica had never told her granddaughter, but Mondo was the name of a woman who had been killed in the nineteenth century by the Native Mounted Police in the Gulf country of Carpentaria.

Jessica was glad to have Mondo staying with her. It was lonely around the homestead these days. Donald had passed away only three years earlier from a heart attack while he was out fighting a bushfire at the edge of Glen View. After his funeral, Jessica and her son, Kim, had gone through a few old things Donald had packed in a tea chest in a shed. Amongst the mouldy items she found a moth-eaten cushion stained with what looked like the image of a man's face. As she held it in her hands, she had a strange feeling the old pillow held an evil secret, and she promptly delegated it to a fire.

Kim was a married man now with a big family, living in a house he had built half a kilometre from the main homestead. He was a country boy through and through, unlike his brother Bryce who was a successful engineer in the city with children of his own.

From the verandah Jessica watched the land around her soften with the coming dusk. Dust hung like a gossamer curtain, stirred up by cattle on their way to a waterhole. The world had changed so much since Jessica was Mondo's age, and civilisation had come to the most isolated regions of the vast outback. Satellite communication kept them tuned to world events in an instant. Air conditioning made life more comfortable, and some of the roads to the property were now tar-sealed for the big road trains to transport Glen View cattle to the markets.

Jessica gazed at Mondo, who was talking to herself again. She was a pretty little girl with a very different spirit to her cousins.

'Nana,' Mondo said, catching Jessica's attention.

'What is it, little one?'

The little girl looked her straight in the eyes. 'What is baccy?' she asked.

The moon was rising, and Jessica could hear the cry of a curlew in the eternal brigalow scrub of the vast plains of Glen View.

AUTHOR NOTES

In 1969 at the age of nineteen I enlisted for three years in the Australian Army. I was posted to the Royal Australian Artillery and in the same year sent to 102 Field Battery. At the Other Ranks canteen I would listen to the gunners who had been with the battery in 1968 tell of experiences the year before in Vietnam. They were recounting the battle of fire-support bases Balmoral and Coral in Area of Operations Surfers.

Almost a half century later, I never thought I would be retelling their stories of courage and tenacity in a novel. My aim is not to provide a historical narration but simply to use a generic canvas to remind Australians of an almost forgotten – but major action and tactically significant – event we fought at the end of the infamous Tet Offensive. Lex McAulay has covered the battle in a very readable way in his book *The Battle of Coral: Vietnam Fire Support Bases Coral and Balmoral, May 1968*. It is his book that I used to gain a detailed picture of early events.

From 1950 to 1972 Australian armed forces were continuously on active service. The longest period of peace came after that era.

After the Korean War, we found ourselves in action in Malaya against the Communist rebels. For this I used Colin Bannister's personal reflections in his very readable book *An Inch of Bravery: 3 RAR in the Malayan Emergency, 1957-59* as a template with author fictional input.

Even as we were sending military advisors of the Australian Army Training Team Vietnam over to what was the beginning of another major and controversial conflict, our troops were engaged in a jungle war against the Indonesian army. It was referred to as the Confrontation – or in Indonesian: *Konfrontasi*. It is a little recognised campaign, and for my canvas I used Lt Col Brian Avery's excellent personal account *Our Secret War: The 4th Battalion the Royal Australian Regiment: Defending Malaysia Against Indonesian Confrontation, 1965–1967.*

One of the most underrated soldiers of the twentieth century was the legendary Colonel Mike Hoare whose Wild Geese campaign inspired many great fiction novels. Colonel Hoare wrote the tactical manual on fighting the war against the brutal Communist forces attempting to take control of Africa in the 1960s. A Communist East German radio report gave him the unearned nickname, 'Mad Mike Hoare', in a desperate effort to discredit his courageous work saving European and African lives. But then the Germans once referred to the troops defending Tobruk as the rats – a label we adopted with pride. His own account *Congo Mercenary* should be compulsory reading for students of a new kind of warfare that has trickled into the twenty-first century. As a young man growing up in the 1960s, I was acutely aware of the news reports concerning the Congo, and Colonel Hoare's efforts in saving so many lives, despite the condemnation by the United Nations. Needless to say, I have drawn significant inspiration from his outstanding efforts for my fictional characters: rescue of the little Belgian girl occurred as portrayed in the book, as well as the bestial actions of the Communist-backed Simbas. Recounting their courage in the face of overwhelming odds is my tribute to a great soldier who fought for African freedom when the Western world turned its back.

Gunner Bryce Duffy-Macintosh in this novel was named in honour of a real Captain Bryce Duffy, 4 Fd Regt, RAA, who was killed in Afghanistan on 29 October 2011. The character is my tribute to all those servicemen and women who followed in the footsteps of the diggers who went before them. The real Captain Duffy constantly displayed courage in his duties. Bryce's wonderful mum, Kerry, and his dad, Kim, are mutual friends of both myself and my author cobber, Tony Park.

Overall, this is a novel about the forgotten diggers of the Malayan and Confrontation campaigns, and I hope that it reignites the fading memories of Vietnam for the younger generations of today.

ACKNOWLEDGEMENTS

My thanks to the great team at Pan Macmillan involved in the production of the last in the Frontier series. My thanks to: Cate Paterson, who has been there for me from the very first, *Cry of the Curlew;* my wonderful editors Libby Turner, Julia Stiles and Rebecca Hamilton; proofreader Kristy Bushnell; Lucy Inglis, my publicist; LeeAnne Walker, who I get to talk to often at Pan Macmillan; and the team of Roxarne Burns and Milly Ivanovic. Thanks also to Tracey Cheetham.

My thanks to Geoffrey Radford for his help on this project.

My thanks goes out to the members of Hardrock Entertainment: Rod Hardy and son, Brett and family, Paul Currie and Suzanne De Passe for their work on the *Dark Frontier.*

Thank you to the ladies at the Maclean Library who supply the diverse research material: Cath, Jolana, Angela, Alison, Maree and Belinda.

Thanks to Kristie Hildebrand for the Facebook site, Fans of Peter Watt Books, and to Peter and Kaye Lowe for looking after my website www.peterwatt.com. Special thanks to John Riggall and his wife, June. John is driving our project to establish a legacy for emergency service volunteers to support families whose loved one has paid the ultimate price while assisting their communities in times of natural and man-made disasters. Also my old cobbers, John Carroll and Rod Henshaw.

To Bob Mansfield and his sister, Betty Irons OAM, thanks for the second Saturday of the month at the markets. For my other family, the firefighters in the Gulmarrad Rural Fire Service Brigade: a thank you for your camaraderie that is well known to those who run towards danger when all others, wisely, run away.

For the ongoing friendship of cobbers, such as Kevin Jones OAM and family, Mick and Andrea Prowse, Dr Louis Trickhard and his wife, Chris. Not forgotten Geoff Simmons, Darren Billett and Dan Butt. A thanks to Jan Dean.

Best wishes go out to my writer colleagues: Tony Park, whose past visits have ruined my liver; Dave Sabben MG and wife, Di; Greg Baron and family; Karly Lane; and an old cobber, Simon Higgins and his wife, Jenny.

A truly big thanks to my relations: Tom Watt and family; my cousins Luke, Tim and Virginia; and my beautiful Aunt Joan Payne, who served her country in World War II. Also, best wishes to the Duffy boys and their families. With thanks to my sister Lindy Barclay and Jock, and to my brother-in-law Tyrone McKee and Kaz.

With sadness I remember two of our World War II heroes who have passed from the ranks since my last book: Vera Montague and Mick O'Reilly. Both served in the Pacific War, and the world has lost another two heroes.

Last but not least, my acknowledgements to my beloved wife, Naomi, who has to review each chapter to ensure I get the romance right.

Next year we march with Captain Ian Steele into the Crimean War, as he serves as *The Queen's Colonial*.